The Physalia Incident

A VIKING NOVEL
OF
MYSTERY
AND
SUSPENSE

ART SPIKOL

The Physalia Incident

VIKING

VIKING

Published by the Penguin Group
Viking Penguin Inc., 40 West 23rd Street,
New York, New York 10010, U.S.A.
Penguin Books Ltd, 27 Wrights Lane,
London W8 5TZ, England
Penguin Books Australia Ltd, Ringwood,
Victoria, Australia
Penguin Books Canada Ltd, 2801 John Street,
Markham, Ontario, Canada L3R 1B4
Penguin Books (N.Z.) Ltd, 182–190 Wairau Road,
Auckland 10, New Zealand

Penguin Books Ltd, Registered Offices:
Harmondsworth, Middlesex, England

First published in 1988 by Viking Penguin Inc.
Published simultaneously in Canada

Grateful acknowledgment is made for permission
to reprint an excerpt from *Poisonous and Venomous
Marine Animals of the World*, second revised
edition, by Bruce W. Halstead, M.D. (1988).
By permission of The Darwin Press, Inc., Princeton, NJ.

Library of Congress Cataloging in Publication Data
Spikol, Art, 1936–
The physalia incident.
I. Title.
PS3569.P535P4   1988   813'.54   87-40291
ISBN 0-670-81222-6

Printed in the United States of America by
Arcata Graphics, Fairfield, Pennsylvania
Set in Times Roman
Designed by Victoria Hartman

To my girls:
Lizz, Vicki and Linda

Acknowledgments

Everything comes from something. This book, while fiction, relies heavily on facts. I obtained some of them from data bases, some from books, and some from people. In certain cases, bits and pieces of those people stuck to my keyboard and emerged in the manuscript, but in every case they all provided aid I would not have wanted to do without.

I would like to thank D. Colin Selley, Bermuda's former director of tourism, a superb host and the best tour guide I ever had, for introducing me to the right places and the right people; Mindy Werner, my editor, for knowing when to put hands on and how hard to push; Linda Parent Spikol, a great first reader, for knowing her husband—and helping him to keep his spirits up, his fingers at the word processor and his distance from the manuscript; R. L. Miller, Ph.D., Temple University Center for Marine Studies, Philadelphia, for his expert advice and his enthusiasm in discussing Portuguese man-of-wars and related curiosities; Frank Bender, a Philadelphia photographer and sculptor, for his knowledge and expertise in cranial reconstruction for law enforcement agencies; Detective Sergeant George Jackson, Bermuda Police, Somerset, Bermuda, a caring professional, for letting me intrude on a busy day; Dr. F. John Rounthwaite, director of the King Edward VII Memorial Hospital, Paget, Bermuda, for the time he gave and the knowledge he shared, and for the Grand Tour; Pete Davis, my pool-shooting buddy, for his help with the initial research; Paul J. Hoyer, M.D., assistant medical examiner, City of Philadelphia; Robert J. Sherratt, inspector, community-media relations, Bermuda Police, Devonshire, Bermuda; John F. Instone, Sergeant, press officer, Bermuda Police, Devonshire, Bermuda; Richard Winchell, the Aquarium, Museum and Zoo, Flatts, Bermuda; Nancy Love, my agent.

Finally, I want to mention a reference book, *Poisonous and Venomous Marine Animals of the World* by Bruce W. Halstead, M.D. (Darwin Press, Princeton, NJ). I found the work most helpful.

The
Physalia
Incident

The item appeared on my terminal a few minutes into my second cup of coffee. That means about 8:30 a.m., me being a creature of habit; I usually pour that second cup when I'm about to check the computer for mail, and I do that about half an hour after I get to the office.

It was a short piece, the type of thing you'd find on page 11 of your local paper—insignificant in a world of nuclear realities, but the kind of story I can't pass up. This is what you get from a guy who is every bit as fascinated with the mating habits of the northern elephant seal as with his own. More important: this is what the readers of *World Magazine* get.

The story: An American had been killed off the coast of Bermuda by a Portuguese man-of-war, a member of the jellyfish family which, if you knew more about it, could make you think twice before going in the water. In fact, I could recall vacationing in Bermuda and seeing signs that recommended doing just that.

I scrolled the copy, trying to figure out how the piece had found its way to my terminal. It wasn't slugged SCI or MED or TEK, the scientific suffixes Stella assigned to the stories that would ordinarily come to me; this item was coded BUS/UPI. Which meant that the piece had come from United Press International—and the suffix, for BUSINESS, meant that Stella had sent it to someone else who had then forwarded it to me. This concern over the origin of a simple news item may seem exaggerated, but when you work in a highly political environment with more than its share of vipers, every little movement has meaning.

The item was dated June 18. This was August 12. Whoever had sent it my way hadn't been in much of a hurry.

I made a hard copy of the piece, listening as the hum of the printer filled my office.

My office gets filled easily. It's small and narrow, like a coffin, but higher than it is long. What happens within it happens on a rectangular gray Formica surface that runs the length of one of the walls, over which there's a corkboard covered with scraps that I once must have found amusing, and at the end of which is home: an L-shaped area facing the window where my computer terminal and printer sit. On the other wall are bookshelves filled with books that I haven't read and never will. The rug is undistinguished and industrial-looking, winter gray. I have two chairs, one of which is so rarely used that everybody thinks it's my IN box. I'm not much for housekeeping.

Me, I'm five-nine, late thirties—as late as you can get and still be there—and in good shape, so I don't take up much room. Black hair, mustache to match. I cut the hair myself and sometimes look it, but the last time I went for a haircut they charged me thirty bucks, and I never went back. Since I met Angelica—that's *An-hel-LEEK-ah,* accent on the third syllable, the way the Spanish say it—I've been looking better, because she cuts the back. Before Angel—that's what I call her—I did it myself.

There is nothing commodious about my office, nothing private: it has a glass wall that faces a hallway and a glass door leading to the editorial department. That glass wall is supposed to give the illusion of space, but if I scratch my balls a hundred *World* employees can watch me do it. As for status: there is nothing to indicate that the resident of this fish tank is, as it says on the *World* masthead, Alex Black, Science Editor. Even less impressive is my staff, the smallest of any department at *World*—Peter Gray, a writer, and Madeline Miller, my secretary. Pete is twenty-five, looks twenty, and runs a little scared, probably because he married young and has a kid and can't afford to lose his job. Also, he has a bad case of hero worship, which I figure familiarity will cure, but in the meantime he *does* tend to tag along, which has a lot of the editorial staff calling us the Black and the Gray. Maddie is a couple of years older than me and has no heroes; she knows better.

Welcome to the world of big-time journalism.

As for my relative position in the scheme of things: *World Magazine*'s Science section usually consists of two pages in each issue—which means once a week. Most of that section is a result of me keeping my ear to the ground, but some of it comes in through the wire services. When that happens, I receive whatever relates primarily to the worlds of technology, medicine and science. But news may overlap. For instance, if there's a technological breakthrough, I write about the scientific implications, but if the implications are mostly financial, my portion will be edited into the other story and appear in the Business section, in which case I can kiss my byline good-bye. And with only two back-of-the-magazine pages to fill, I'm not exactly on the fast track.

I'm not complaining. I like the narrow focus, always have. But it means that I'm an anachronism, and so I've become the dumping ground, a sort of object lesson to those folks at *World* with the lean and hungry look—as if to say, *this is what happens when you don't care enough about the things that really count, like sports and fashion and celebrities.* Science editor isn't just a title, it's an epitaph—they anoint you expecting it to be permanent, one less thing to worry about in putting out a weekly magazine. It was like that for the former titleholder, a loner who died of lung cancer at fifty-five. I used to do some free-lance writing for him; when someone mentions his name I can still smell the cigarettes.

And now I was looking out the same window that Ralph had looked out of for all those years. Most of what I could see was the building across the street, a weather-worn, soot-darkened, turn-of-the-century monstrosity with opaque windows and sills covered with pigeon droppings. But if I positioned myself just so, I could see a vertical sliver of the green treetops of Rittenhouse Square in the distance, and among them the high rise in which I live. The sky over Philly was cloudless and powder blue, and heat shimmered up from the window ledge.

I reread the article as it zipped off the printer.

Dies snorkeling

An American businessman, thought to be the victim of an attack by a Portuguese man-of-war, was found dead yesterday in shallow water off Church Bay by members of a fishing party.

Vladimir Zaychek, 68, a resident of West Chester, Pennsylvania, and a guest at Fontana, was spotted floating face down by Carlton Chew of Somerset, owner of the fishing boat *Pound-Foolish.*

Albert M. Augustus, M.D., an American tourist, and Det. Sgt. Earl P. MacLeod, both on the beach at the time, were unable to revive Zaychek. Dr. Augustus pronounced the man dead at the scene, attributing the death to a Portuguese man-of-war sting.

The article had been picked up from the *Royal Clarion,* a Bermuda daily that seemed to get its international news items from UPI and Reuters and then edit them to make them incomprehensible or incomplete or, at the very least, dull. In its coverage of local news, however, it started out that way. Its editors, with typical Bermudian insularity, would assume that islanders knew enough about the islands to understand who Det. Sgt. Earl P. MacLeod was and what he was a Det. Sgt. of, and if they didn't, they weren't Onions (as Bermudians good-naturedly call themselves) and they'd soon be gone anyway.

I have a love-hate relationship with the ocean. I'm a threat to myself when I'm in it. Yet I'm fascinated by what lives there. So I found myself right down there with Zaychek, the victim, wondering what had gone through the poor bastard's mind in those last few seconds. Had the shock of the sting stopped his heart? Cut off his breathing? Set his skin on fire? Or had it knocked him unconscious, maybe buying him a pain-free ticket out?

It was not a journalist's curiosity that made me want to know. It was fear. Twice I had almost drowned. The first time had been on the Chesapeake, when I jumped from the side of a yacht and tried to swim to shore; later I would say, in my landlocked vocabulary, that it only looked about a block away. A teenaged girl had saved me, towing me as I gagged and choked to a point where I was able to touch bottom—less than twenty feet from where my arms gave out.

The second incident took place, I remembered with a shudder, off the coast of Bermuda. A more experienced snorkeler asked me if I wanted to swim out to a far-off reef. Well, sure, I said—after all, I had snorkeled before. Yesterday, in fact. For half an hour. But I didn't tell him that.

So we went. I did fine until we got there, thanks to my extra buoyancy in the salt water. But once there, once beyond my initial amazement at being able to look down several stories into an undersea world, I suddenly realized that the other guy was a good thirty feet away and I was alone and vulnerable with nothing in my ears except the sound of my own breathing, a rhythmic whoosh echoing through the snorkel. The land was a distant ridge speckled with tiny umbrellas; below me, around me, were only water and the silent, darting fish that now seemed to be waiting in ambush. I felt a wave of something close to nausea. Don't panic, I told myself, just get to the reef and use it to steady yourself.

But the reef was not the place to be. It was there that the water met resistance, there that it was forced to twist and shove and rush. My environment turned hostile; I was caught in the turbulence. Water filled my snorkel and my mouth and my lungs. Instinctively I tried to breathe through my nose—impossible in the face mask.

I surfaced, my lungs bursting; I ripped off the mask and gulped the air. But I had panicked, and I grabbed for the end of a large coral that stuck several feet out of the water, inflicting long diagonal cuts on my legs and knees as I tried to steady myself. I tried to get upright to clear the snorkel, readjust the face mask. But the current was relentless, and now I was pummeling the water with both hands, out of control . . .

My phone rang.

"Black? Colin Chase. I sent you something—about a guy killed by a Portuguese man-of-war?"

Well, that explained it, and my stomach felt suddenly empty, the way it does when you're walking down the street and you spot somebody you don't want to see because you're supposed to be somewhere else, and there isn't a damned thing you can do about it.

"Let me tell you why I sent it," Chase continued briskly, having sensed my apprehension.

One thing I was sure of: he had a reason. Colin Chase was one of those lean and hungry types, only leaner and hungrier than most, and better at satisfying the hunger. A perfect bureaucrat. I say that with a certain grudging respect—so few people are perfect at anything—and with a certain fondness, since I really had nothing against the guy. In fact, he could be friendly on occasion—I remember how he once smiled and said "Merry Christmas" to me on the elevator. Of course, back then he didn't know who I was.

Chase told me he'd known the victim. Vladimir Zaychek, he said, a local millionaire and an acquaintance of his, had been an interesting guy in a couple of areas. One was scientific: Zaychek had an ability to recognize undercapitalized inventions and the companies that owned them. Back in the late forties, he applied that ability—backed some research and marketing efforts, got rich. Later, when he saw the computer age coming, he moved toward high tech; he bought companies that lacked only management, made them profitable, then sold them. The other area in which Zaychek had apparently been interesting, I inferred, was his wife, now a widow, whose welfare seemed to be of some concern to Chase, and somehow all of this had conspired to bring the news item to my terminal. Chase asked if we could discuss it at lunch. I said yes, which is an appropriate answer when it's the associate publisher doing the asking.

Colin Chase was *World*'s heir apparent to the top job, and well packaged for it: trim, handsome, Harvard, late forties, salt-and-pepper hair and mustache, a head taller than me. He was marked for success, often aloof and humorless and political, but with an ability to turn on the sincerity and charm like a tax-shelter salesman.

Chase did not mention that there was any urgency in the situation; in fact, he sounded almost casual about it. But as I hung up the phone, Maddie, who after twenty years at *World* could always tell which way the wind was blowing, stuck her head in my door. "I just got the word that Colin the Terrible was down here looking for you—at, get *this*, seven-thirty this morning." She blew a clump of red-tipped brownish-gray hair, overdue for a coloring, out of her face. "That's why you'll never amount to anything, Black," she said, infusing her voice with authority, "you're never here when we need you."

I laughed, but I wasn't enjoying the joke. I was having lunch with Machiavelli.

It had been three years since *World* had convinced me to leave my newspaper feature-writing slot at the *Chronicle,* a move I never regretted—the *Chronicle* went under soon after that. In those three years Colin Chase hadn't had much to say to me. That was understandable. Chase was on the twenty-fourth floor, I was on the fourteenth; I was a writer and editor who, on the job at least, moved about in a carefully circumscribed world—a paramecium in a drop of water. Chase was a creator of policies and budgets as well as *World*'s hatchet man, the cause of many a large tree falling.

As a result, no one from my part of the organization met casually with Chase: pleasantries were next to impossible; everything was loaded with implications. That was the nature of his job and, some said, since he fit the job so well, the nature of the man. I wasn't too quick to buy that; I believe it *is* lonely at the top, and I always figured that there were some human characteristics in Chase's gene pool.

I'd been up to the twenty-fourth floor maybe half a dozen times—budget meetings, policy meetings, meetings about the redesign of the magazine. It's amazing how much time people can spend talking about a 1/72nd-of-an-inch difference in a typeface. I yawn, I tap my feet, I make little drawings on my yellow pad. I can't help it. I feel like I'm back in third grade. When I first get up there, I sort of like it: we sit in these big leather chairs at an enormous teak table and there's lots of room to move around, and the whole city is outside the window. Because I rarely get to see the top of my own desk, I like the pristine neatness of it, too; it's like going on vacation.

That feeling, which is mixed with awe and longing, stays with me for about three minutes, and then I start feeling sorry for the animal that died to make my chair.

But rank has its privilege. On the twenty-fourth floor the rugs are thicker, the wood is richer, the chrome is shinier. Even the sky is brighter.

Down on the fourteenth, where I work, people have less of everything—except spontaneity. Okay, there's an occasional hole in somebody's upholstery, and maintenance is a little slower at removing the graffiti in the men's room, and if you spill coffee on the rug you *own* the stain and will, by the time they get it out, feel naked without it, and when things are new they look like they were brought in by mistake—but it's like we're all in the same foxhole, like we're *part* of something, some kind of spirit or tradition.

And it's there in spite of the computers. I know lots of people who work at computers all day in other organizations, and they tell me that it's tough to feel the camaraderie. People don't interact as much. They don't ask Mimi Bains or Fred DiNuccio; they ask the computer. Computers are so much *better.* And yet at *World*, despite the fact that everybody on the fourteenth floor spends the day looking at monitors, the camaraderie comes through, and we take what we can get from the situation and mostly we like it: the kind of work we do and the kind of people we do it with.

That's what they didn't have on the twenty-fourth floor, and I was going to try to remember that when I went to lunch with Colin Chase.

At noon, which is earlier than I like to eat, we arrived at Leslie's, a chic little French restaurant that embalms everything in sauces of at least three syllables.

The hostess greeted Colin Chase like a brother, blinked at me, and led us through the front room to a pillow-cluttered banquette in the *good* room. Jesus, I hate being chic. Chase made small talk, mostly about the financial realities of producing a national newsweekly. He sipped a glass of white wine. I nursed a margarita and waited to find out why we were eating lunch together.

I knew and he knew that he was expected to get down to business. But the conversation took an unexpected turn toward editorial matters, more my area than his, and Chase found himself trapped in the subject. I use the word appropriately: it wasn't that he didn't know anything about the editorial end, or simply that he felt more competent when talking about budgets instead of journalism. It was perhaps the fact that he had to look like he was enjoying himself having lunch with someone who earned a lot less money than he did. So rather than let him squirm and then resent me for it, I shifted gears.

"I read the piece."

"Oh. Right." Like it was the furthest thing from his mind. "What do you know about those things—Portuguese man-of-wars?"

"Not a lot. They're jellyfish with long tentacles—I've heard they can be a hundred and fifty feet or more, although that may be one of those sea-monster exaggerations you get— and the tentacles are covered with, uh, *nematocysts.* That's where the sting comes from, and it's used primarily to paralyze fish. Which it eats." I sounded like a freshman digging through his Biology 101 notes, which I was, to a degree, but I also didn't want to sound too bright until I knew why I was here. I knew it wasn't to write a story about jellyfish; if that was what Chase was looking for, he didn't need an expensive restaurant to get it.

"But people get stung, too, on a pretty regular basis— scuba divers, snorkelers, swimmers—it can happen just by stepping on one at the beach. The result can be pretty unpleasant, a burning pain that can knock the hell out of the heart and the lungs. Not to mention the skin and flesh, which can get really messed up, scarred—the tentacles may have to be torn off. And if you panic and use your fingers to do that, you'll end up with stings on them, too." I buttered a piece of bread and looked across the table at Chase, who was staring blankly. "Sometimes victims go right into shock."

"This can be fatal?"

"Well, I think you'd have to get quite a dose for the *poison* to kill you. But if you're out snorkeling and you're alone and you go right into shock, or if your vital functions are affected—well, you can drown, and *that*'ll kill you. Of course, you don't hear about that happening much, because these things aren't hard to spot and avoid."

"That's one thing that's tough to figure," Chase said. "Zaychek was experienced. He had lifesaving certification. He knew scuba, snorkeling—he was a water *specialist*. He even wrote a book about some aspect of undersea exploration."

"Well, obviously he screwed up. Maybe he got overconfident."

"Maybe. He was pretty far offshore—out beyond where the tourists were snorkeling. Nobody saw what happened, but some guys were going by in a fishing boat and they spotted the body. He hadn't been in there all that long, I'm told."

"Uh-huh."

Chase leaned forward. "The Zaycheks were friends of mine—Maria, she's the widow. She has it in her mind that . . . there's more than meets the eye here."

"Why?"

Chase shrugged. "First of all, like you said—these man-of-war things aren't hard to avoid, so she can't imagine how Vladimir would have allowed himself to get so close to one. But that's not all. She says he had enemies. He was very powerful, very well connected. Rich, reactionary—some say ruthless. And secretive. I knew him for years, played tennis with him—he was in great shape for a guy his age, until his heart problems started, anyway—and I still know very little about the way he made his bundle."

"This guy wasn't Mafia, was he?"

"No, nothing like that. Totally different. He was brilliant, literate, highly regarded by the movers and shakers. He didn't have to make his money illegally.

"Considering that he didn't share much during the ten years that Maria was married to him, I can understand just about any suspicions she might have. He kept her like a hothouse flower—went off to work, came home at all hours, and just left her there. She didn't seem to mind; she's an oddball to begin with. But now her imagination seems to be running away with her, and I'd like to help her get over it. I think it's what Vladimir would've wanted me to do."

I still didn't know what he wanted from me, and I said so.

"Just talk to her, help her see that there's nothing illogical about her husband's death. Give her some facts about man-of-wars—is that the plural?—whatever."

"Why don't I just fix her up with a marine biologist?"

"No. I mean, I'd like you to do it. You're somebody she'll relate to. She's a foreigner, not very sophisticated but with good instincts. She's hard to get close to. Vladimir kept her isolated. She distrusts academicians, distrusts doctors—they read too much, they don't know the real world, et cetera. I've already been down that road. But I think she'll trust you. It's a hunch." He rotated his wineglass, streaking its sides with the California chardonnay.

Chase didn't say why he had that hunch, but it wasn't hard to figure out. I'm the kind of guy that hotel clerks ignore. Like, some guys put on a tux and they look like prime ministers; I look like a waiter. I am, in a word, *unthreatening*.

And so, for the purpose of Maria Zaychek, I guess I made sense. I managed not to be offended.

"I know this is an imposition," Chase went on. "I wish I

didn't have to ask you, and I don't even know if she'll go for it. But I'd like you to try."

So I said okay, I would do it. He knew I would; he signed my checks. He didn't smile or say thanks. He just sat there and looked down at his plate, twisting his teaspoon and wondering what to talk about from then to the end of the meal, while I sat there nodding and picking at my salmon, which had, in a way, suffered a fate similar to Zaychek's. Only in butter.

The next morning I didn't go to the office. Instead, I took the elevator from my apartment to the subterranean garage of the Dorchester, the Rittenhouse Square high rise where I live, slid into the worn seat of the Great Unwashed, and drove out into a misty, unseasonably cool summer morning.

Rittenhouse Square doesn't depend upon the weather; it wears all the seasons well. Now, with the fog rising from its sidewalks, obscuring the tops of the chestnut trees and wrapping the still-burning street lamps in halos, it might have been a square in London. It would especially look like that through the windows of the cocktail lounge of the Barclay Hotel, the Square's grande dame, on the southeast corner.

I rolled down my window and followed the Square to Walnut Street, listening to the hiss of the tires on the damp asphalt. I made a left toward the Schuylkill Expressway, turned on the radio and went east toward I-95.

"Maria," Colin Chase had said, "there's somebody here I think you should talk to." It had been a hard sell; she'd been reluctant. But finally, Chase held out the phone to me. "Here," he said, lifting his eyebrows.

Her voice had been tired and mechanical—the voice of a woman who did not care to be charming. But Chase had done his job convincingly, and now she was sold on me—so much so that I felt conscience-bound to explain that my knowledge of marine biology wasn't all that Chase had said it was, but mostly depended upon what I could find in data bases. But I didn't. At least, I figured, I'd know more about the subject than she would. She gave me directions to her home in a very slight accent, maybe Greek or Italian.

The expressway was empty eastbound; all of the morning traffic was heading toward the city, and so in just a little over half an hour I found myself in a fashionable area of country estates, where I pulled into a long drive fringed by tall poplars. Had the directions been any less specific, I could easily have missed it—it was a sharp right turn into a blind driveway through a heavily curlicued wrought-iron gate with an ornate 100 at the top. Right after that, at the end of a short winding drive, the large stone house presented itself, a lone, pale mansion with a stand of trees on either side, surrounded by the same type of iron gate through which I had driven. I parked my six-year-old Volvo next to a small yellow Mercedes on the front drive.

The housekeeper, a diminutive gray-haired woman, greeted me by name and invited me in; I followed her through a towering center hall and down a long oriental runner that traversed the center of the house. To the left and right were twin sitting rooms—a grand piano and some expressionist paintings, probably real, in one, and a fireplace and over-stuffed furniture in the other—then a large, formal dining room and a kitchen and pantry.

The woman led me through French doors that opened onto a huge terrace, extended her palm to the right, and disappeared back into the house.

The terrace was perpendicular to the center hall. On the right side, a considerable distance away, a woman in a yellow silk robe sat at a patio table under an umbrella of almost the same color. In front of her on a linen tablecloth were a newspaper and a tall silver coffeepot. She had long coal-black hair that seemed to float on the breeze, partially obscuring her face, and her posture was almost regal—or maybe just rigid. She looked tired and drawn, and her failure to turn toward me—although I knew that she knew I was there —made the quality of the misty morning, in which the yellows were the only bright colors, even more surreal. In this strange translucent but dense light, Maria Zaychek looked quite at home, although she might have looked at home nowhere else—the way certain complex, highly developed plants can look artificial when they're not surrounded by jungle.

She was looking at something, a small greenhouse at the end of well-manicured gardens. Then: "Come sit down, Mr. Black," she said, turning only her head to do so. She said *sit* almost like *seat,* and she said it like someone who was used to giving instructions. A monarch.

When I reached the table, she leaned forward to shake my hand. Hers was both strong and delicate, and cold—a hand, its white skin stretched taut to show prominent blue veins, that looked and felt like sculpture. She had a firm grip; her lips were thin and tight, and her eyes were deep green and impenetrable and without humor. But she appeared less unfriendly than sad. She smiled, and was beautiful.

"My husband raised orchids," she said, nodding toward the greenhouse. "He spent a lot of time there. Do you want coffee?" She was already pouring it into a small peach-tinted china cup. "You're the science editor at *World.*"

"Yes."

"That's very impressive."

I couldn't tell if she meant it. "Not because I'm a regular reader," she added, sensing that.

I could tell that she never picked it up.

"But my husband used to read it. He was impressed with your section. He said that you really did your homework."

I nodded appropriately. It was hard for me to get all worked up about being *World*'s science editor when I found myself in a palace like this. I felt like saying, *You, too, can work at* World. *Of course, you'll have to give up your house and your maid and your Mercedes. . . .*

"And you obviously know quite a bit about marine life."

"Well, something."

She looked surprised. "Modest, too?"

"Trying to be accurate."

"Why didn't you try to be accurate on the telephone?" There was an edge to her voice now, an air of formality that reflected former disappointments. She was good with the language despite her accent, obviously well educated, although when she used phrases such as *really did your home-work* she sounded like Ninotchka.

"Maybe I should have. But I figured that you would've wanted to see me anyway. And I really felt that I could help."

She relaxed, nodded, dipped a sugar cube halfway into her coffee and watched it turn dark brown. "Tell me, what do you know about the Portuguese man-of-war?"

"What do you want to know?"

"I want to know if my husband was really killed by one."

"The evidence seems to suggest it." I sipped my coffee, using the moment to study her. She studied me back.

"Well," I went on, "he was snorkeling in an area in which they were known to exist. And *something* killed him while he was in the water there. A doctor on the beach diagnosed the cause of death, which was apparently corroborated. Death from that kind of sting is not unheard of, and Colin Chase says your husband had a heart condition. It seems to hang together." I looked at her for affirmation.

"I think my husband may have been murdered."

I searched for a good answer. I said: "Oh?"

"Yes. A month ago I wasn't so sure. But the more I think about it, the more convinced I am."

"What is it that—"

"Nothing I can put my finger on. Just little things. For instance, my husband never went into the water alone. Never. It was his rule; I heard him say it many times. So I've been asking myself, 'Who was he with?' When they found him, there was no one else. But there had to be someone. I'm sure. And I think that when I find the person, I'll find out quite a bit. Perhaps it was unfair of me to have you come here, your orientation being scientific, but I didn't know how else to begin."

She had finished her coffee and was now folding and unfolding her hands. They fluttered about on the table, straightening out the silver, folding the napkins—all things she obviously did not have to worry about—until finally the slender fingers found comfort in her lap.

"My husband was involved in . . . many things. He was a strange, complicated man, one who cared deeply about those close to him, his country, his business. But he could be . . . ruthless. I know some of this by living with him, the rest I—absorbed; he never confided in me about his affairs. Even now, while I know that most of his estate will be coming to me, it will take me months to learn just what it is that I own.

"Perhaps it's because of the difference in our ages. He was sixty-eight when he died, and that made it easy for him to behave more like a father than a husband. And for me, more like a daughter than a wife." A breeze tossed some strands of her hair into her mouth and carried the smell of her my way—not quite perfume, or at least not only perfume. I wondered what she was wearing under the yellow robe. Then I tried not to.

"Just a day or two before he left for Bermuda, my husband seemed preoccupied. I sensed that something was wrong. I mean, Vladimir often behaved as though he lived on the edge of danger. He was suspicious of strangers, and when I would question him about that he would only say that money

makes its own enemies. That was the behavior I lived with and got used to.

"But this last time he seemed almost nonchalant. He said there was nothing specific that he had in mind, but just in case anything ever *should* happen, he told me, he had provided for me. This last time he did not seem . . . melodramatic at all. He was calm, soft-spoken. He said, 'I don't want to frighten you. Nothing to worry about.' This time there was no implication of danger. He told me to call Colin Chase if I needed anything. Mr. Chase has been a close family friend. And he left me an envelope."

"You opened it?"

"Yes."

"What was in it?"

"Money. A list of things I would need to know in case of his death, like the fact that he had asked Mr. Chase to be executor of his will. But he'd never done anything like that before, Mr. Black. So even though I was shocked when I heard of his death, I wasn't surprised. I'd had a premonition. I *sensed* it was coming. And somehow I knew that Vladimir knew it, too." She had moved forward to the edge of her chair, animated for the first time, waiting for my reaction.

I thought she was a little off the wall. I remembered my mission, remembered what Chase had said. But she was convinced, and that helped her be convincing. "Well," I repeated, "the problem with all this is that we have no evidence that it was anything but an accident."

She looked at me and smiled—a sad, wistful smile. "I don't want to imagine things, Mr. Black. I have been tortured trying to separate what is real from what is imagined. And I *need* a more objective outsider to say what you're saying. But I want you to listen to me, too. I think that once you learn a little more, I'll know that you're looking at every side of the situation.

"I will tell you this: there were others in the ocean doing what Vladimir was doing; no one had seen any Portuguese man-of-wars. Despite his age, my husband was an expert swimmer, an expert diver; snorkeling, in fact, was as easy as pie. And again, where was the other person?"

I listened as she repeated the litany, ticking off the points one by one with a bright red fingernail against her open palm. Despite her own convictions, there was nothing—at least nothing that I could see—to justify her suspicions. It could have been an accident. Vladimir Zaychek could have made a mistake. He would not have been the first expert to die of carelessness. I told her so.

"There was one other thing I noticed. Those orchids. He was fanatical in his dedication to them; they were the only things for which he had any patience. In fact, as a so-called captain of industry, Vladimir was fond of making things happen; he moved worlds, controlled lives, demanded instant gratification. Except for the orchids. It fascinated him that no matter what happened, he had to wait six or seven years to find out whether he was successful in developing a particular hybrid. 'I admire orchids,' he used to say, 'not just because they are beautiful, not just because they are inscrutable, but because they do not respond to threats.' "

I remembered Chase's comment about Zaychek keeping his wife like a hothouse plant.

"Then, quite recently and rather suddenly, he stopped going to the greenhouse. And when he left for Bermuda, he didn't even call Jeanette to come in and care for the orchids. Was he letting all those years of work go down the drain? Or was he simply convinced that he was not coming back? He was behaving like a person with a terminal illness.

"All of this may seem silly. But there are things that one learns by living with someone that nobody else can know. Are you married, Mr. Black?"

"No. But I was."

"Divorced?"

"Yes."

"How long were you married?"

"A few years. Long enough to know what you're talking about—about learning by living with someone."

"And now? Are you with anyone now?"

"Sometimes. I mean, there is someone," I said, and I told her about my current state, and the way I was living, and my job, and we sipped the coffee until it was cold. She told me more about her husband, and about the moment she learned of his death. I asked about the funeral; there hadn't been a formal service. But Vladimir's body now lay, as he'd always wished, in an old cemetery on Bermuda. Maria had not attended the burial. She said it wouldn't have made anyone feel better. At least not her.

At last she said, "Mr. Black, thank you for coming here. In a strange way, I'm relieved that you're not getting all emotional about this like I am. I have great faith in scientific inquiry. Maybe I *am* overreacting. I don't think so. But time will tell. In the meantime, I think I can trust you—a certain chemistry." She smiled tentatively.

That quickly, it was over. The sun had burned through the early-morning mist; soon it would be hot. Maria Zaychek accompanied me down the long hallway, her backless yellow slippers causing her to walk a little clumsily. The effect of that walk, I had to admit, was not lost on me.

S tella lives in a small, otherwise uninhabited room on the twenty-second floor of the World Building. Her terminal looks pretty much the same as any other terminal in the place, but the large metal container alongside her is different. It is within that box, which houses Stella's vast memory, that the programs, the networking and communications capabilities—and the detritus of the past itself—reside. A few years earlier those contents would have required fifty times the space; a few years before that, five thousand times.

I spend a lot of time with Stella, not there in that twenty-second-floor office, but wherever I have a computer and a modem—my office, my apartment, even my briefcase, in which I always have my lap-top computer. Give me a phone line and I can link up with her no matter where I am, and in doing so have access to pieces of information almost infinite in number. I've been working with Stella for two years. I'm still learning. I'm still amazed.

Within Stella's gray metal exterior is a warehouse of computer capabilities called Standard Telecommunication, Editing and Library Link; even before her packing case had been opened, the *World* staff spotted the acronym that became her name. Stella does all the easy stuff: she receives and transmits everything from electronic mail to articles that have been scanned, a neat trick in which actual copies of the printed page, pix and all, are committed to memory; she enables on-line conversations during which large quantities of written information are exchanged; and she searches thousands of data bases worldwide, including every piece of information processed and stored by *World* on a continuing basis, for a name, a subject, a single word. More important, Stella functions as an artificial intelligence: she solves problems by asking questions, uses the answers to compare data, then narrows down the possibilities by asking more questions.

Under normal circumstances, this is far more than anyone at *World* needs. Take me. All I have to do is present complex scientific issues in terms that my Aunt Bessie can understand. Using Stella, I can access much of the world's recorded knowledge, including anything added to a data base almost anywhere within the last ten minutes, with a few taps on the keyboard and in the space of a phone call. I use Stella to absorb knowledge which I then clarify, rewrite and pass along—which is a lucky thing, since editors are the ultimate armchair adventurers, people who know far less from experiencing it than from reading about it.

Because of that, Stella's become my colleague, almost alive—only better. She doesn't bitch, doesn't take coffee breaks, doesn't get sick and works around the clock. Other than that, she's practically human; ask anybody who loves high tech. And it's difficult to avoid that feeling when you can speak to something in English with only minor adjustments for protocol, especially when it starts your day with GOOD MORNING, ALEX BLACK. YOUR PLEASURE?

Today my pleasure would be information about jellyfish.

I thought about Maria Zaychek as I fought the noon traffic back toward the city. There were certain things about my meeting with her that surprised me. *She* surprised me. Part of it was that she simply didn't fit my preconception of a rich widow, a demographic entity that was beginning to have pleasant new connotations.

The other part was the small mystery she presented. I had been sent to quash the fears of a woman who, with nothing much to go on, believed that her husband had been murdered. She had presented very little evidence to that effect. And yet . . . and yet. She had been tentative; I ended up feeling that she hadn't told me everything worth telling in this first encounter. But there was something about her that reminded me of certain puzzles of logic that I find irresistible—puzzles in which the answer is given, and the solver must find the question.

Unfortunately, it turned out, the man-of-war would have to wait. Back at the office, I found a piece of copy by a freelance writer waiting for me in Stella's memory, an article about a cancer-causing food preservative that needed considerable editing and fact checking; and my own column, which appears once a month and which I enjoy writing, was due in a week and hadn't been started. I decided to attack the work immediately and put in an hour or two on the man-of-war on my own time in the evening.

I had told Colin Chase I would call when I got back. But it slipped my mind, and when I remembered, I was in the middle of writing and didn't want to interrupt the flow. I figured that if I didn't call him, he'd call me.

By the time he did, I had at least revised my thinking and picked the subject for my column: a species-by-species comparison of methods of self-preservation—skunks, lionfish, rattlesnakes, black widows, jellyfish. A quiet little essay which, if done well, could raise issues about the Pentagon version of self-defense and, for me, kill two birds with one stone.

I sat down at my terminal, typed STELLA, and entered the prefixes of a few data bases—mostly newspapers to start with, in case there was anything similar to the Zaychek death to know about—then the search phrase PORTUGUESE MAN-OF-WAR. I put Stella in an automatic save mode and began to edit some copy.

That's when the phone rang. It was Chase's secretary. Then Chase was on the phone. He seemed edgy, probably because I was supposed to have called him and he'd ended up making the call. At *World*, the pecking order is preserved as carefully as a bone sliver at the Vatican.

"Just calling to check, Alex—did you see Maria Zaychek?" Studiedly nonchalant. Underneath it, a twitch.

I told him I had.

"How'd you make out?"

"Well, it's hard to say. She really believes that all the pieces don't hang together, and she's asked me to look into it."

"Well, I guess you can see she's sort of overreacting."

"Maybe."

"Oh?"

"Probably."

"You . . . think there's some reason to take her seriously?"

"The evidence isn't particularly convincing, but she is."

"Mmm."

"She says that her husband behaved like he *knew* he was going to die—"

"You're kidding."

"That's what she says. And then, she knew her husband's habits. Knew that he didn't go snorkeling alone. Felt that he was too good at what he did to get finished off that way. And she says nobody remembered seeing any Portuguese man-of-wars in that area. Of course, all of this is the kind of stuff that can be explained in several ways, but if you believe in circumstantial evidence—"

"Damn her," Chase said, but not without affection. "And do you?"

"Do I what?"

"Believe in circumstantial evidence."

"Sure, sometimes. I mean, when a guy's wife disappears, and he says she went to see her mother, and then they find the plane tickets in the trash, and it turns out the mother's been dead for two years and the guy took out a million-dollar insurance policy on his wife's life and—"

"Enough."

"Anyway, Maria Zaychek doesn't sound ready to give up the ghost. So I told her I'd look into it."

"I don't know," Chase said, pushing a little harder. "The more attention this gets, the more likely it is that Maria will blow it out of proportion. Maybe it was a lousy idea. Maybe if we leave her alone, she'll forget it. Sometimes, just by paying attention to something, you give it credibility."

"Well, I can't just drop it. I told her I'd look into it."

"Then get it over with as quickly as you can." Chase started to add something, then changed his mind. "Where will you start?"

"I don't know. Probably on the computer. Look, you never know—she wouldn't be the first wife to have a good antenna."

There was a brief silence. Then: "Well, of course, you'd be a better judge of these things than I am. Just let me know what you come up with."

"Sure. It's your party."

"Right," Chase said.

I spent the better part of the afternoon looking for Albert M. Augustus, M.D., the doctor who had cited the man-of-war as the cause of Zaychek's death. A reporter at the *Royal Clarion,* the Bermuda daily in which the death had been reported, stated—with the geocentricity characteristic of a British Crown colony—only that the doctor had been an American; for their purposes, city and state had been unimportant.

The American Medical Association proved more helpful; there was an Albert M. Augustus with a Cincinnati address among the organization's members. I got through to Bermuda Customs, which in an unbelievable display of cooperation got back to me in less than an hour and confirmed the Cincinnati name and address as being that of their June visitor; upon arrival, he had indicated his intended length of stay as about two weeks.

It was late afternoon by the time I called Augustus's office. A woman there said, in a voice with a midwestern twang, that the doctor was no longer practicing, and asked if I wanted to call a Dr. Edgars who had taken over.

"No," I said. "Can you tell me how to reach Dr. Augustus himself?"

"Well," the woman replied, her voice turning respectful, "I'm afraid Dr. Augustus has passed away."

I know lousy luck when I hear it. Only two months before, the doctor had declared dead the victim of a Portuguese man-of-war attack. Now the doctor himself had died, a medical practice had switched hands; it was that old journalistic tragedy, a lead turned cold.

"I'm sorry," I said. "I guess it happened right after he got back from Bermuda."

"Bermuda?" A pause. "Albert was never in Bermuda."

I repeated the name and address.

"Well, that's certainly us. But Albert—I'm Katharine, his wife . . . widow, now—Albert was never in Bermuda. In fact, he never went near the beach or the water anywhere because of the sun. He said it caused cancer. Still, it was cancer that got him."

"Could he have gone to Bermuda without your knowledge?"

"Of course not." It was the wrong possibility to suggest, and now she asked with a trace of indignation, "Who *is* this?"

"My name's Alex Black. I'm an editor at *World*."

"Oh, yes. We subscribe to it." Still in the first person plural.

"Okay. I'm working on a story that involves the death of a man named Vladimir Zaychek. He died in Bermuda. Now, a doctor who was on the beach at the time identified himself as Albert M. Augustus. An Albert M. Augustus, M.D., of your address in Cincinnati, supposedly went through Bermuda Customs a few days before that."

"It's impossible. My husband died in New York on June twenty-ninth."

About two weeks, I thought, after the death of Zaychek. Plenty of time for him to have been in Bermuda to make the diagnosis.

"Were you with him?"

"Say, I don't know about all these questions. I mean, I don't *know* you."

"I understand exactly how you feel. I really do. One of the least attractive parts of my job is asking questions like these, and I'll tell you, I don't like doing it. My mother

didn't raise me to intrude on people's lives, and I know I wouldn't want it to happen to me." It came out sounding like I spent my life interviewing plane-crash survivors instead of technocrats, but she started to relax. "Look, Mrs. Augustus, I know this phone call came from out of the blue. How about if I give you the phone number here—or you can have the operator give it to you—and you can call me collect, just so you'll know that I am who I say I am."

"Well, I don't know if that's necessary." She hesitated, but her voice had softened a little. "Just what is it you want to know?"

"When your husband died, were you with him?"

"No. He was in a medical facility in New York, a place called the Doan Institute. It was a next-to-last hope for us. If that didn't work, he'd heard of a place in Denmark with some new experimental therapy. But we never got the chance. Too little, too late."

"I'm sorry."

"So am I." She let out a sigh. "Anyway, he failed suddenly. I would have been there, but there was no time. They called me and told me he was dead. When I got the news, I had some kind of anxiety attack, and they put me into the hospital for fear that it was my heart."

"Were you with him before that?"

"No. He wanted to be alone. To work it out, he said. Then he was supposed to come home. But he never got that far."

"Look, I hate to ask this next question, but I have to. Please understand that I am not implying anything—"

"Go ahead."

"Could your husband have gone out of the country for even a day without your knowledge?"

"No. You had to know Albert. He was really quite predictable. And he was really in no condition to do that anyway. He was undergoing various cancer treatments, terrible treatments. I felt that I should have been there with him,

but you couldn't argue with Albert, not even when he was
dying, and he made me promise not to come. It was something about his not wanting me to remember him—that way.
I couldn't break a promise to Albert, but I wish I'd never
made it." Her voice trembled and she paused, then added,
"Well, he's with me now. He was cremated, which is what
he wanted, and his ashes were shipped to me. And I scattered
them over our garden. He always felt that it was so beautiful
there."

"Did Dr. Augustus have a passport?"

"Oh, yes. We traveled some, especially once the children
were grown. The problem wasn't traveling; it was the sun."

"Do you—I know this may seem silly—do you know where
his passport is?"

"No. At least not offhand. But I might be able to find it."

"I wonder if you would try, and then call me collect?"

"I already told you that he wasn't out of the country, if
that's what you're wondering about."

"I believe you. But if he wasn't, somebody used his name,
and I'd like to try to find out who and how. And it'll be
a lot easier with the real Dr. Augustus's passport and passport photo. Naturally, you don't have to do anything you
don't want to, Mrs. Augustus, but I'm sure that if someone
was using your husband's identification, you'd like to know
about it."

"You can be sure of *that*," she said, sounding a little feist-
ier.

"I'll give you my phone number. I'll be here all day tomorrow."

She agreed to get back to me.

"One more question. Was your husband ever interested
in marine biology? Forensic pathology? Did he specialize in
anything like that?"

"Oh, heavens no. Albert was sort of a small-town family
doctor. Like Marcus Welby, if you remember him."

I hung up and sat back in my chair and stared out the

window at the office building across the way. It was an older building, its brick yellowed by exposure to the weather and pollution, a once-famous hotel covered with tons of gothic gingerbread. Now, in the evening sun, its gargoyles threw long shadows.

Stella beeped.

She had come up with several hits on the Portuguese man-of-war search, the most recent of which was datelined Atlantic Beach, N.C., about a year earlier. "Hundreds of Portuguese man-of-war jellyfish," the AP wire said, "floated ashore on beaches during the weekend, and swimmers were warned to avoid the water. . . . More than 30 swimmers were stung . . . two victims were being treated at Carteret County General Hospital." By the following afternoon, the item said, a shift in the wind had apparently eased the threat.

Another incident had taken place a year before that: "An eight-mile-long slimy mass in Washington's inland marine waters," the article said, "is made up of velellas." The item explained that velellas, though closely related to the Portuguese man-of-war, pose no threat to humans.

Most recent was the man-of-war invasion of southern Florida beaches a few days before Christmas, which left hundreds of sting victims in its wake. The item pointed out that the creatures are traditionally washed ashore in large numbers by strong east winds from December to May, and that "ounce for ounce, the man-of-war's protein-based venom is almost three times as toxic as that of the Asian cobra. The stings, however, seldom are serious because the bladder-like creature doesn't inject large doses of its poisons into the victim's bloodstream."

Outside of that, there wasn't much. "The bizarre and beautiful organism," as one on-line encyclopedia called it, rarely made any significant news.

A man had died, that was certain. So far all parties seemed to agree that he had died of unnatural causes. The question was, what causes? The Portuguese man-of-war theory was at least plausible. But if one could assume Maria Zaychek to be an accurate barometer of the customary behavior of her mate, Zaychek would not have been swimming alone in the first place. And the doctor who supposedly ascertained the cause of death was a man from Cincinnati who was himself dead, and according to *his* wife, was not even in Bermuda to make the diagnosis.

I began jotting a few things down. And then it hit me.

How could a physician from Cincinnati, particularly one who avoided the beach, be familiar enough with a Portuguese man-of-war sting to name it as a probable cause of death? Augustus had probably never *seen* such a case.

Stella was glowing at me; the time had gone so swiftly that I was now sitting in semidarkness. It was after seven; only a few people were left in the editorial department.

I switched on a desk light and typed in a command telling Stella to open a new file designated *Physalia,* the scientific name for the Portuguese man-of-war. And then I started typing everything I knew at this point, everything that wasn't making sense:

> Based on what his widow says, Augustus couldn't have offered an immediate opinion as to the cause of death.
>
> Katharine Augustus claims her husband was not in Bermuda at all. Check with Doan Institute as to Augustus's whereabouts on 6/18.
>
> If Augustus was not in Bermuda, could someone else have been traveling on Augustus's passport? Not logical—why would a person traveling illegally make himself public by offering help at a drowning?

To these I added Maria Zaychek's suspicions.

What I ended up with was a list of inconsistencies, things that simply didn't hold together, and I was now beginning to see the incident through the eyes of Maria Zaychek. Of course, life isn't always consistent. It was like what they say about medical students; teach them enough of the symptoms and they begin to think they have the disease.

But it was more than that. I had only just begun, and it seemed I was already finding a few possible holes in the official story.

Or maybe it was just fun to take a break from the writing business.

I decided to go right over to the Barclay and have a drink and think about it.

There is no way of determining with any degree of accuracy the actual annual incidence of coelenterate stings. On the basis of the published reports from 1836 through 1960, there have been >502 stings with >46 fatalities, giving a crude case fatality rate of about 9 percent.
　　　　　　　　—Bruce W. Halstead, M.D.,
　　　　　　　　　　Poisonous and Venomous
　　　　　　　　　　Marine Animals of the World

S tella spoiled me. After you've used computerized data bases for a while—after you get dependent upon them— you begin to think that all the world's knowledge is waiting to be tapped. It was only after weeks of using Stella on a regular basis that I had to admit there were things she didn't have and, even more disappointing, some things she couldn't even tell me where to find.

When that happens, Stella sounds like an overworked lover: SORRY, ALEX BLACK, YOUR SEARCH TERM CANNOT BE SATISFIED. If the traditional 0 DOCUMENTS SATISFY SEARCH is what they call user friendly, then Stella is user intimate, with hundreds of "human" responses in memory, one for every occasion, and sometimes—like when I'm alone in my office late at night, and a response I've never seen before appears on the terminal screen—I realize that I'm smiling. Which makes me feel like an idiot, because a computer programmed to sound sincere is by definition anything but—like the parakeet pet of a childhood friend who used to say, "I'm Chipper Berman. Wanna kiss?"

Because Stella is far more dependable than any human being, learning about her fallibility was for me sort of like learning that your brain surgeon's last patient became a vegetable. We want our computers—like we want our physicians—to be *beyond* human. Computers *are* that, but they're only as good as the hardware, the software, and what they can handle in memory; in fact, a vast amount of what has been committed to paper is still not in data bases. Sure, with just about all of today's news and stock reports and the like being handled by computers, almost every scrap of every major newspaper and news service goes into a data base. But try to find something that happened ten years ago. There may be references to the article and indices, so you can learn where to find it or even order it, but the article itself may exist only in hard copy, the actual publication, until such time as somebody gets around to making it part of a data base. This is not so tough—there are optical scanners that can "read" data into memory from hard copy—but there have to be commercial incentives.

And you can count on one hand—and still have enough fingers left to imitate Scott Joplin—the number of people who are preoccupied with physalia, the Portuguese man-of-war.

I told Maria Zaychek that I wasn't one of them. But I probably knew as much or more than the average science buff, and I knew that I would be better at employing the scientific method than just another guy looking through a data base. Chase knew that, too, and I was in no position to decide not to help out.

But most important, I was interested. I'd had years of interviewing and researching and writing, and I couldn't remember writing anything that hadn't come from somebody else's experiences. I knew of the war against cancer, but I never fought in it; I knew of animal society without ever observing it firsthand; I knew the leap into space without ever witnessing a live launch. This time it was different, first person singular, something waiting for *me*. I liked the taste and the smell of it.

Besides, I could never resist a puzzle. Even as a kid, I was a fanatic. Give me a tough one and I'd sit there for hours working at it. Some kids got competitive on the football field, but I never cared for contact sports. I was a shrimp until I was fifteen or so, the last guy picked when they chose up sides, so I ended up in arenas that took a different kind of talent—chess, pool, the science club. I wanted to test the limits, loved the act of discovery and had to find out things for myself—the kind of kid who would touch the wall to make sure the WET PAINT sign was right.

So I told Chase yes.

But first things first: signs on the beach notwithstanding, I had no real evidence that a Portuguese man-of-war actually *could* cause death, nor how common it was. I knew what I believed, what I'd heard, but empiricism starts at home. I'd have to *confirm* the deaths.

And when I asked Stella to provide some actual stats, she came up empty.

That's why I was about to do it the hard way—in the library on the second floor of Philadelphia's Academy of Natural Sciences, a VISITOR tag clipped to my shirt. I had called Dr. Arnold Vogel, the Academy's mollusk expert, whom I'd met while doing a piece on mercury concentrations in clam and oyster beds. "All I know about jellyfish," he said, "is not to step on them"—but he recommended a comprehensive work in the Academy library: *Poisonous and Venomous Marine Animals of the World,* by Bruce W. Halstead, M.D., director of the World Life Institute and one of the world's heavyweights on the subject. The work filled an enormous volume with a cast of characters that could make you swear off salt water forever.

The Academy had been my childhood stomping ground. I grew up fascinated by the natural world; the idea that dinosaurs once roamed where there were now traffic circles gave me, even as a child, some idea of my place in time, of the continuum, although I had to stretch my imagination to encompass a future that would not include me. I loved saying words like *brontosaurus* and *pterodactyl* and—my favorite, because it sounded so scientific—*Tyrannosaurus rex*. Under the covers at night I often pictured myself (with the kind of inaccuracies you'd expect from a little kid who pictured a prehistory that lasted about ten years) as early man trying to survive on the same planet with these incredible giants while playing hero to several female pithecanthropi.

From the outside, the Academy hadn't changed much since I roamed those rooms filled with luminescent beetles, glow-in-the-dark minerals, and stuffed birds and zebras and low-land gorillas. It was still an imposing red-brick institutional-looking building with block granite trim and two entrances, one facing the Benjamin Franklin Parkway, the other on 19th Street. These days there were huge banners over the arches of the entrances to call attention to the treasures that awaited therein, and the building itself seemed to have grown a little smaller as I had grown larger. But to me, it was essentially what it had always been: a place where my pulse quickened at the very sight of a skull, a chunk of pyrite, a feather. When I was a child, the simple anticipation of a visit was almost too much to bear. As a grown-up, I still leave there with a residue of scholarship and curiosity that won't wash off, and feel the tug to immerse myself in the exploration of uncharted territory for many days afterward.

I got off the elevator at the second floor and walked through the glass-windowed double door of the Academy library.

The library was a large, square open room with high windows; through those windows, around the room's perimeter, light poured and was deflected by the high, dark, polished wooden bookcases, then caught the dust hovering like a microcosmic Milky Way high above my head. There were cozy little reading areas, culs-de-sac with rectangular tables and chairs insulated from one another by heavily stocked shelves of volumes that varied in size and age. In the center of the room stood an oak card catalog, and except for an anachronistic copy machine that groaned and clanked as it ran, the room seemed relatively untouched by time, the way old libraries with old books do. There were more workers on this particular morning than visitors, scattered about at a few desks, each of them seemingly engaged in work that required neither speed or human interaction.

I filled out a slip for the Halstead book. Once I had it in front of me, I felt a little better about Stella, because reports of Portuguese man-of-war stings were far less common than the occurrences. Hospitals generally didn't bother keeping accurate or detailed records of such events, and quite often attacks would be attributed to specific jellyfish with no real evidence that those particular animals were responsible.

But the case was made: jellyfish could kill. In 1927, four people were stung, two fatally, by "jellyfish" in the Philippines. Between 1937 and 1951 in North Queensland, Australia, ten deaths from physalia were reported; in 1958, a physalia death in the Philippines; in 1960, two deaths from chironex in Australia. The list, which was erratic and incomplete, went on, including some of the more widely publicized mass stingings, all of them a matter of record, but it was offered with apologies; it was only as accurate as poor record-keeping would allow. Today the activities of jellyfish are still widely misunderstood, and most people can't tell a Portuguese man-of-war from a pair of water wings. Reporting is catch as catch can, with even the best scientific literature contradicting itself. In fact, while the Halstead book claimed over forty-six recorded fatalities, another source speaks of at least sixty deaths from jellyfish stings along the northern Australian coast alone.

I spent as much time reading as I could—what the book lacked in reports of actual occurrences it made up for in its historical references and medical and toxicological observations—then photocopied the rest.

There was a cool breeze blowing in from the south when I left the Academy, so the six-block walk back toward center city—what Philadelphians call the downtown area where I live—wasn't bad. I have something in common with the late Dr. Augustus—a sensitivity to the sun that makes my skin resemble the surface of Mars when I'm crazy enough to let it get burnt. Despite that, I like the heat and don't sweat easily. That should have been perfect for my ex-wife, who couldn't stand natural body fluids of any kind—blood, sweat, tears or what have you. Or what had I.

Seven years after the marriage was over, I understood. Carol was fashionable above all, sleek and tanned, with a nose job, copper hair and a space between her thumb and forefinger labeled INSERT CREDIT CARD HERE. I was part of her wardrobe, a piece of intellectual camouflage she pulled out whenever she felt the need to prove that she was not merely chic. I, on the other hand, was so out of touch with her world that I might've thought Bill Blass played shortstop. Those were the days when my hair was "professionally styled" and when Carol went with me to shop for clothes, but the guys in *GQ* always ended up looking taller than me. Maybe because they were. Once, after I'd bought a pair of knee-high canvas boots at Carol's insistence, she said they would look better with my trousers tucked in. Anybody who's ever seen a guy in that kind of getup knows it takes a certain something to pull it off, and I didn't have that certain something; that same day I was in a hotel lobby and somebody thought I was the doorman.

At first Carol laughed. I was counterpoint, she thought, an oboe to play against her flute. But in time I learned that she was no flute. She was a piano, a solo instrument at heart, and what she really needed, although she didn't know it, was a string section, a chorus, all the right costumes and one hell of a stage set.

I don't say it was all her fault. Maybe she was my camouflage, too.

Our mistake was in getting married. I liked the way she looked and she liked the way I looked, and we were young enough to let it go at that. Because we didn't have the same admiration for each other's intellects. Things were swell when we weren't thinking, before Saks became more important than sex, but after a while we both knew I was the wrong guy for her. I needed somebody with brains to make me happy. She needed somebody with purchasing power.

And she was just traditional enough to not be able to understand why I didn't want to get it for her. She wanted me to go into business for myself—start an ad agency, make real money. I couldn't understand why she'd want me to do that when she knew that I liked to write, and that I was happy at the time putting out an unprofitable alternative weekly called *Street Sounds*. Is that any way, I would wonder, to treat someone you love? If she wanted all that, I would tell her, why didn't *she* start a business? I would certainly do anything I could to help her—short of finding another career.

Carol thought that was ridiculous; after all, she would say, I was the man of the family. She sounded like she was trapped in the 1950s, despite the fact that she hadn't been born until then. It turned into a strange marriage, maybe because I didn't grow straight and erect like all the other guys—I didn't *want* a BMW, didn't *want* the expensive suits. When I walked down Walnut Street I'd feel like all the shops, the SALE signs, the boutique displays, were for other people, people of another species. I'd see a mannequin in a men's store window and it wouldn't occur to me that somebody put it there so that I would maybe buy something. Before I'd spend money on socks, even, I'd go back two, three times to make sure I really wanted them. I had no sense of fashion. I still don't. But now I have some sense of proportion. Now I realize that it isn't the tie around your neck that chokes you, it's the situation.

We separated peacefully; Carol married a guy with more money. That didn't last, either; they could afford to go anywhere they wanted, but Carol couldn't enjoy herself once she got there. Not with that joker.

These days when I see her, which is usually on the street and always by accident, we chat like ex-college-roommates who have nothing in common except the room they once shared. Her business is going well, she always says, and I tell her what little there is to tell about me, and then we shake hands, which I find preferable to kissing her cheek while she kisses the air, for which inconvenience half my face gets to smell like Secret of Venus for the next four hours. Carol was when I stopped liking perfume.

I was almost back to Rittenhouse Square when I realized that I'd been thinking about the marriage since leaving the Academy of Natural Sciences. For a moment that unnerved me. But I chalked it up to the fact that I was on my way to a little second-story salad-and-sandwich place on Sansom Street to meet Carol's polar opposite.

I walked into the air conditioning, then took the steps two at a time. I was looking for Angel to be sitting at the little table in the corner.

She was.

Six months had passed since the first time I saw her—at an American Bar Association seminar on libel in which I was a speaker. I wasn't the ABA's first choice, but nobody else at *World* could make it and I love the subject. Angel asked a couple of smart, tough questions from the audience. During the coffee break, she stood on the fringes of the crowd of questioners and waited, and I became increasingly aware that every time I looked up, she was looking into my eyes. That's unusual even when you're the center of what's going on; when people are listening to you, their gaze normally shifts from your eyes to your mouth. It's a very subtle eye movement, perhaps, but it's perceptible if you're looking for it, and it's what makes the difference between someone who's paying attention and someone who's doing something else entirely. Angel was doing something else entirely, and soon I was, too, glancing up and then down and then shifting back to one or another questioner.

She had below-shoulder-length dark brown hair and a full mouth, but a thin nose and pale skin—products, I would learn, of a Spanish father and an Irish mother, respectively—and dark green eyes from which shone not only intelligence but a variety of wonders: a certain intensity, a brooding passion, curiosity, all of it quiet and serious and unstudied. I can spot an enigma at ten feet, and Angel looked like a combination of librarian and hooker and little girl lost. Unbeatable.

She wore a midnight-blue dress that hugged her gently, with a ruffled front that was open to where her cleavage began. That dress wasn't entirely appropriate for an American Bar Association meeting, she told me later—something I hadn't noticed—but it was all she'd had at the time due to an unsteady income resulting from her fast burnout rate on practically any job.

"Hello," I'd finally said.

"Hello." A quick smile.

"Are you a lawyer?"

"A paralegal."

"Uh-huh. And you're interested in libel?"

"Well, actually, in writing."

"What kind of writing?"

"I'm not sure yet."

It could have been an awkward, painful conversation, but it wasn't.

"Well," I shuffled, "is there something you wanted to ask me? Something I can help you with?"

She shrugged, smiled a quick, nervous smile, bit her lip. And then got businesslike. "I think I'm a good writer, but I'm operating in a vacuum. I think maybe it's time to involve a professional . . ."

I was a sucker for the pitch and for whatever else Angel had, and the subliminal flirtation didn't hurt. She could've done it in front of a dozen witnesses and nobody would've seen it except me. And I liked the ambivalence, the way she was fighting it while doing it, pulling her eyes away, fumbling with her notepad.

She wasn't a bad writer, but she turned out to be a terrific photographer. In the following months she saved up her money and put a darkroom into her basement, and in a relatively short time, through a lot of lunch-hour pavement-pounding, she began to get some photojournalism assignments. But she was still a long way from being able to support herself at it.

Now we sat across from each other in an unchic restaurant about a block from my apartment, a place we liked because the food could never attract a crowd, and I was bringing her up to date on the events of the last week, a period during which a death in her family had taken her out of town. I told her about the column I was writing, the research I was doing, the Portuguese man-of-war. She told me how she had finally decided to start redecorating her house.

She lived in a low-income part of town, a mostly white neighborhood—Irish, Polish and Ukrainian—with a smattering of blacks and Hispanics. It was not, she had initially warned me, a feast for the eyes; from her tiny front porch it was only a block to the huge monolithic structure of Interstate 95, and in the early-morning hours, when the sun came up over the Delaware River, she literally lived in its shadow. Because of her proximity to the river and to the piers of the Port of Philadelphia, and because her one-way street was an alternate route that let the truckers cut out a traffic light, the block was constantly vibrating from the noise and weight of huge semis. That, and traffic from a dozen surrounding arteries, blanketed the area with a gray pall; fresh white paint quickly became jaundiced. Because of the income level of the neighborhood, and because the only businesses there served the people who lived there, storefronts were tired and worn-looking before their time, not unlike the men and women who spent their lives waiting for buses and trolleys on the corners there, and all but the best-intentioned store owners soon stopped repainting the exteriors. It was a place of heavy drinking and hand-me-downs, of little Irish bars with neon shamrocks and a handful of regulars to keep them alive, of women who either used too much makeup or stopped trying, of men who shaved twice a week. And all the time, traffic.

But there were compensations; the house was large inside and well insulated and cheap to maintain, and because of where it was, it had been easy to buy. While the neighborhood might have looked less than desirable to a visitor from center city, to Angel it was home—she had grown up just two blocks away—and the people, the trucks, the hand-lettered signs, the trolleys, the men who ran the markets and the women behind the restaurant counters, were hers; I wondered if they would become mine. At night, sometimes, after we made love, I would lie there and watch through the bedroom window the distant lights of the traffic on I-95 as it moved in its measured pace, the headlights glistening like tiny bubbles in an intravenous tube.

It sounds wonderful, and sometimes it was.

We talked. I told her about my conversation with Colin Chase, with Maria, with Mrs. Augustus.

"You're excited about this," she said. "I would be, too."

I could tell from the way she said it that all was not well.
"What's wrong?"

"The job. You know."

"The job?"

"It's boring. There's no challenge. This morning they offered me more responsibility, and it's still going to be easy.
I'm not using . . . me. My mind, my creativity. I feel like
every day is a waste of time."

"Why not coast for a while? Tick the days off and use the
evenings and weekends to really get down to the writing and
photography."

She shook her head. "I go home tired. I mean, the work
is work, whether it's hard or not. Besides, I'm not disciplined
like you, Alex," she sighed. "Listen, can we talk about something else?"

This was our dilemma. I could be only certain things to
Angel; there were places I would never reach because the
furies that lived within her had long-term leases, and I didn't
know how to evict them. Despite her intelligence, despite
how easily she absorbed facts and applied concepts, she had
come of age in the streets, where people were identified as
friends or enemies, and was a combatant of that arena. She
had little understanding of such things as supply and demand.
If someone declined to buy her talent, that was a hostile act.

She was a good but unpolished writer, a diamond in the
rough who might never be anything but, because she could
not accept the fact that everybody begins like a beginner,
and it usually shows.

Sometimes Angel would do some writing and then ask me
what I thought of it, and I would tell her. Sometimes she
would even listen to me, but if this resulted in her selling
the piece to a newspaper or a magazine, she would attribute
the sale to my input, not to her talent. And sometimes she
would decide, after a rejection slip or two, that rather than
follow my suggestions, she would destroy what she had writ-

ten, assuming that to change it was to destroy it anyway. She couldn't be edited; she took it too personally.

The funny thing was, she knew it. She recognized what was happening while it was going on, with the same clarity of vision with which she saw practically everything else. And she couldn't do anything about it. Sometimes she would use sex to chase the feeling, replacing her failure with some kind of acceptance and success—and not just with me.

It was hard to switch gears. I just talked. Eventually I found myself drawing a diagram on a napkin, showing her how a nematocyst injected its venom.

She made a good stab at being companionable. "It's an interesting name," she said of the Portuguese man-of-war, "an animal named after a human invention instead of the other way around. I mean, there are all kinds of products named after animals—like Cougars and Pintos—but I can't think of any animals named after products."

Neither could I.

As Aesop knew and as Angel reiterated, the diversity of the nonhuman world provides endless metaphors for humans; if they are now all clichés, that testifies only to their universal applicability. We have our sharks and gorillas and vipers, our pigs and weasels, our wolves in sheep's clothing and snakes in the grass. The passive among us are lambs or pussycats, but then there are tigers and Dobermans, too. We play possum or fight like cornered rats, and sometimes we even find ourselves in the doghouse. And despite the fact that our least attractive traits are particularly human, we use *animal* as a synonym for the worst among us.

The Portuguese man-of-war is an exception, an animal named after one of man's early messengers of destruction— in this case, a heavily armed ship that roamed the seas from the fifteenth century until ships of wood became obsolete, depending upon the wind in its huge sails to deliver it to and from its enemies.

"Perfect name for it." This was a day or two later, Dr. Schmidt speaking. I had finally located her office at the Bio-Life Sciences Building on the eastern edge of the Temple University campus, found it despite several encounters with students who didn't know where the building was—one of them while he was standing in its lobby. Schmidt, in a white lab jacket, peered up at me and withdrew a gloved hand from an aquarium, one of several large tanks that surrounded her, waved and put it back in.

"Anemones," she said, nodding down at her submerged progeny. "One day happily paralyzing little fishies in Australia, a few days later in a tank in a university science building." She shrugged. "That's life. Are you Alex Black?"

I was, and this was Inga Schmidt, Ph.D.: late twenties, tall, bookish, thick lenses in tortoiseshell frames, nice nose, reddish hair knotted in the back, good legs encased in blue jeans, and bubbly about her specialty, which was invertebrates and zooplankton, the latter being a group of animals identified by what they *can't* do—swim against the current. The Portuguese man-of-war is one of them.

"So it puts up this tinted translucent sail and uses it to navigate," Schmidt said. She had led me from her lab to an adjoining smaller room which looked something like her office, and which had the aura of a place in which guests were less common than mollusks. There was clutter everywhere: papers, magazines, scientific journals, bookshelves to the ceiling, and Schmidt's small desk covered with what looked like the papers of students currently under scrutiny. If the red scrawls on those papers were indicative, Schmidt could be tough.

She sat down on a leatherette desk chair, her longish legs pressed together at the knees, her toes pointed slightly inwards at the base of the triangle they formed. I sat just a few inches from her—we were in cramped quarters—on a small folding chair with a flat, unforgiving wooden seat. On the walls around us were color photographs of sea creatures, some visible only where the light struck them, hanging in the water as amorphous as ghosts, others solid and spiny with saw-toothed edges like medieval weaponry.

"Of course, it's *not* a sail," she went on. "It's an inflatable bladder that catches the wind and adapts to it, constantly changing its shape—*trimming* itself, to use a nautical term—and in this way traveling hundreds of miles at a time. In schools of thousands."

Schmidt, it turned out, had been delighted to have the

opportunity to talk about jellyfish, and had fallen into the mode she used on her first-year biology students, spending a lot of time on the basics. I didn't stop her; if she enjoyed the process, I figured she wouldn't mind doing it again later, when the questions would be tougher.

"Picture a mass up here." She pointed to her hand, which, now poised in midair as though afloat on an imaginary sea, obviously represented the man-of-war's bladder with its bubblelike chambers; the fingers of that hand, one of which had a thin gold band, were curved into a sinister umbrella. "With a red crest running lengthwise here." She used the index finger of her free hand to draw a line across her knuckles.

I asked for an indication of size, and she moved her hands to define a shape about the size of a football. "Sometimes this big. And fairly colorful—it can range from deep red to greenish blue." Her hand became a physalia again.

"But the man-of-war appellation goes further, Mr. Black," Schmidt said with great relish. "Physalia belongs to a group of what we call colonial siphonophores. The man-of-war is an animal, yes, but it's really a *colony* of animals—like the crew of the ship." She seemed delighted by her metaphor and smiled. She had an attractive overbite.

"Now, this contradicts many of the preconceptions people have about life. Imagine yourself as not just one individual, but several—a head individual and a right-arm individual and a left-arm individual and a mouth individual and a digestive-tract individual and so on, each of which is born and dies and regenerates independently. You lose your head, another grows. Your parts function together, and they're dependent upon one another, and yet they're different from *you*. How? Why? That's the puzzle. It's not enough to say that you are the colony, or they are your inhabitants. There is no *you* without the colony; there is no *they* without the colony.

"A Portuguese man-of-war, for instance, includes as its

crew a variety of creatures called hydrozoans, each group of which handles a particular life function and gradually becomes modified so that it can better handle that function. Some polyps modify themselves into the gas-filled bladder; some modify themselves into long tentacles; some of them retain the ability to ingest and swallow and digest food; some of them are simply reproductive. And some—the nematocysts—just do the killing."

"Pretty efficient."

"Yes, and as time goes by, the coordination between the individuals becomes better and better, just as it would on a real sailing vessel. It's not that they *know* anything; it's that the nervous systems become more and more integrated as these individuals become more and more specialized. And the more the individuals become coordinated, the more the colony acts like a single organism."

"Suppose one of these individuals dies? Do they all die?"

"No, but a good question," Schmidt enthused professorially. "The colony is not *just* its individuals; it has a collective self. Even though some individuals die and others are born, the colony has a life span separate from its individuals and, in fact, outlives its individuals. So nobody really knows how old the colony is. The life and death of the colony's individuals are not the life and death of the colony."

Imagining this, if you imagine it correctly, can make your brain ache.

"Now, under the float here"—Schmidt was gesturing with her index finger—"are gastrozooids, the polyps that do the eating, swallowing, digesting. Lots of them here." She pointed under the umbrella of her fingers. "Each one has a mouth, with tentacles hanging from the base. Not tentacles like you'd see in an octopus—"

"More like ribbons."

"Yes. Sometimes scores of them. They don't need strength; they need flexibility. They're very contractile and extensible.

And very long, some of them—sixty feet or so in physalia, and some say more than that, although I've never seen them quite that long.

"Okay, the gastrozooids eat the fish that are paralyzed by the nematocysts, which are the stinging polyps. And it's in the tentacles that we find the nematocysts." Now the fingers of her right hand were drawing imaginary strands down from the fingertips of her left. "They're tiny, but each one contains a long, threadlike stinger—very thin, but capable of penetrating a surgical glove. Okay, along comes an unsuspecting fish"—she wiggled her hand toward the imaginary tentacles—"and *whomp*." Her hand went palm up. "All except for a fish called *Nomeus gronovii,* which lives within the tentacles of physalia in a symbiotic relationship. You know, another fish comes along, sees the tasty-looking gronovii, and takes a shot. Next thing you know, physalia is eating the intruder, and gronovii is getting the table scraps."

"What's your experience with humans and physalia stings?"

She waved at the walls. "See those books?"

I nodded, getting up to look.

"Don't bother. Almost nothing there. It's underreported, underresearched. For a number of reasons. First, it's not the kind of research that attracts funds, so that limits it. Second, it's hard to get good data. For instance, your specific interest is physalia. We think that there have been deaths due to physalia stings, but we don't know how many. Maybe more than we know about, maybe not. Statistically, it's not the most dangerous hydrozoan, but it's the one people often think of first. Probably because it's so exotic. Or maybe because it's so visible."

"Not the most dangerous—"

"For two reasons. Partly because you have this bladder floating on the top of the water. It's very easy to spot, and if you saw it you'd probably be inclined to give it a wide berth. It's unpleasant-looking. *Weird.* Like those pods in *The Invasion of the Body Snatchers.* Sinister, not beautiful. Except, of course, to somebody like me. And then, a single physalia—we're talking about *Physalia physalis*, I presume—"

"Yes. Not the bluebottle."

"Okay. And what you're dealing with here, I think you said on the phone, is a death due to a toxic sting, and statistically physalia isn't nearly as likely to be responsible for that as some other kind of jellyfish. It's not the most toxic— it would take a pretty hefty physalia sting to kill you. Unless, of course, you already had a weak heart or a respiratory problem or were particularly allergic. Or so we think; as I said, a lot of this is based on limited data.

"On the other hand, there are some of the cubomedusae, particularly chironex and chiropsalmus, that are extremely dangerous."

"I'm not familiar with them."

"No reason why you should be. Chironex occurs from Australia to Asia, chiropsalmus around the Philippines. Although I've always felt that they're wider spread than that, and that some of the stings attributed to physalia could well be from other members of this family.

"I'll tell you how toxic chironex is," Schmidt said, leaning forward. "If one of these things no bigger than this, and probably smaller"—she made a circle by touching her thumb to her index finger—"stung you, you could be dead within seconds. They're hard to spot, almost invisible in the water, extremely toxic—and there's no antidote."

"You know where I can see one?"

"Alive? Hard to say. They're rarely taken, and when they are they sometimes end up in aquaria for photographic purposes, but they don't keep well. And out there in the water where they belong, they're extremely hard to see—small, virtually transparent. I wouldn't suggest you go looking for them." She laughed.

"You mean nobody's raising them?"

"Not in these parts. It's almost impossible. You can rear

a tiny polyp through part of the life cycle, but raising one to adulthood isn't easy. You'd need a huge tank. And some of these animals are so toxic, it's like handling radioisotopes. You can't bring the tentacles into contact with bare skin without tempting fate. People have to wear protective clothing to handle them. I've talked with some people who've worked with them in Australia, and they have a great deal of respect for them, to say the least. It's like working with cobras. In fact, it's worse, because they look so benign."

Schmidt had, she said, recently come back from Australia, where she'd spent the Christmas season—it was late spring and early summer down under—doing research.

"Part of the difficulty in collecting data is that bathers get stung and, in great pain, either drown or stagger onto the beach and fall over and die there if they're not given first aid immediately. CPR is the only thing that would be meaningful, since these stings tend to affect respiration in just about every case; often the lungs fill with mucus and you suffocate or choke to death, pulmonary edema. But CPR doesn't guarantee anything, because sometimes other organs become involved. These toxins can cause anaphylactic reactions—sort of like an allergic reaction to a drug. And there's no cure, no antidote, if you get enough. Nobody actually knows how much it takes, or how much gets into people when they're stung, but it's very fast-acting, like a fatal heart attack. Causes an almost-instantaneous shock reaction. In some cases the bite is so small it's hardly more than a fleabite, and you might feel almost nothing when it happens, but in a short time, sometimes just a few minutes, there's pain. There's *always* pain. In a worst-case scenario, it can be so excruciating that victims become irrational, screaming, dying in agony."

"In other words, the person's on the beach but the animal's still in the water."

"Right. But it's usually fairly clear what happened. Sometimes there will be tentacles adhering to the body. Almost always the body will show marks. A lot depends upon the species and the sting and the allergic reaction of the individual—different people react differently. But it's usually apparent that there's been a jellyfish sting, and the configurations of the markings depend upon the type of jellyfish. Physalia generally doesn't leave massive wheals, but the cubomedusae do. And despite my comment about fleabites, they're not really like an insect sting. They're more commonly like welts left by, say, a whip, although more veinlike in appearance. Sometimes they can look as if they've been tattooed onto the body."

"Jeez."

"My sentiments exactly. In most cases nobody asks questions—the coroner sees it as an open-and-shut case—and frankly, I'd say that most times the death, or the attack if the person survives, is probably attributed to the wrong animal. Rarely does anyone see the jellyfish inflict the sting. Rarely does anyone properly preserve the tentacles, which can be helpful in identification. If somebody has a little knowledge, that's what goes on the medical report, right or wrong. They call it a Portuguese man-of-war sting, or a jellyfish sting, and let it go at that. And why not? The person is dead or the person survives. There's nothing to be done about it. There's no way to prevent the next occurrence. It's not exactly a public health menace. They post signs on the beach warning people to be careful, and that's it.

"Me, I don't go into salt water for pleasure. It's strictly business. I'm like the surgeon who's removed too many lungs to be able to enjoy a smoke."

"Maddie asked me to drop this on you," Pete said, tossing a package onto my IN chair. It was a little after ten on a Monday morning; with my door open, I could hear the soft click of fingers tap-dancing on keyboards. "She said to make sure you saw it. What's it all about?"

People always took Pete for younger than he was, partly due to his appearance, short and pudgy with dimples and a thick mustache and hair cut in a sort of pageboy, and partly due to his enthusiasm. He hadn't had enough of the business to grow jaded, and he could greet the most innocuous slip of paper—in this case, a hand-addressed brown kraft envelope—with the curiosity of a journalism-school freshman, his cheeks always in a state of anticipatory semi-blush. On the one hand, I envied him that; on the other, it could be a pain in the ass—even now, his eyes remained fixed on the parcel.

"For Chrissakes, Pete, it's an *envelope*. What makes you think it's all about anything?"

"I dunno." He shrugged and smiled. "Something about the way Maddie reacted when she saw it, I guess." He hitched up his pants, which tended to disappear under a stomach far too large for his years. I talked to him often about exercise, but the closest Pete came to any cardiovascular activity was playing blackjack against his computer between articles.

"I think it's a passport," I said.

"You going somewhere?"

"It's not mine. It's some guy's." I changed the subject. "What are you working on?"

"I just finished that microchip piece."

"And now, no doubt, you're looking for something else to do."

"Right," he said. "You need help?"

Like I said, enthusiasm.

Maddie stuck a disheveled head inside the glass door. "You guys gonna want more coffee? . . . so I'll know how much to make."

"Yeah. Thanks. I'll do the next."

"Don't sweat it," she said with a wave of her hand, but before she could leave, I motioned for her to come in, and she did.

"So what can I work on?" Pete said, still not entirely giving up on the envelope.

"Forget that for a minute. Suppose you were an elderly guy dying of cancer. Would you want to die at home, with your loving wife, or would you want to go out trying to make every minute count?"

"I dunno. I'm just a kid," Pete said. "Why? What would you do?"

"I'm asking you. I figure you two are as normal as we get around here."

"Okay," Pete said. "Right now, from my perspective, I'd say that I'd probably want to raise hell, go out with a bang, catch up on what I never had time or the guts to do. But statistically, I know that most people who are dying are too weak to do that. So I don't know. And I don't know how I'd feel looking back on thirty or forty years of history with the same person, so it's hard for me to say how I'd feel. I love my wife, but right now, I think I'd want to jump in a van or on a ship and just go." He looked at Maddie. "How about you?"

"Well," Maddie said, "I'm about as old as Alex, shave off a year or two, and I'm glad you asked me now, because this is as close to elderly as I'm going to get. Now, my first reaction is to jump into the van with Pete here, but that's because I'm divorced and fancy-free—"

"It'd cost you," Pete said.

"You should be so lucky," Maddie shot back. "Anyway, that would be my first inclination under the current circumstances. But ultimately, assuming that I had people I shared my life with, I imagine I'd probaby want what most people end up wanting, and that's to die in bed surrounded by those who adore me. Sounds pretty square, but—"

"That," I said, "is a logical answer."

"That's gonna be a pretty empty bed," Pete joked, and beat it. Maddie gave me a look, shook her head and followed him.

Logically, everything inside me told me that Maddie was right.

I figured that the contents of the envelope would tell me at least one thing: whether Augustus had been in Bermuda. If he had, it would mean that Augustus had for some reason kept the trip a secret from his wife—not unheard of in healthy husbands, but unusual behavior for a dying one. On the other hand, if Augustus hadn't been in Bermuda, I was back to square one.

I let the envelope wait and took a manila folder from the corner of my desk.

I now had two files on Zaychek's death—one in Stella's memory, and one in that folder. Stella held the soft copy—everything that I'd pulled from various data bases—and the folder, thickening by the hour, held the hard copy: photocopies that I'd made at the Academy of Natural Sciences; a dozen articles on the medical and toxicological aspects of coelenterate stings; a copy of Augustus's statement to the police that I'd gotten from a reporter at the *Clarion*; some of what I'd edited out of my essay on animal defensive and offensive weaponry (which had turned out to be about venoms and toxins and chemical warfare) inspired by all this, now on the newsstands in the current issue of *World*; a few names I'd scrawled and hadn't gotten around to adding to Stella's PHONE.DIR file, and so on. Halstead had, in his book, warned that the state of the art regarding coelenterates—statistics, stings, rates of incidence and death—was lousy, and he was right; for that reason, even his own book, or at least the parts dependent upon that kind of data, was limited.

This meant, thanks in large part to the resources Stella made available, that at this point I was probably more current—not more knowledgeable, but more current—than practically anyone when it came to Coelenterata. I had given myself a two-week crash course and was now the kind of guy who could tell you enough to make your eyes glaze over at a cocktail party, if I had time for one.

And I felt it. It was the dull ache in my back, my neck. My own eyes were glazing over, and I had reached that semicatatonic state in which—having, in addition, produced my own feature copy for one issue and being up to my ass in copy for the next—I needed some time off.

But the contents of my files wouldn't let me. Nor would that three-inch-high glass jar sitting on my desk: "Yours for a week," Inga Schmidt had said when she handed it to me. "For inspiration."

It was a young specimen, its "head" smaller than the top joint of a human thumb, and it was in fairly good shape, its small tentacles intact. It had turned from its naturally transparent state to a translucent white in the solution in which it had been preserved, and now it hung suspended in the water like a tiny ghost. Back in its natural habitat, poised a scant few inches from the surface of the water, the tiny chironex would have been almost invisible, but even at this size it was capable of inflicting a sting so severe that its popular name, the sea wasp, made it seem far less dangerous than it actually was. I held it up to let the light from my window pass through it.

It was shaped like a thimble, only with squared-off sides,

giving it the cube-like appearance that led to its family name, cubomedusae; on each side was one tiny dark spot smaller than the period at the end of a sentence. These were the eyes, and with them it could see a full three hundred and sixty degrees without moving.

It was hard to reconcile the now-harmless contents of this jar with the picture I took from the manila folder. It was of a child, thirteen, photographed from the chest down, legs spread. He lay on a table, naked except for a small gauze dressing that had been tossed over his crotch. The body looked dead, not only because of the granite whiteness of the flesh but also because the picture had all the warmth of a typical homicide snapshot: shot with flash, hard-edged, black-shadowed, cropped to focus on the gory details.

The dark discoloration started at the boy's thigh, a thick, angry band that twisted into several thinner bands and became more veinous as it ran down his leg, eventually covering half of it in fiery welts. The thinner of these welts formed wormlike random trails on the leg, a circular shape here, an arc there, overlapping; but the heavier ones reminded me of lightning, the way it appears in photographs taken at exactly the right moment: jagged-edged, tearing the darkness in half in its erratic, broken-field run to the ground.

The caption attributed the sting to chironex, and it said the child survived, but that the scars on his leg would be with him for life; I pictured him as an old man—if he lived that long, considering the respiratory and organ damage that might have been done—retelling the story, showing the lightning to his grandchildren.

In the small specimen jar in front of me was the type of creature that had done that—profoundly dangerous, but still not the champion. That title belonged to a sea anenome called palethoa found only one place in the world—an area in Hawaii—which is so toxic that virtually any amount of its venom, palytoxin, if introduced into the bloodstream, can cause death. And if by some chance the venom doesn't go directly into your bloodstream—if it just gets absorbed through the pores—it can destroy the body's immune system; in fact, one marine biologist who received enough of it just by working in the waters around palethoa now has to avoid crowds for fear of contracting disease.

"Here you go," Maddie said, leaving the steaming styrofoam cup.

I took a sip and opened the envelope. It was postmarked August 23; two weeks had gone by since the physalia incident had first come across my terminal. In the envelope was Augustus's passport, issued three years before.

The doctor stared at me, half smiling, from a two-inch-square photograph. He was—had once been, anyway—an amiable-looking man with white hair and a bushy white mustache, and he wore what would be better described as spectacles, not eyeglasses. He looked slightly overweight, although it was hard to tell; besides, that had probably changed with the cancer. According to his date of birth, he died at seventy-seven, and if that was the case, Augustus had been well preserved. The photo didn't show many wrinkles, but then, there had been a lot of light on the face when the photograph had been taken, which would have tended to bleach out detail. Passport photos are notorious for their flatness and lack of chiaroscuro. Furthermore, a slight frown, a pout, a knitting of the brow, a parting or compression of the lips can in an instant change a face into something that it may actually be for only a few seconds a day in real life. This can make the likeness quite different from anything customs officials will meet, but they're used to it, and at only twelve bucks a throw, passport photographers aren't losing any sleep over it.

I flipped through the pages, looking for the rubber-stamp imprint that would tell me that Augustus had been in Bermuda. I didn't find it. I laid the passport aside.

Then, my coffee cup an inch from my face, something jangled in my brain, like what happens when you're only half paying attention as the guy on TV reads the six numbers that will win a multimillion-dollar lottery for somebody, and you suddenly realize that those numbers might have been yours. And when you try to recall them, there's nothing left but a sort of echo.

In my case, I wasn't hearing the numbers of the winning lottery ticket. I was seeing the signature on that passport: Albert M. Augustus.

And I wondered if I had actually seen that signature before. I *should* have. In the manila folder was a statement signed by Albert M. Augustus, M.D., the physician who had witnessed Zaychek's death.

I put the passport and the signed statement side by side.

The signatures were similar, but there were inconsistencies. On the statement, Augustus's hand was stronger, more angular, more controlled. On the passport, it was shakier, perhaps more spontaneous. I would have expected exactly the opposite from a man dying of terminal cancer—that the disease would afflict the handwriting to the degree that it afflicted the body. And there were differences in the individual letters, in the way those letters were made.

I mentally flipped through half a dozen scenarios, even picturing Augustus with an injured arm at the time of the issuance of his passport, or in a particular rush—that would explain the seeming lack of control. But it wouldn't explain the difference in the letters themselves: after all, the same brain that operated the right hand would have been telling the left what to do, so any differences should have been limited to those caused for external reasons.

There was another possibility—that what I received from the police was not a photocopy of the original signed statement, but a copy typed and executed by a clerk and signed by someone else to act as a legally acceptable copy. I quickly rejected that: for that scenario to be plausible, the signatures were too *similar*.

Could Augustus's signature have changed in the three years

from the time of issuance of his passport? It was possible. So was forgery, but as forgery it seemed inept. Besides, why suspect forgery? Forgery to what end?

I don't know how long I sat there looking at those two items, but by the time I called Maria Zaychek, my coffee was as cool as my desktop.

"Interesting," Colin Chase said, staring at the documents on the polished mahogany in front of him, "but I think you're exaggerating the significance. What you're saying is that a passport fails to show that a person was in Bermuda, and that a signature either looks similar enough to refute that or different enough to confirm it. Is that what you're saying?" He shrugged. "What? Which?"

"I don't know. But those signatures—don't you see what I'm talking about?"

"Sure. But so what? What's the significance? Why is it important in any way? It's not as if there are no other possibilities. After all, we're not handwriting experts—"

"Why don't we call one in?"

"Because it's not important enough." Chase flipped through the passport and turned the photocopy of the signed statement over and over in his neatly manicured fingers, even inspecting its blank side as if he expected something to magically appear there. "Maybe somebody made a copy of the document and then signed it because the signature didn't come up—you know, if maybe this doctor, this Augustus, signed the statement in blue ink."

"Makes no sense. Besides, the signature is part of what was photocopied."

"Or maybe his signature changed over the course of the three years. You say he's an older guy, you say he had cancer.

Hell, the bank sometimes questions *my* signature when I go to cash a check."

I shook my head, but in the rational businesslike atmosphere of Chase's office, worlds removed from Maria Zaychek's obsession, it was easy to feel that the real explanation would end up being more simple than sinister.

"Of course, the problem is that now you've called her, and she thinks her suspicions are well founded. You know, she called me all excited about this, like it was a real breakthrough."

"Why is that a problem?"

Chase looked at me as if I were a lunatic. "Because that is exactly what I wanted to avoid. Exactly why I involved you. Bad enough to have Maria Zaychek deluded. Now you?"

"Look, wait. I didn't ask myself to get involved. And *I* didn't sting her husband." I could feel myself losing it.

"Don't get your back up. All I meant to say was, I didn't expect the science editor to turn detective; it was the scientific stuff I was after. The idea was to help Maria understand—"

"Well, I tried. But the lady thinks her husband's death doesn't add up. I would've talked her out of that if all I'd had to do was explain the man-of-war's role. But it's the *human* behavior that needs explaining. So where do I go with that? On the other hand, if we eliminate all the things that don't add up, we can mark it case closed. That's what I thought you wanted. But I can't help it if I find something that just doesn't seem to make sense. I can't help it if things haven't followed your timetable."

"Well, I don't know, Alex. Somehow you received a message other than the one I sent. I'm not saying that it's your fault . . ."

The hell he wasn't.

The conversation was rapidly turning into a pissing contest. If I got Chase to grudgingly admit that I had a point, he wasn't going to like it, and he was the kind of guy who kept score of minor slights. If I dropped the point entirely, Chase would know that I'd backed off just to keep the peace, and he would never forget that, either. Whichever, the outcome would ultimately make my life miserable.

Furthermore, Chase was the consummate politician, and what he said was so often buried in nuance that it wasn't always possible to reconstruct it using language alone; while I could recall the words and phrases—I was good at that—I couldn't be sure that I hadn't misinterpreted his intentions. Did he care how Zaychek died? Or did he just want to get Maria to stop thinking about it? I had no idea. With Chase, there were too many strata between the message and its true meaning.

I'd started out in a plain chrome-and-cane chair in front of Chase's desk, but I didn't like it there; I found myself remembering the attempted brainwashing in *Darkness at Noon*. Now I was walking around the office as we talked, letting Chase's possessions distract me: the thick Persian rug; the imitation-imitation Jackson Pollock from one of New York's lesser galleries; the deep-blue antique dish that served as an ashtray on the marble table in front of the leather couch in his sitting area. I picked up a cigarette lighter that had been made by boring out a piece of old scrimshaw, opened and sniffed and closed a cigar case filled with long thick Belindas smuggled in from Havana, flipped through a magazine, seeing nothing. Flush-mounted windows that started a foot off the floor wrapped around two sides of the corner office, creating the unnerving effect that you could easily walk off the twenty-fourth floor and drop to the street below.

The sky was overcast; rain threatened. On the roofs of the surrounding buildings, huge air-conditioning units, most of them below where I stood, sent up squiggles of heat.

I wondered what it was that made it somehow appropriate for people like Chase, who didn't need the room, to have offices like this.

"Besides," he said, daring to push a little further, "I'm somewhat concerned about you getting distracted from the editorial product."

I felt that one in my shins. "What do you mean?"

"Well, not that there's anything wrong. Although there was some talk that your little essay this week didn't live up to what we've come to expect of you. And I wondered if perhaps I didn't do you an injustice by pulling you away from your work."

"Somebody said something?"

"Well, nothing in particular. Nothing *concrete,* that is. But you know, you get a feeling; you get vibrations."

He was lying. I know when I'm good and when I'm not. But I could feel myself getting defensive, because he was hitting me where I live. *My little essay?*

There was a small antique mirror on the bookshelf in back of his desk, enabling me to see myself while I was facing Chase, and it was clear why Chase, just as a physical specimen alone, was destined to be more successful with the big boys. I looked like my job the way he looked like his: I had the pallor of a guy who lived in a fluorescent-light solar system; I had a do-it-yourself haircut; my sports jacket had, like atrophied muscle, given up the fight, and for all I knew the slacks I was wearing were shiny in the seat and my shirt was frayed at the collar.

No, the verdict was in: I was a guy who could look at home at a keyboard or a concert, a poolroom, a library, a bar, but not in a boardroom. I seemed to reflect all the occupational hazards of a writer.

Not that I felt bad about that. The guy in the mirror was familiar, somebody I liked and trusted. I was, I thought, a nice guy who didn't hurt anybody, never had trouble sleeping and usually had somebody to sleep with. I was not particularly happy, but I felt that I had the potential for happiness, that it was worth shooting for.

Sitting across from me was Chase. He wore $700 custom-

tailored suits and $200 shoes. He could have been designed
by NASA—his face as smooth as the hour he'd shaved
it, salt-and-pepper hair and mustache trimmed to space-
program tolerances, nothing out of place. He never unbut-
toned his jacket, never had to. If the two of us went to a
board meeting as strangers, even *I* would want to listen to
him. And yet he was, ultimately, an idiot savant; he did his
job well, but it wasn't much of a job. I was smarter than
Chase and more substantive, but he was living proof of what
every successful politician knows: voters will cast their ballots
for a *look,* a *style,* a *theme*—because looking beyond that
makes the choice impossible. Look too closely and you won't
want to vote for anybody.

"What did you hear?"

"Forget it, Alex. It was probably just an irresponsible
comment." Sincere, like somebody selling insurance.

What was I doing having this conversation with this bastard?

"How about Maria Zaychek getting a private detective to
do this," I said, "and letting me get back to my work."

Chase didn't hesitate. "Well, I have a lot of confidence in
your opinion, and so does Maria, obviously. But is that a
real request?"

I had tipped my hand, damn it, and he knew that I was
far too interested in the case to give it up so easily.

"I'm not used to being on the carpet."

"Oh, hell"—he tried to look sheepish—"that's not what
this is." And then he told me how much he appreciated my
efforts, and did all the squirming and shifting and readjusting
that fence sitters like Colin Chase do when they figure they
might have leaned too far in the wrong direction.

"Let's give it a few more days," he said. "Let's see what
happens."

I left his office knowing, at least, what was expected of me.

Stella's white-background monitor was glowing, its blinking black cursor where I'd left it in the middle of an article

about hazardous waste disposal. On the wall above it was a framed reproduction of John Singer Sargent's *Madame X*, probably his best-known painting and a thousand times better than any cover portrait that had appeared on *World* since its inception. The painting violated a prohibition against hanging things—with walls of glass, the backs of frames are not particularly beautifying—but then, this was the fourteenth floor, the editorial department, and *World*'s policy-makers had long ago thrown up their hands in despair over it.

Maddie called in sick, something she did occasionally when we were far ahead in terms of deadlines. I thought about doing some editing in Rittenhouse Square, but little droplets were hitting my window now, turning black at the edges from the city's grit. I sat back in my chair, folded my hands on my chest and stared at the monitor.

I remembered a high school biology class experiment. It involves planaria, a very small dark gray flatworm that lives in water and is best known for its trick of regenerating: you cut it in half and its tail grows another head and its head grows another tail, so you get two planaria for the price of one, ad infinitum if you like, until you have more planaria than you know what to do with. For that matter, if you cut its head into six sections without detaching it from the body, it grows six heads.

In this experiment, planaria is transferred through a series of petri dishes. Each time it is introduced to a new dish, it will not eat for at least forty-five minutes to an hour after food is introduced. But once acclimated to the dish, it will again eat immediately as soon as food is introduced. Over and over again, whenever the planaria is moved, it will ignore its food until it feels at home in its environment even if the petri dishes are identical and the water is transferred along with the planaria.

But planaria know. Even the surfaces of identical petri dishes have their own distinctive differences to eyes that see microscopically; those glass bottoms, smooth and similar enough to the human eye, become distinguishable terrain; a topographical feature the size of a pinpoint can look like a boulder to planaria. If planaria could hang a little sampler in the petri dish, it would read: THERE'S NO PLACE LIKE HOME.

I understood that. I prefer my own bathroom, my old broken-in clothing to new; I stick with tried-and-tested seats in restaurants. My old industrial carpeting may have felt thin after my visit to the twenty-fourth floor, but the place had the benefit of being home, and the added benefit of not being Colin Chase's office.

Planaria would have felt the same way; the only worm that belonged up there already had the job.

To me, Vladimir Zaychek represented the least interesting part of the puzzle, or what little there was of
one, anyway: an aging tycoon, incredibly rich, engaged in
an activity that was probably better suited to younger people
with sounder hearts. I was tempted to believe that if he'd
stayed home and fertilized his orchids, he'd still be alive.

On the other hand, Zaychek had apparently been in extraordinarily good shape. Before his heart attack, he'd been
able to give Colin Chase, who was something of a health
nut, a good game of tennis. True, Chase never lost, but the
fact that Chase worked up a sweat—which he did—said a
lot for an opponent almost a quarter-century his senior who
should have been worrying about arthritis.

Further, Zaychek had been not just a diver, but an expert.
He had been a creature of habit, too, with certain ironclad
rules about not going it alone, and I understood how rules
like that came about and how carefully they were adhered
to—I could remember my own panic, the feeling of isolation.
We can *go* out there, but we don't *belong* out there.

So what did I have? A guy who died earlier than necessary.
A woman who felt that her husband had been "different"
before he died, and so had misgivings about his death. And
a man who wanted that woman to forget her misgivings,
maybe because he was in love with her. A soap opera with
a weaker-than-usual plot.

But for me, the interest went far beyond Maria and Vladimir Zaychek and their human quandaries, whatever they were or remained, to the supposed killer, the jellyfish. My fascination with that strange little creature far outstripped anything else I felt, and here was an opportunity to look into the dark side of the animal world: a seldom-seen creature, unfathomably different from almost everything else on earth, with a killer instinct. It was, for me, the perfect story.

The human component, if the mystery needed one, was Augustus: a doctor, a cancer patient near death who conceivably went to Bermuda just weeks before he died without telling his wife, and who while there diagnosed as a cause of death a situation that he had probably never seen before. And signed a statement to that effect in a signature that wasn't indisputably his. Now, there was a guy I would've loved to talk to.

I was doing everything but. I'd asked Mary Anne Warrick, *World*'s Cincinnati stringer, to find out what she could for me, and she came up with enough to give me a pretty good picture. Augustus was born, raised and educated in Germany, where he began a medical career. His family was not fond of the Nazis, and after the Gestapo arrested his younger brother in the late thirties for so-called crimes against the state, Augustus saw the handwriting on the wall. He escaped to the United States, changed his name, took the additional training he needed to practice here, married an Ohio girl he met in college and settled down to general practice in Cincinnati.

Between Mary Anne and Stella, I found out which magazines he subscribed to, the limitations that appeared on his driver's license, and the amount he owed on his mortgage before the life insurance paid it off. I knew about his children: his son, a lawyer in Minneapolis; his daughter, a housewife in L.A. He belonged to several organizations, was a registered Republican, drove a Buick, had served on a state medical advisory board, had several hospital affiliations. He hadn't been news, really, but he got a few mentions along the way because of his board involvements and a few locally interesting medical situations that made the papers in the course of his career.

What was emerging from this dossier was a portrait of the kind of guy who keeps the United States from coming unglued. A caring professional, a taxpayer.

"Don't move." The voice was in my ear, next to me; I froze; I heard the click.

"Great."

Angel advanced the film. We were on her front porch, each of us in one of the big wicker rockers that had been left by the previous owner. The sky had turned luminescent, the blue sunset bleached to bright gray by the summer storm. The rain was hitting the street in sheets.

It was dinnertime; none of the neighbors were out. No kids, no traffic, just the lull and the downpour. At the end of the block, on the cross-street, a bus picked up some umbrella-shrouded passengers. We could see the traffic of I-95, its hum lost in the sound of rain, carrying the last of the homebound city workers toward the northeastern suburbs.

I liked it here; it felt more like home than my own place. I saw that as a sort of trap; I didn't want to be that comfortable *anywhere*. Besides, there were many times when I preferred to be alone, and times when I didn't even mind being lonely. You can learn a lot from both.

The contrast between center city, where I lived, and Fishtown, where Angel lived, emphasized the isolation of the upwardly mobile. Here on Angel's turf, people were visible as entities connected to something larger than themselves: to other people, to families. On front porches and through windows you could watch life unfold, getting to know who belonged to who, hearing tiny scraps of conversation that would eventually flesh out a relationship. After a while you could know that the long-suffering Mary Scott down the block had had a good reason for taking up with her boyfriend, since, with her own husband hardly ever sober, all of the responsibility for the kids fell to her—and certainly she was entitled to some fun in life. Maybe you'd be better off not knowing—you could see the faces in the process of aging when you got too close—but it was real.

Where I lived, residents got on elevators, avoided eye contact and watched numbers blink, then went to apartments like mine—little hamster dwellings with small terraces looking out onto the roofs of a thousand houses and ten thousand strangers you could never look in the eye. Often I liked it; sometimes I wished there could be more.

My walls were stark white and empty; I'd never gotten around to hanging anything on them. I moved in and got used to them that way. Visitors would ask how long I'd been there, and they'd be shocked to hear me say five years. The interior that apathy decorated, a friend once called it, although it wasn't that at all. If, once you get used to the way things look, you stop really *seeing* them, why put anything up in the first place? On the other hand, that's inconsistent, since I have several prints and some memorabilia that I've been thinking about getting framed for years.

"Is this color?"

"Black and white," Angel said. "Just stay there." She backed up to the edge of the porch and refocused. "I want to get the whole works."

"Another picture where I look like an idiot."

"More like an aging nerd, I'd say." She crouched down, tucking her arms in close to her body, and clicked again. "This light is wonderful."

I pictured it from her side of the lens: a guy just beginning to look not so young, glasses, dark hair and mustache—well, maybe a hint of gray—sitting on a rocker with a portable computer on his lap. Nice face. Silly smile, which I removed immediately. White shirt, open at the neck, sleeves rolled up. A hint of a roll at the beltline, now being sucked in; no point in giving it to posterity. What Angel wanted was the dichotomy of the computer and the rocking chair; she had an eye for things like that.

She noticed the cable that ran across the porch and through the front door. "Dialing for data?" she asked, snapping me.

"Looking for stuff on the doctor—Augustus. I've been through all the Cincinnati papers, the county medical publications, the AMA Journal." Through Angel's phone line I was connected to Stella, who networked me to just about any data base, including her own. It was one of the great advantages of the job; *World* would bitch about costs, but the data-access costs were not broken out by department, so on-line costs for research didn't affect Science's budget.

"No luck?"

I shook my head. "Not what I want."

"And what's that?"

"You don't know until you find it. Whatever it is, it didn't make the papers."

Distant lightning, then a rumble like a passing truckload. The shutter clicked again; I saw the legs of the boy on the table.

"Want a beer?"

I didn't, but Angel did. "Disconnect the modem," I called after her.

Through the lace curtains on the window—they also came with the house—I could see her maneuvering, on tiptoe, around the furniture that had been moved away from the walls. She was doing the painting herself; the floor was covered with a tarp, cans of paint, rags, rollers. The living room air conditioning had died, so she was painting in her underwear when I arrived. There were pale blue specks on her knees and her breasts. I thought about helping her clean up.

Angel disappeared into the dining room, then into the kitchen. She was now wearing shorts and the slippers she called her tramp shoes, exposing a stretch of flesh that ran for miles from just below her buttocks to the bottom of her

foot. Blue-collar sensual, with her long brown hair—grown
longer since I met her—tumbling halfway down her back,
she could walk out in traffic and cause the kind of horn-
honking Philadelphians usually reserve for the Stanley Cup.

I knew it was more than that kind of stuff that kept me
coming back, but most of it defied definition. Put simply, I
was nuts about her. She was complicated, which I liked, and
screwed up, which I didn't, although you can't always get
one without the other, but that wasn't it, either. It was everything, all the indefinable things that constitute being knocked
on your ass by someone, and all the problems that went
with it.

Nevertheless, I forced myself to be wary, because Angel
was an emotional gypsy. If you got too close, she moved her
tent. I knew it without experiencing it; it was there, unspoken.

Angel was a puzzle. And I was hooked.

She was feeling particularly good tonight. She laughed a
lot, cracked a few jokes, complained good-naturedly about
the city and the trash collection problems.

"What's up?" I asked, knowing something was.

"I quit my job today."

"You're smiling like you just won a spelling bee."

"I feel terrific."

"What did Maury say?" Maury was Maurice Kline, her
boss and a senior partner in the law firm.

"He offered me a raise to stay. I told him it just wasn't
me. I gave him two weeks' notice."

"And then?"

"He was great. He wished me luck, and gave me a photography assignment."

"You're kidding."

"Nope. He needs portraits of the staff for a newsletter."

"You don't have a studio."

"I won't need one. We're shooting on site, available light."

"He took it well."

"Yes. I mean, no, too. He hasn't given up. He still wants

me to change my mind. And I'm still invited to the staff splash party at the Society Hill Club next month."

"Hmmm."

"Oh, come on."

"Come on what? He's not human?"

"He's married."

"Oh, that's different. No married guy could possibly look at you and feel anything. Especially if all you're wearing is a bathing suit."

"Is this jealousy? From Alex Black?" She was being facetious; she'd seen it before.

"Forget it. But I'm glad you quit."

"Well, we'll see. I think I'm good."

"You are. I'll try to open a few doors for you at *World.* And I can always loan you a few bucks if you're short."

"I've quit jobs before. I'll survive." She took a swig of beer, and I knew I shouldn't have offered the money. Patronizing, she'd think. Caring, I thought.

That's what I mean. You couldn't get too close to Angel, couldn't let her know you were thinking that maybe she'd need help. She didn't want to give up the smallest piece of her independence. Or she was afraid to. I couldn't tell which.

She didn't even like staying at my apartment. She had a house; she didn't need me to put her up. I would've worried, but she was always asking me to stay there. Anyway, the arrangement kept me from asking her to move in with me. The words sometimes tried to come out of my mouth, but I stifled them. Besides, I suspected I would be sorry if I did that.

I'm as quick to choose a mate as I am to buy a suit.

Inside the house, the phone rang. I hoped it would be her mother.

A few seconds later, she was at the screen door. "It's for you," she said. "It's Maddie."

If it was for me, it *had* to be Maddie. She was the only one with the phone number.

"I'm sorry to bother you," she said. "I tried you at home and got the answering machine—"

"No problem. What's up?"

"Colin Chase called me at home looking for you."

"You're kidding. What'd he want?"

"He didn't say." She read me his phone number.

I could think of only one thing—a problem regarding something that had appeared in the Science section. What? I'm careful. I couldn't think of anything I'd written or edited that was even close to libel. My stomach was twisting.

"Hey, don't jump to conclusions," Maddie said. "Maybe he just wants to have breakfast with you tomorrow morning or something. He didn't sound upset."

When I called Chase, he was actually pretty decent. He apologized for tracking me down, hoped he wasn't interrupting anything, asked me if it was raining much where I was, and told me I wouldn't have to worry about that for the next week or so.

I was going to Bermuda.

From the taxi's window, I watched Bermuda go by. The islands are seven hundred and some miles from Philadelphia, long and narrow with a fishhook-shaped western end that seems to be angling for South Carolina. The long, narrow shape is one of Bermuda's natural resources; it means that you're never far from the water. And despite a tourist traffic of half a million annually, not even the public beaches are crowded.

Bermuda's airport is at the eastern end of the islands, and Fontana, the resort where I would be staying—where Zaychek was staying at the time of his death—was far west. To get there I would have to traverse most of the island; I told the driver to take the shore routes so that I could see a little water. The three major roads are logical if nothing else: North Shore Road is north, South Road is south, and Middle Road runs between them.

A lucky son of a bitch, Maddie had called me. She couldn't remember the last time anyone from Science had been assigned to go anywhere interesting. She didn't begrudge it to me—hell, she knew how many hours I put in—but she also knew she'd have to pick up some of the pieces while I was gone. It would be up to her to make sure that Pete and the free-lancers were meeting deadlines, up to her to keep an eye on production schedules. Meanwhile, an associate editor from Financial had been plugged in to keep the copy moving once it hit my desk.

Both chores had been underestimated, as usual—a fact I did not find particularly comforting—but I tried to put myself into a my-ass-is-covered mode and not worry about it. Nevertheless, I decided to take along a bunch of revised galleys just to be certain that some last-minute changes had been made.

Before I left, Maddie came into my office. "I think Pete's upset," she said. "You know, you're the only real editor he's ever worked under, and now somebody else is going to be editing his copy. He's afraid he'll be crucified."

"Yep. Goes with the turf."

"Okay, tough guy. But a few words from you would make his day. I said all the right things, but I'm not the right person to say them."

A little later, I called Pete in and asked him to sit down, having cleared the IN chair for that purpose. It was the first time he'd seen the seat empty, and he put on his jacket for the occasion.

"Hey," I said, "you feeling okay?"

"Sure." He shrugged. "How do you mean?"

"Well, you'll be working under another editor, and I thought you might have some concerns."

He grimaced; it made his mustache bushier.

"Eloquent." I smiled, and his face relaxed. "Look, Pete, you're a good writer—better than anyone they're gonna send in here. Now, this editor is going to make some decisions, and that's his prerogative. And they'll probably affect you. But I want you to keep one thing in mind. You and I, we have a good relationship, but it happened gradually. When you started, I used to tear your copy apart, right? And today you can practically read my mind. But you can't read *his* mind, and that probably makes you nervous, right?"

"How do you know it'll be a he?" he asked.

"If you knew Financial, you wouldn't have to ask. They still use hand-cranked calculators."

"Not really."

"No, not really."

"Yes, I'm nervous."

"I thought you might be. And I'm telling you to keep it in perspective. There's no threat to your job. You may encounter a different point of view. On the other hand, he may have some good ideas. All you have to do is the best you can, plus"—I leaned forward to give it weight—"keep an eye out for potential disaster. Like, if a really dumb story idea comes up, maybe you can slip in an appropriate recommendation and make him feel like it was his idea not to do it. By the same token, if you think an idea's good, tell him so."

"No problem," he said, beaming, pleased to have been suddenly catapulted into the upper levels of editorial expertise. "I appreciate your confidence."

"You earned it."

He shook my hand and went out quickly with a little bounce in his step; a few minutes later, I heard him chattering to his wife.

Now I was in Bermuda. I knew why, but I didn't know *why*.

"Twenty years I've been around here, Alex," Maddie said, nodding sagely, "and I've never seen anything like it. I mean, there's no *story* here—unless it's something that nobody's talking about." Not that it was unusual for *World* to send people globe-hopping; for a lot of our reporters and writers, it was de rigueur. But rarely for the science department, and never for the science *editor*. If anybody got to go anywhere, it was Pete, who enjoyed the advantage of being dispensable.

I figured I was here because Chase had a thing for Maria. Simple as that.

Of course, I had prerogatives, and my job had parameters. Had Chase asked me to go to some industrial center in North Jersey, I might have told him to kiss off—unless he had a damned good reason, and then I'd have sent Pete. Generally speaking, management kept its nose out of editorial, and there was a sort of knee-jerk reaction to any infringements. But this was not the kind of thing you jerk the knee about. I'd been in Bermuda. If you didn't like the water and you weren't on your honeymoon, it could be the most boring place on the face of the earth, but it was a wonderful kind of boredom, the kind anybody can use once a year. As it is, I happen to like the water, so Chase didn't have to twist my arm.

Furthermore, this was the first time Chase had asked me to do a favor, as opposed to a duty, and I knew it would be less expensive to say yes.

It was Sunday and quiet. The Toyota station wagon snaked through parish after parish, Devonshire and Paget and Warwick and Southampton, sleepy in the afternoon sun—past high stone walls that kept Bermuda's tropical foliage from clotting the roads, past docks where men were cleaning their catches, past long rows of shiny white fiberglass decks glistening in the sun, past the hulls of pleasure boats flashing against the blue water, past a bus stop where two black girls stood in pink dresses, their Sunday best. And then there would be an occasional main intersection with a food market or a post office or a bar and restaurant or a gift shop.

We saw it all at a leisurely pace. Bermuda's speed limit is twenty-one miles an hour, often exceeded, but not by much or for long. The roads can twist sharply, sometimes dangerously. And then there are the mopeds, thousands of them, which slow things down. Only compact cars are permitted on Bermuda, and they're governed by strict regulations; an unsightly dent can keep you off the road. As for *selling* a used car, forget it. By law, they can't be sold; they're cut in half and used for landfill. The only exceptions are station wagons, which can be sold to cabbies.

Not that it matters to Americans. On Bermuda, visitors can't even rent a car, because only Bermudians are allowed to drive. The only alternative to taking a cab is driving a moped. And so the tourists, many of whom have never been on one and are confused to begin with by having to drive on the left, get wiped out on a regular basis; as many as half a dozen a week are airlifted home in plaster casts. But there's no choice: a hundred thousand more cars would turn the island into a tropical parking lot.

Bermuda is probably the only place in the Caribbean that isn't to some degree at war with American tourists. It's not so much that they like us as that they value us; we make the economy go. In the Bahamas you'll find an undercurrent of hostility and hatred; despite a government campaign to motivate its citizens to act like humans, surly waitresses will unceremoniously toss silverware and dishes down in front of you—settling for that mild an act of rebellion only because it's illegal to slit your throat.

Bermuda is light-years away from all that, one of the few British colonies left where they don't want to pee on the queen. Sure, they had some trouble back in the early seventies, when a disgruntled black bumped off the commissioner of police and the governor—and then was formally executed a few years later, which touched off some racial violence (rioting and arson, to be exact) that had to be quelled by British troops—but everybody seems to feel that was a fluke; those things simply didn't happen in Bermuda, as indeed they probably wouldn't have if they hadn't been happening everywhere else in the world. And besides, after a Royal Commission published its report on those events and made recommendations to improve the position of the primarily black Progressive Labor party, Constitutional amendments were enacted to do just that.

Most Bermudians today say there's no racial hostility on Bermuda. They're wrong, but they've gotten used to taking the temperature of things by looking at them. Bermuda is civilized, and people behave, but the racial tensions are there. Once in a while the paper will print a letter to the editor from somebody who says as much, but nobody pays much attention. Most people are concerned only with how they're treated, not whether they're loved. Besides, the black and white populations—60 percent and 40 percent of the colony, respectively—do get along better in Bermuda than they do just about anywhere else.

The cabdriver, a black guy, spent a third of the trip telling me about black cops and black Jamaicans, and particularly about black Jamaican cops, who from the cabbie's perspective were the worst species on the island. "They lord it over us, you know, like they're better than us." But he described his experiences in the same tone of voice that he used to describe the scenery, just another hill on the Bermudian landscape.

The island's fifty thousand or so inhabitants, for the most part, live decently—the government is benevolent—but they go crazy with island fever; the hospital for the mentally ill has about two thirds as many beds as the general hospital. Living on Bermuda is a little like being a prisoner in paradise. The only changes are seasonal ones, and they're not much. There's no real variety. And the whole deal covers only twenty square miles. You could probably stick something that size into most American metropolitan areas and have enough room left for Nantucket.

To escape the sameness, many of those who work even in the more menial jobs save their money and go to places like New York City for vacation. There they can overpay and maybe get mugged and, if they're particularly unlucky, get treated the way American tourists do in the Bahamas. It's their way of eluding the boredom, the quiet, the inertia, that damned blue sky and crystal-clear blue water and coral beach wherever they look—that eternal sun; those predictable temperatures, which during the day average between winter's 68 and summer's 86.

We drove on for a while until we swung off the road through a stone-pillared entrance and through the dark underside of a high wooden bridge covered with a thick growth of sage; we then wound upwards, following a narrow road edged by stone walls, aloe sprouting from their crevices, past manicured lawns and a croquet court.

I had a bungalow waiting for me at Fontana, a place Chase said is the island's premier resort, stretching every syllable. It might have been at that. Although *World* was pretty good about shipping its employees around in comfort, it wasn't normally this generous, and it wouldn't have been this time, either, except that Fontana was Zaychek's address at the time of his death.

As we followed the twisting road, I could see a smattering of various-sized cottages and bungalows, none of them very close to any other, some of them having the appearance of being privately owned, and some broken into upstairs and downstairs apartments. The foliage, thick and varied and higher than eye level in most places, seemed to ensure relative privacy. In just a few more seconds we drove under the overhang of the main building.

On the other side of the drive, a few ducks watched my arrival from an enclosed pool. It was late afternoon.

I checked in. During the process, I casually asked the young woman at the front desk if they'd had any problems with Portuguese man-of-wars since the Zaychek incident. She shook her head.

"He was a business associate of mine," I said.

"Yes, it was terrible." She nodded mechanically, scribbling something on my room registration card.

"Were you on duty here when it happened?" I asked.

"No, I wasn't." A vacant smile. "You will be here for how long?"

"A week or so. Do you know anyone who was around when it happened?"

"No," she said pleasantly, and hit the bell on her desk to summon the bellhop.

I suspected I would've done better with a computer, and

I confirmed that when I tried to interrogate the bellhop. Somehow he started out assuming that my concern was for my own safety, and no matter what I asked him, he merely answered the one question I hadn't asked at all. "I've been swimming in these waters since I was two"—he laughed— "and I was *never* stung. Don't worry."

Fontana was built on a slope overlooking the Great Sound, the inside curve of the fishhook. It was much steeper than it looked or felt, thanks to a variety of footpaths that tacked back and forth instead of going directly to their destinations; in fact, the small wooden bridge leading from my bungalow to the main building was the same bridge high above the dark road on which my cab brought me.

My bungalow looked like a single dwelling. Actually, it was *two*—one upstairs, one downstairs—but the entrances were on opposite sides, and the earth had been contoured to enable the entrance of each bungalow to be at ground level, so each looked like a single bungalow with its own outdoor patio. Mine was the upstairs unit, and the only in- dication that another bungalow was attached was a spiral staircase connecting the apartments, separated by a locked door at the bottom.

I set up my lap-top computer in the living room on a coffee table in front of the sofa, wondering if I would have any trouble reaching Stella; on a nearby desk was a vase of scar- let hibiscus in full bloom, apparently having been put there just prior to my arrival. Amazing what three hundred a day will buy. Off to the right was a kitchen, well appointed, large and clean; in front of me, opposite the sofa, a fireplace that had probably never been used; a large bedroom with a kingsize bed; and a bathroom. The air was damp but not uncomfortable, typical of an island with a small land mass.

I unpacked, putting most of the business end of what I had brought next to the computer. I'd worked out a rough itinerary that started the following morning, and I'd left plenty of holes in it—to see the island, do some snorkeling, have a few drinks.

I slept, woke up, threw on a pair of slacks and a jacket, and walked over the bridge and up to the main building for dinner.

"Eating alone?" He was a thin, nice-looking guy, maybe forty or so, but balding prematurely, a characteristic that made his forehead prominent. He wore horn-rims and a corporate-America look, and he was smiling at me, his hand extended.

Even if my lack of a dining partner wasn't obvious, it soon would be, so I nodded.

"I'm Jeffrey Little."

"Alex Black," I said, and shook his hand. He had arrived at Fontana's dining room right after me; we were both waiting at the entrance to be seated.

"I don't mean to intrude," he apologized. "But I followed you here. Oh, not intentionally, I assure you"—he laughed, raising his eyebrows—"although of course you never know these days. It's just that I was coming in the same direction, through the woods and over the bridge, et cetera, and apparently from the same bungalow. I'm the lower level."

"Oh," I said, accepting that as the kind of coincidence that legitimized further discussion. "Well, nice to meet you."

Little looked pleased. " 'Well, Jeff,' I said to myself, 'maybe you won't have to ruin your eyes trying to read the newspaper by candlelight tonight—there's a fellow who looks like he might be in a similar predicament.' "

"Predicament?"

"I mean, eating alone. This is the third night in a row for me."

The maître d' approached, put up two fingers inquiringly, and so Jeffrey Little and I were seated together. Actually, I didn't mind; if it hadn't happened, I would have had to read through dinner, too, almost impossible by the single candle that lighted each table. The sky was now turning from blue to deep purple, darkening the dining atrium, which was actually a greenhouse, and the only other light, of hardly any consequence, came from the illuminated bunches of artificial grapes interspersed among the real plants that hung from the roof.

"Well, this is a treat," Little said. "Alex Black, right? Are you here on business, Mr. Black?"

"Call me Alex. Yes, sort of. I'm researching a book." I had decided not to tell the truth to anyone who didn't have to know it. One thing journalists learn early: announce what you do for a living and the public relations people crawl out of the woodwork, and the first thing they usually do is tell everybody you'd like to question to refer you to them. I don't hold it against them—we all have our jobs to do, and the media rarely comes for good news. Besides, for every obnoxious PR type I've ever known, there's been a journalist who was willing to quote out of context to make a story a little spicier. But the journalists have the upper hand. Nobody ever talks about freedom *from* the press.

"Ah, a writer. Wonderful. What's it about? Can you talk about it?"

"Actually, there's not much to say yet. It's in the scientific arena, anyway. Computers." As soon as I said it I was sorry; you would no sooner visit Bermuda to research a book about computers than you would visit Jersey City to do one on Venus flytraps. "I mean, most of the research is done," I fudged. "I'm sort of getting away from it all to start putting it together."

If it sounded implausible, Little didn't seem to notice.

"I'm with AT&T up in Basking Ridge, New Jersey. Not far from Princeton, if you know where that is."

"Sure. I'm from Philly."

"No kidding! Well, small world. And we have something else in common, too. What I'm doing here is, I'm trying to bring Bermudian corporations up to speed in terms of using phone lines for various kinds of transmission. You know, voice, data, image."

Little talked a lot, mostly about AT&T and data access and his wife and kids. The wife and kids were the most interesting part, so that gives you some idea. He asked me a lot of questions about myself, which helped, and I had a double shot of Glenfiddich, which didn't, and by the time we were on our after-dinner coffee it had become hard to keep my mind from wandering.

Nevertheless, I figured it was worth investing a little false attention. I hadn't tried to connect to Stella yet, and had never done it from outside the U.S. before, and here was a telecommunications guy who probably knew every wrinkle. When I brought it up, he volunteered to hook me up, show me a short cut or two. By this time, he knew who I was and where I worked, although he knew nothing about the specifics of my visit. I stuck to the computer book story.

"Say, some of the folks around this place have been talking about some fellow who was killed by a jellyfish here a while back—he was from your neck of the woods, right? Whaddya know about those things?"

Warmed by the Scotch, I warmed to the subject. I had no intention of telling him the real reason why I was in Bermuda, but I figured that *Physalia physalis* had to be more interesting than Doris and Stephanie and Timmy Little, so I spent the rest of dinner impressing us both with my jellyfish lore. As for Vladimir Zaychek, I said, I knew only what I'd read in the papers.

The next morning I ate breakfast alone. Then I hired a moped, got some directions from a transplanted young American who ran the cycle shop, and took off. This last thing I did slowly—I'd just read in the morning paper about a tourist in a Syracuse hospital, still there months after his moped lost an argument with an Austin at a Bermudian intersection.

I was on a back road, a narrow place with soft curves, quiet enough, if it hadn't been for the moped, to hear the insects buzz in the early-morning sunshine. The road, a narrow one where cars were prohibited, followed a hill as it wound along the coastline; below it, maybe a quarter mile away, the hill gradually leveled off and met the blinding early-morning glitter of the Great Sound, while on the mainland side of the road, depending upon where you found yourself, it ranged from fairly level, sparsely populated by private homes behind thick foliage and ancient wrought iron, to quite steep, its highest such elevation logically being at Fort Scaur, now a rarely used picnic ground but in the nineteenth century a fortress used to defend the Royal Navy's dockyard at the island's western tip.

Up ahead of me small lizards, interrupted from the rigid pose of predator, darted into the thick tangle at the side of the road; I wondered if they could feel the vibration as I approached. A moped driven by a Bermudian overtook me and whizzed by, but other than that I was the only vehicular traffic. At one point a heavy black woman with a basket on her head noticed me smiling and smiled back.

In just twenty-four hours, it seemed, Philadelphia and *World* were gone, and all I could feel now was the me of the moped: firm grip, forearms relaxed, knees bent and calves flexed, teeth slightly clenched. I was learning the feel of the metal between my legs, moving against the warm air, the sun on my back and the comforting weight of the helmet on my head. And, reverberating within it, only the steady snore of the moped—no telephones, no bureaucracy. I was untouchable, out of reach, free. I concentrated on the moment as if it were possible to save it to disk, like a piece of data, just in case I would ever want to recall it when times got tough.

I reached Somerset Road, checked my map and headed toward what Bermudians call the Sandys police substation. It turned out to be impossible to miss, a wide, proud-looking two-story building freshly painted in white with sky-blue columns and arches, separated from Somerset Road by a low wall. Its entrance was a single wide door on a landing at the top of a set of steps half as wide as the building itself.

I pulled my moped into the parking area.

It could have passed for a small hotel had it not been for the little things: the two official-looking flags on the front lawn, obviously cleaned at least once a week, that flapped lazily in the breeze; the thick-looking paint, which gave the impression that the building might have been painted over every time it needed a washing; the wrought-iron gate around the edifice that was painted in the same white as the building with less regard for aesthetics than for the cost-efficient use of a painter. And then there was the glass-paneled bulletin board that stood just outside the entrance, with its admonitions against drugs and moped racing.

If it had the official bearing of a well-scrubbed, spit-and-polish municipal institution outside, it soon became clear that nobody had given the same thought to the interior. Everything was floor-to-ceiling imitation-wood paneling that collided unhappily, sans baseboard, with a sickly yellow polyester wall-to-wall carpeting, and that was it wherever you looked. It was the kind of decor that a bunch of middle-aged hockey fans would throw together if they were designing a place as a refuge from their wives, a place where the most important piece of furniture might be a refrigerator. The individual offices had been created with the same kind of architectural integrity: What, you needa office? Gimme a hand, we'll stick up a few walls. . . .

There was a front counter. Behind it was a large open

area with desks where a couple of cops were looking through some file cabinets. A woman at a desk sensed my presence and, without looking up from her work, asked if she could help me; I gave her the name.

"Sergeant MacLeod," she called out sharply.

This was a place that didn't do much entertaining.

A short black guy slowly filled the doorway. *Filled* it. Wide enough to cause an eclipse. He wore dark blue shorts, a white shirt, a loud, skimpy tie and a gold sports jacket with a faint plaid, all of which were appropriate for the island climate, but not for somebody built like him. He was one of those people who look ridiculous in clothes, like a sumo wrestler—bald, with no neck.

"Alex Black," I said. My hand disappeared into his, made a pumping motion and was abruptly dropped. Detective Sergeant Earl P. MacLeod mumbled something and turned around and went back through the doorway. I followed him.

If he turned out to have all the charm of a Philadelphia postal clerk, he was in the right office. I remembered a huge insurance company I had visited, a place that did its business in an enormous room with little glass enclosures wedged in around the perimeter and open-topped cubbyholes everywhere else. In the cubbyholes worked about a million secretaries, and the company rules were that no one could display anything personal—no photos, no birthday cards, no little pieces of anybody's life. It was depressing, but MacLeod would have been right at home. His office looked more like an interrogation room than a workplace, and it was impossible to tell anything about the man—except, perhaps, that he wasn't sentimental. There was nothing on his walls but the fake grain of the paneling. Not a photograph, not a clipping. Not a cartoon, not a calendar.

I thought about my own apartment and decided not to jump to conclusions.

MacLeod got behind his desk, settled into a large chair without arms and looked at me. "You're here about that jellyfish incident," he said. "The American who got killed."

"That's right," I replied.

"Well, I don't know what I can do for you." He shrugged. "What's all the fuss about?"

"No fuss. It's just that the victim was a sort of important person—"

"Important people die, Mr. Black, and some of them even die here." He was looking down at his desk, not at me, holding a pencil between thick finger and thumb and tapping it against his palm.

"—and he died under unusual circumstances."

"Unusual?" Now he looked straight at me. "Well, that's true enough. Statistically, you could even say *rare*. But not unheard of. The man died of a jellyfish sting. It happens. Most people *don't* die of that; he did.

"Of course, that's not exactly natural causes, so there was probably a pathology report. And if there'd been anything unusual, there would have been an inquest. There wasn't, so you can draw your own conclusions. But what do I think? I think if it had been a heart attack after dinner, no American reporter would be here asking questions. Furthermore, why hasn't there been? Why are you the first?"

"Because an accidental death isn't news on the face of it. There was no reason for anyone to come here. The media— the papers, *Time*, *Newsweek*—they took the story off the wire services, maybe made a few phone calls, and they had the story. *Their* story. In fact, we did that ourselves.

"But there are two parts to the story as we see it. The first part was the news of a dead industrialist. Then there was the story that nobody covered—death by jellyfish sting. We often go in after the hot news value disappears, sometimes months after, to get the story that wasn't covered.

"This story, of course, has an important victim, but it has that additional dimension from my magazine's point of view. And from my point of view, as science editor. It's the kind of freak occurrence nobody ever gets the chance to read about—indeed, few people even *know* about—and that in itself makes it worth writing." I didn't mention Chase and Maria Zaychek; there was no percentage in it.

"Science editor." He nodded. "Well, Mr. Black, the problem with stories like the one you'll write is that it will appear in a major American magazine, the effect of which will probably be to keep tourists away from our beaches in droves. Which could hurt our economy. And for nothing—for a story. I guess I have no control over that, but I want you to know how I feel.

"On the other hand, I do have great respect for science. It lets us learn things we might otherwise never know—the identity of a poison, the origin of a strand of hair, that sort of thing. But I tend to be a, you could say, God-fearing person. A religious person. Now, you might wonder what such a person is doing in such a job, Mr. Black," he said, placing both hands on his chest.

"Well, actually—"

"I'll tell you. I consider myself God's tool, here to help him bring the guilty to justice. As for jellyfish stings—or heart attacks, or death from old age, or what have you—all the same. I look upon them as acts of God."

"Well, yes. But then you could argue that everything is an act of God, including the acts of men. Have you ever worn a bulletproof vest?"

"Yes." He looked puzzled.

"Despite the fact that your fate is in God's hands?"

"Ah. God helps them that help themselves, Mr. Black." MacLeod smiled.

"I agree," I said. I didn't, but I wasn't going to get anywhere telling MacLeod that everything he believed in might just be a figment of his imagination.

"But what does that have to do with us?" MacLeod asked.

"Zaychek—the victim—did some things that were out of character for him which may have contributed to his death. He used to take certain precautions, let's say, to help God help *him* in case he ran into trouble. Like never going into the water without someone to help God pull him out." I was getting edgy, and so was he, but this wasn't the conversation I'd expected to have with Bermuda's finest. "So there are elements of this that are . . . suspicious, I think."

He didn't like me, and I needed him. I couldn't afford to sit there and discuss whether I had good reason to be there. I decided to confront the situation.

"Okay, Sergeant. What's the problem?"

"Problem?"

"From the moment I walked in here, you've acted as though I was taking you away from your job."

He smiled, but there was nothing pleasant in it. "You're perceptive, Mr. Black. Yes, this *is* my job, and you *are* taking me away from it." MacLeod backed up from the desk, opened a drawer, pulled out a wide loose-leaf and flipped it open to somewhere around the middle. Each spread was filled with precise, small ink entries in columnar fashion running from far left to far right.

"Each of these is a complaint," he said, flipping through the pages. "Sometimes I spend the whole morning filling them in. For instance, we have a growing narcotics problem that, left unchecked, could eventually turn this island into the Bronx. The world, you know, was always trying to make Bermuda catch up. But catch up with what?

"Take the cars. They didn't get here until 1946. But it wasn't because we wanted them; it was because the world couldn't fight its war without vehicles, and so we got used to them, and improved roads for them, and now we have cars.

"Or take the guns. Nobody on Bermuda is permitted to own a gun, Mr. Black. Not even me, and I'm in charge of the CID branch here. There is one special police detachment here, and only they can use guns, and then only under very unusual circumstances. No police official carries a gun. But guns are being carried on Bermuda all the time by a group of people who don't follow the same prohibitions. Now, Mr. Black, would you like to guess who those people are?"

I shook my head.

"The drug pushers. And once again, we'll eventually be forced to adapt. We've already had police officials beaten. We've had near misses. So here I am, trying to keep a lid on all this, when an American tourist gets careless and is killed by a Portuguese man-of-war, and then I receive a phone call from Inspector Blake asking me to spend some time with a journalist from a big-time magazine who thinks that event is for some reason . . . *interesting*. That makes *you* my job as well. Now, I know it isn't my job to wonder if an American businessman who is beyond help is more important than the children of this country who could someday be dying of overdoses or committing crimes to support their habits, but somehow I can't help doing that.

"Furthermore, I don't know what it means, *spend time*. If it's fifteen minutes, that's one thing. But if it's hours and hours, my timetable—on which results of my own investigations are based—is thrown off. This because *you* work for *World*. But *I* don't work for *World*."

I almost swallowed it, and MacLeod certainly believed it. But after you've worked around bureaucrats for a while, you know how they work, and they get to believe their own publicity. They talk about how much they have to do so they won't have to feel guilty about collecting a paycheck. And so that nobody will ask them to do more. But nobody works so hard that they don't have time for a crossword puzzle or a forty-five-minute telephone conversation or a couple of beers. And if MacLeod had time for that, he had time for me.

I had to think all that in an instant, because it wasn't easy to avoid feeling intimidated by somebody as physically imposing, as unfriendly, and as convinced of his own point of view as MacLeod.

"It's gonna be more than fifteen minutes, Sergeant," I said firmly. "I'll be here about a week. I may need you off and on."

"A *week?* What can take a week? A dead tourist, a jellyfish—"

"If it takes less, I'll let you know. In the interim, I'll cooperate with you. If I get in the way of your saving a young life, just tell me and I'll step aside. But I am here with authority. I was sent here, as you pointed out, by your inspector over in community-media relations, and he got it from whoever's on top of him, and so on. I have to do this. One way or the other I will, even if I have to go right back up the chain of command. Naturally, I'd rather not."

He started to say something, then stifled it, and instead looked at me for what seemed a long time. Then he nodded slowly. If he'd been white, he would have been red.

"Now, I'd like to hear it from you. What happened on the beach. Everything."

MacLeod sighed. "The fishing boat brought him in. He was dead. It was rather ordinary." He sat back and waited.

"What did he look like?"

"He looked like a dead person looks."

"Yes?" He was lucky he wasn't getting paid by the word.

"His eyes were open and back in his head."

"How about the rest of the body?"

"You could see the things on his legs—"

"Pieces of tentacle?"

"Yes. And purple discolorations, like welts. A zigzag pattern."

"You've seen this kind of thing before?"

"Sure. Only this was worse."

"What made it worse?"

"He was dead."

I let it pass. "What were you doing on the beach?"

"Eating my lunch."

"It was a workday for you?"

He nodded.

"Did you see the guy go into the water?"

"No. I don't think he went in where we found him."

"Why's that?"

"The ocean current moves to the west at that time of year. We figured that he'd have to have been drifting for a while. There are a few places along the shore there where people go snorkeling."

"Okay, what then?"

"A crowd collected. I ran up. That doctor ran up. It was pretty clear what had happened."

"Anybody try CPR?"

"I did, but as soon as I touched him, I knew it was too late."

I took Augustus's passport from my knapsack, opened it to his picture, and pushed it across the desk to MacLeod.

"Is this the doctor?"

He glanced at the picture. "Yeah, that's him."

"And what did he do?"

"You know. Took the pulse, listened for a heartbeat. Said the man was dead. Said it was a Portuguese man-of-war sting."

"How did he know that?"

"It was obvious."

"Suppose I told you Augustus had never seen a jellyfish sting."

"Doesn't matter. A dozen people there recognized those marks on his legs."

"Did anybody see the man-of-war?"

MacLeod shook his head. Then he glanced at his watch, hoping I would notice.

"How about witnesses?"

"I have a few names here." He tapped his notebook.

"Good. We may need them. I want to get in touch with the owner of that fishing vessel, too."

"Why?"

"I want to find out exactly what he saw, that's all. That Portuguese man-of-war bladder is fairly easy to spot; I want to know if anyone saw any that day. I'd appreciate it if you'd set it up, sort of give it an official stamp."

I gave him the phone number where I was staying and offered to clear it all through his superiors if necessary. It was my way of telling him not to fuck around, and he understood instantly; I could, after all, put his name in print. He wet his lips and waited.

"One more thing," I said. "You took Augustus's statement, right?"

"That's right."

I showed him the passport and the statement and asked him if he could see any differences between the two signatures.

"I don't know. They look similar." He kept looking. "They do and they don't."

"That was my feeling."

"What's the point?"

"I don't know."

MacLeod moved his massive shoulders into a shrug and let his demeanor take a more official turn. "Well, I wouldn't attach any significance to it. This Dr. Augustus was upset by the death, upset at being in this office. He sat in that very chair. I heard him dictate the statement, saw him sign it. Maybe he was just nervous. Maybe his signature changed. Why worry about it?"

"Another thing. The passport. It doesn't have a Bermuda stamp in it."

"And?"

"Well, how did Augustus get into the country without getting his passport stamped?"

"Did you use your passport, Mr. Black?"

"Of course."

"And you're a United States citizen?"

"Right."

"You could have used your birth certificate, voter registration, even an outdated passport. That's our arrangement with your country. You don't need a passport to get into Bermuda."

Alex, you shmuck.

"Do you have a business card, Sergeant?"

"I used to have some." He opened a drawer, then another, then another, then gave up. "Nobody ever asks."

MacLeod didn't show me out, and I thought he shook my hand harder than necessary. Or maybe that was normal for him. I walked out of his office and went the wrong way. When I passed his door again he was standing behind his desk with his hands in his back pockets, shaking his head from side to side. I saw it, and he knew I saw it, and I knew he wanted me to see it.

That afternoon I went to a small supermarket and bought enough to strain the moped's basket. If I was going to spend a week in Bermuda, I didn't want to have to make the hike from my bungalow to Fontana's dining room every time I got hungry. Besides, the place came with its own kitchen—stove, refrigerator—so I thought that I should have all the comforts, including a six-pack. I had already decided to spend the rest of the day quietly, part of it at work on my agenda.

At Fontana, as you move down the hillside toward the beach, the bungalows and buildings give way to more open spaces—lawns, a grassy plot defined by a little circular roadway, and a beachside cocktail lounge and restaurant. Before the beach there is an outdoor freshwater pool with chaises on three sides and, on the fourth, white-columned and of not much use except for the shade it offers, a sort of poolside Parthenon. In the pool's center, a brass frog spits water in an arc. And beyond the pool, on the edge of the Great Sound, lies Fontana's small, sunbaked private beach and dock, never heavily populated.

It was on that beach that I spent the afternoon, under an umbrella and covered with a double-digit sun block, without the slightest bit of guilt about violating the work ethic.

That evening I decided to stay in. There were a few calls I wanted to make, and besides, Bermuda dies at night except in Hamilton, where some retail establishments stay open to capture the tourists from the ocean liners that dock in the harbor there. I was miles from Hamilton and not experienced enough on the moped to try it after dark.

That limited my options to dinner and to the lounge and terrace outside the dining room at Fontana. The place had its moments; there was always the possibility of striking up a conversation. But I had no illusions about anything more exciting—the songs they played out there under the stars were not for me. Singles were rare here, and so were people traveling without spouses, Jeff Little, I assumed, being more typical than any members of the other sex.

Although there was a possibility that Little wasn't *that* typical. When I left the supermarket earlier that day I'd caught a glimpse of him—I was almost sure it was him, anyway—at a table at a roadside café in a little shopping strip on Somerset Road, and he was with a very attractive, curly-haired redhead. They did not look like they were strangers.

Little looked like a natural resource. He knew his way around; he did business in Bermuda; he seemed to be well connected. And even if all the rest turned out to be unimportant, he understood telecommunications. I'd probably do fine without him, I knew, but it couldn't hurt to have someone available who could save me from overlooking the obvious—an occupational hazard when it comes to computers—if I ran into trouble accessing data from the United States.

I opened a box of spaghetti and a can of clam sauce, put up a pot of water, sat down on the living room sofa and called Maddie at home.

"Hi, kiddo," she said. "No person to person?"

"I figured it was you or no one. Who else could have answered?"

"Christ, that's insulting."

"Well, who?"

"My answering service, that's who, if I'd been out. You

think I have nothing better to do with my Tuesday evenings?"

"How's my replacement?"

"Bernie? Boring, like his name. Bernard J. Bernard. His parents didn't have much imagination either. But so far that's his biggest fault. He keeps busy, keeps his mouth shut and doesn't drink much coffee."

"Good. I pay six bucks a pound for that stuff."

"He also doesn't offer to make it."

"Well, explain to him how the coffee maker works, Maddie. Say, 'Look, I'm sure you've been wanting to pitch right in—' "

"Yeah, right. He already thinks I'm a goddamned revolutionary. Remember, this guy's a *financial editor*. That's like a Republican or something."

We went on like that for a few minutes, after which I read her a few errors I'd caught in the Science galleys. Pete caught them, too, she said, so relax.

"Right. Anything I should know about?"

"Mrs. Augustus called."

"Oh?"

"She said she received the copy of the statement you sent her. The one her husband dictated to the police."

"That's it?"

"That's all I know. Says you should call her." Maddie read me her number, and I wrote it down on the corner of the desk blotter.

"Okay. I'll talk to you tomorrow. Hope I didn't interrupt anything."

"No. But it was close. I just finished chaining some guy to the hot tub."

I didn't bother calling person to person for Mrs. Augustus, either, and there was that midwestern accent again.

"Mr. Black, I looked at the signature you sent."

"Yeah, what do you think?"

"Well, it *does* look like Albert's signature."

"But?"

"I don't know if there *is* a but, except for the fact that I find it unbelievable that he could have been there to sign it. There is a real similarity, and I have to point out that Albert's handwriting had a tendency to vary. I mean, you know how doctors write prescriptions."

"Right, I do—"

"But just to make sure, I looked around. You know, checked some places where he'd signed his name—his driver's license, last year's tax return—"

"And?"

"If I hold the two signatures next to each other, the one on his statement doesn't look *quite* the same as the others."

"No?"

"Now, that may sound crazy to you, but to me it means that somebody else may have been traveling under my husband's name. . . ."

"Maybe. Hold on a second." I took the passport and the statement out of my briefcase and put them on the coffee table in front of me. She had picked up the same thing I had, but I didn't want to put words in her mouth. "Okay," I said. "What's different about the signatures?"

"Well, as I said, there is a strong similarity. But some of the letters are different. On the statement, the *l* doesn't have a space in it. In every signature I have, Albert writes with kind of an open loop. Same for the *g*. Then there's the *r* and the way it runs into the *t*. Also, in my examples Albert crossed his *t* lower. And finally, Albert's handwriting was never this good. This handwriting is, ah, *nicer*."

I knew what she was feeling. If the handwriting was Albert's, he had lied to her during the last days of his life. She sounded exactly like a wife trying to convince herself that her husband really *had*, so to speak, been working late at the office.

"How about the slant of the letters."

"Now that you mention it, Albert's slant less."

"Okay. Now suppose Dr. Augustus had taken his time. Suppose he wanted to make a better signature, a more careful signature, the way he might if he were signing a legal document—like that statement. Is it possible that he could have signed his name like that?"

"I suppose so. But can't you ask the policeman whose name is on the statement about it?"

"I already did. He thinks there's nothing to it. He says he saw your husband sign it. And I showed him your husband's passport and he identified him."

There was a long silence.

"I don't understand. The signature may have some inconsistencies, but basically it looks like Albert's signature. And the policeman says he *saw* him."

"That's what he says."

"Well, frankly, Mr. Black," she said resignedly, "it sounds like he was *there*. Like he *was* in Bermuda. Doesn't it, Mr. Black?"

"It sounds that way."

I wanted to be wrong. She sounded so upset by the idea that her husband could have gone anywhere without telling her—even in the final stages of a terminal illness—I wanted to give her something to cling to.

"Darn. I was coping so well until all this happened." She sounded close to tears. "But if Albert held anything back from me, he must have had a good reason."

"Maybe we'll figure it all out, Mrs. Augustus. But back to the question. If he had been under stress, or considering the nature of his illness—is it your opinion that he could have modified his signature?"

"I don't know. I don't think anybody can change the basic nature of their signature. I read that somewhere, Mr. Black," she added, as if to explain her sudden expertise. Hell, I didn't care how she came to her conclusion; the important thing was that it was the same as mine, that I wasn't just imagining a more interesting scenario.

"One more thing. Didn't you tell me that you spoke with your husband regularly by phone while he was at that hospital—what was the name—"

"The Doan Institute."

"Yes. What kind of place is that?"

"I really don't know, Mr. Black. Albert talked about it as if everyone had heard of it as a cancer treatment and research center."

"Maybe it is." Although it sure as hell wasn't any Sloan-Kettering, or *I'd* have heard of it. "Anyway, you used to talk to him? When?"

"He would call me most nights—that is, they would place the call for him if he was able to talk. They had him on chemotherapy and radiation, so sometimes, like right after a dosage for two or three days, he'd be too sick to talk. Or he'd sound very confused or tired."

"Did you ever call him?"

"The nursing staff told me not to because there was no way to connect an incoming call to the ICU, which is where they had him."

"What was the longest period of time you went without speaking to him?"

"Let me see." She mulled it over. "Not more than three days."

"Then it's safe to say that if he did spend a week or so in Bermuda, you must have spoken to him while he was there."

A long pause. "If he was there, that's true. I'd never even thought of it."

"He certainly didn't sound like he was in any condition to be on the beach or giving medical opinions, did he?"

"No. It just doesn't make sense, any of it."

I could see the water boiling from where I sat, and I'd asked just about all I had to ask for the moment anyway, so I told her I'd keep in touch. Then I made my spaghetti.

Later that evening, between calls devoted to setting up appointments for the week, I tried to call Angel, and this time I did get an answering device. "This is Angel," it said, a soft voice with a hint of her Hispanic heritage. "Please leave a message."

"It's Alex," I said. "I'm in bed. I'm alone. I can hear the lizards screwing in the grass outside my window and the guy downstairs is carrying on with some lady. I had spaghetti. The nights are very exciting here in Bermuda. Angel, I miss you."

In fact, the guy downstairs may well have been enjoying some after-dinner exercise; Jeff Little had, for certain, *some* female company, and while the voices were indistinct and conversational, it did not sound like a business meeting. Or maybe it was all my imagination. Maybe, I reflected, Angel had some company, too, and while my attitude was supposed to be, what the hell, it's her body and she can do whatever she wants to with it, I found myself hoping she was as lonely— and as alone—as I was.

There was a knock on my door at eight-thirty the next morning—first a tap, then more insistent. I looked out the bedroom window; Jeff Little was on my doorstep. If his evening had been more exciting than mine, it didn't show—his face appeared well scrubbed and well rested, and now he was wearing a pair of dark blue Bermuda shorts with matching jacket and over-the-knee stockings, a tan shirt and a tie.

I slipped on a pair of jeans and answered the door.

"I thought I'd try you early," he said, "you know, get your computer up and running—just in case you were going to need it today." He saw that I wasn't wearing a shirt and noticed my bare feet. "Didn't wake you, did I?"

I shook my head and tried to look grateful, then offered him some coffee.

"I have to go to Hamilton, but not for an hour or so. Won't take more than a few minutes to hook you up, anyway. This piece of equipment we're talking about—Stella—is it always on-line?"

"Except for when they shut her down for maintenance," I said, "but that's usually between three and four in the morning. She'll be up now."

"Great. You'll be able to use it today."

"Maybe later. I have to be out of here by eleven myself."

"Oh. Business?"

I nodded.

"Well, I'm cabbing it. Can I give you a lift?"

"No. I'll need the moped to get back, anyway."

While we sipped our coffee I connected the line from the lap-top to the phone. Little dialed an access number unsuccessfully, flicked a switch in the back of the lap-top computer, dialed the number again, scratched his head once or twice, called up the computer's terminal program and made an adjustment, dialed again, got a connection, then typed in Stella's code, which I gave him, and hit the return key and got up. "I think you're just about there."

I sat down at the computer and typed in my password, and the familiar GOOD MORNING, ALEX BLACK, appeared on the computer's red plasma screen. YOUR PLEASURE? I typed M for menu, pulled up a file and made a fast test access to make sure the information would travel, watched the sentences and paragraphs spill across the monitor, saved it, then went back to Stella's main menu and hit GB. On the screen of the portable, Stella asked me to confirm the sign-off, yes or no. I typed Y.

GOOD-BYE, ALEX BLACK, Stella said.

I thanked Little. There was no question that he had saved me time; I would have had to consult the manual. The hookup worked without a hitch, just as it would have in the States.

"Any time." He got up and slapped his hands on his thighs with an air of finality. "Now I'm off to blaze the path of the telecommunications revolution. Sure I can't drop you?"

He took a couple of steps down the path, then turned around and, as if it were an afterthought, said, "Hey, I hope I didn't keep you up last night."

When people say things like that, they usually mean just the opposite.

"No," I answered.

"Good." He gave me a boys-will-be-boys wink and then turned and bounced down the path, too thin to be a sensation in his Bermuda shorts.

                    *   *   *

There are always bathers at Church Bay, but dozens or fewer, never hundreds, spread out over a beach that is in city terms about two blocks long; the place is a mecca for snorkelers but only marginally popular with the tourists. You can't rent a cabana there, can't rent a beach umbrella, can't get anything to eat without climbing a hill, and most tourists—Americans, anyway—would rather visit beaches that require less effort to get a hamburger and provide more relief from the heat of the powerful Bermuda sun. Those who do show up at Church Bay either bring their own sources of shade or find refuge within the beach's natural sand formations, structures ranging from clifflike to totem, deep green to black, sharp-edged, carved by the ocean from the coarse sand to create a surface as accommodating as a dentist's drill.

Further, getting down to the beach—and up from it—is not something everyone can do at Church Bay; the main road, the only access by land, is high above it, and to reach the beach you have to walk over a grassy knoll to the crest of a hill where the composition changes from earth to sand and pebbles, then down a steeper path, made treacherous by the sliding, shifting surface, which gradually levels off as it approaches sea level. It isn't all that difficult—in fact, it's typical of Bermuda's shoreline in many places, and if you slip, you simply come to rest on nothing more serious than your rear—but the trip is easier in sneakers, and the less agile usually go to Horseshoe Bay.

The people who come to Church Bay do so to avoid crowds, but on that September morning the place was far from deserted; there was already the sprinkling of bright primary colors and pastels of bathing suits, towels and umbrellas, and the human confetti of flesh tones from city white to red to dark brown, and then the occasional bright blue or jet black of a face mask or snorkel. Where I stood, at the top of the hill in a stand of tall trees, a family selling hot dogs and hamburgers and soft drinks from an old trailer did a lively business, less from the bathers below than from the passing road traffic. It was there, I assumed, that MacLeod had bought his lunch on the day that Zaychek died.

It was a quiet, pastoral place, but not without reminders that humans were less well equipped to survive here than almost any other species: they had to deal with the coral, which introduces an enzyme to retard healing when its ragged, razor-sharp edges tear the flesh; with the small voracious blackflies that instantly swarm over the smudges and trickles of blood from the cuts or from the scratches resulting from encounters with nettles; and with the marine environment in which one was always an intruder, a place ruled by moray eels and barracuda. There were signs bolted to the thick trunk of a tree at the top of the hill, one of which read CAUTION! and told of dangerous riptides, the other whose large letters said WARNING! and contained a Portuguese man-of-war alert featuring an artist's rendering of the creature at its least attractive along with the cautionary message "Recogniseable by a purple coloured balloon-like float structure approximately 8″ or less in size. Can be seen floating in the water or washed up on the beach . . . a mass of tentacles armed with powerful stinging cells." And on the sign, instructions for first-aid treatment of both wound and shock.

It was as Inga Schmidt had said: being in the water is like being in the sky; technology can take you there, but it can't make you *belong* there.

You could tell that the humans came late to Bermuda, although not latest. That distinction belonged to the lizard population, brought to the islands by the British at the turn of the century to control the insects in a stroke of ecological inspiration far ahead of its time.

I stared at the beach from above. It was here that the passengers of the *Pound-Foolish* had plucked and dragged ashore a lifeless Vladimir Zaychek from the water almost three months ago, on this beach that Augustus had pronounced him dead, to this grassy hilltop that the ambulance had come, without urgency, to pick up the body and take it to the morgue at King Edward VII Memorial Hospital. It was quiet now. It had probably been quiet then.

A flash of reflected sunlight drew my attention to a white Subaru bouncing across the grass in my direction. Behind the wheel was MacLeod; in the passenger seat was a guy of about fifty in a captain's cap. That would be Carlton Chew, owner of the *Pound-Foolish*. The car came to rest and the two men got out, Chew dressed entirely in white, MacLeod in the same limp clothing, including the gold sports jacket, that he was wearing when we first met.

I thanked them for coming out; MacLeod grunted. Chew, wiry and suntanned with an expensive look about him, looked at me through tinted bifocals, squinting in the sun.

"We might as well start here," I said, referring to our position on the hill that gave us an overview of the coastline. "Can you show me where the action took place?"

"Okay," Chew said, walking to where the hill crested slightly and then pointing out to sea beyond a promontory that defined the eastern edge of the cove. "If you'll look to your left over there," he said, "we were coming down that way. And we were just past that piece of land when we spotted, uh, what's his name—"

"Zaychek."

"Right."

"You couldn't see the beach at that point?"

"No. Not *this* beach." He took off his captain's cap, revealing a few strands of sandy hair lying flat on a reddish scalp, and absently polished its shiny black peak on his sleeve. "Of course, there are a series of other beaches you pass as you head west. At any rate, my boat is for hire—fishing, snorkeling and scuba—and that day I had a party of six, tourists, who were primarily interested in snorkeling. So we were hitting some spots, gradually working our way west toward Pompano, stopping here and there, you know, and I was heading toward that reef out there—see it?" He pointed out toward the middle of the cove to a point about a quarter mile offshore where three large natural formations protruded from the water.

"It's deeper than it looks out there," Chew said. "That piece of rock actually goes down about forty feet. Of course, you can't see anything but the tips from here. But underwater it looks like a building. Great place for snorkeling.

"Anyway, we were moving in the direction of that reef when we spot this chap all alone out there in the middle of nowhere, facedown. Well, that's not *that* unusual, although we were pretty far out—and I thought to myself, that's a funny place for a snorkeler. But we could see the snorkel, so I figured everything was okay. But one of the women in the party—there were three women and three men—finally says, 'I think there's something wrong with him. He hasn't moved.'

"Well, her husband starts talking about how she has this overactive imagination, you know, but then we all start taking a closer look, and I figured we'd better investigate. We got alongside him, and by that time, even though I could see that his face mask and snorkel were still in place, I was pretty sure something was wrong. One of our guys dropped into the water and touched him on the shoulder, then shook him, but he didn't respond. So we knew we had to get him to shore. We took him into the boat, took the snorkel out of his mouth. One of the men in the boat tried to give him artificial respiration while I brought the boat as close to shore as I could, then we dragged him through the water the rest of the way. We really moved. It was only a matter of seconds. But he was dead."

"Any idea how long he'd been dead?"

"Only what the doctor said—"

"You mean Augustus?"

"I don't know his name. The doctor on the beach."

"Augustus," MacLeod confirmed.

"Anyway," Chew continued, "he said that the guy might have been floating out there for as much as two to three hours."

"What's the tide like there? Can we determine where he might have gone into the water?"

"No way to tell. He was staying at Fontana—the hotel name was stenciled on his snorkeling gear—and that's on the Great Sound. To be in the ocean here he'd have had to cross the island and come down the coast aways. If I had to guess, I'd say he could've come in around Warwick Long Bay, maybe. But it's hard to know."

"I wonder why nobody saw him earlier."

"I'm sure they did. But as I said, at a distance it would've been easy to think he was just another snorkeler. Around here there's nothing unusual about people facedown in the water."

MacLeod had been silent—no surprise—but he managed, with body language or an occasional shift of the eyebrows, to affect disinterest with a thin-lipped tolerance of the amateur with whom he'd been saddled. Now he looked at his watch and asked, "You want to take a look around down there?"

We walked to the path. At the crest of the hill, the trees thinned out and the sky opened above us. Chew pulled his captain's cap firmly back on his head, and we started down the steep path. I went first, half worrying about MacLeod falling behind me and crushing me like a boulder, but looking back I could see that he was extraordinarily light on his feet for a man of his build, taking the descent with the grace of the fat girl who turns out, to everyone's surprise, to be the best dancer at the high school prom.

The heads of the sunbathers pivoted slowly, like turtles startled into vague interest. The children, wondering at the sudden incongruous appearance of men in street clothes, seemed particularly taken with MacLeod, who caused them to giggle as he sank into the soft surface, accompanying each step with a grunt.

"Okay," Chew said, stopping by a large round boulder half submerged in the sand a healthy distance from the water's edge, "this is where we laid him down."

"Why up here?" I asked.

"It wasn't up *anywhere*," MacLeod said edgily. "This is late morning. That was midafternoon. The tide was up."

"Right," Chew agreed. "We got the boat about twenty yards offshore, then anchored and dragged Zaychek the rest of the way to the beach.

"Well, a crowd collected right away, and then Sergeant MacLeod here came running down that path, and he tried to give him CPR, but it didn't work. And then that doctor came up and put his head on Zaychek's chest and took his pulse and lifted his eyelids and, you know. But he said he could tell by the body temperature that he'd been dead for a while, so Sergeant MacLeod gave up."

"Do you remember where the doctor came from? Was he on the beach?"

"I don't know. There was so much excitement. . . ."

"Well, how was he dressed?"

"Bathing suit, some kind of shirt on top. Nothing unusual."

"He might've been up there," MacLeod said, pointing to the spot we had just left. "I was up there eating my lunch, as I said. And when I saw Augustus on the beach a few minutes later, I thought I remembered seeing him up there by the food truck. But I can't be sure." He gave me a let-the-cops-do-the-work look. "What's the difference?"

"Maybe nothing. I'm just trying to get events in the right sequence." I turned to Chew again. "Do you remember what the body looked like?"

He shrugged. " 'Course, I don't see a corpse every day, so the most significant thing to me was that it was *dead*. You don't expect this. It's as though someone you might talk to about the weather or about the way fish are running has suddenly left his body and gone off somewhere. It's a very strange feeling, to touch a dead person. It doesn't *feel* like a person." He puffed out his cheeks.

"How about the legs, the thighs?"

"Well, that's something I never saw before, either. All these years of running charters and I never saw a man-of-war sting. But I knew what they looked like, all those zig-zaggy purple lines. You could see just where the tentacles had attached."

"Did any of the tentacles remain on the body?"

"Not that I noticed."

"They were there," MacLeod insisted. "I saw them. And I remember the doctor wiping them off with a beach towel."

"But we don't know for sure that it was a man-of-war."

"What do you mean?" Chew responded.

"Well, I mean it could've been some other species of jellyfish."

"I guess. I don't know much about them, except to throw 'em back if I net one. To me, one's as desirable as the next."

"Not to Mr. Zaychek," MacLeod said. Chew laughed, and so did MacLeod, with a loud coughing sound and a sudden grin. It was the first time I saw his facial muscles do anything remotely like that.

"Okay, you pulled Zaychek to shore and laid him down here."

"Right," Chew said. "We had him up on the beach in, I'd say, less than a minute. We moved very fast."

"And the snorkeling gear—where is it now?"

Chew looked blank for a moment, then said, "Probably still aboard the *Pound*. I don't recall that anyone ever asked for it."

"Do you think you can find it?"

MacLeod, who had by now shed his jacket to reveal large stains around his armpits, looked at me with a combination of scorn and genuine curiosity, waiting for an explanation.

I let him wait. "Sergeant, you administered CPR. Mouth to mouth?"

He nodded.

"Notice anything unusual?"

"Like what?"

"Like anything around the nose and mouth?"

"Right. Some kind of slime. I thought it was from the salt water."

"Well, it wasn't. It was mucus."

MacLeod's face looked like he'd just swallowed a rotten oyster.

We left Church Bay at about one o'clock; during the time we'd been there, MacLeod had looked at his watch no less than half a dozen times. I gave Chew my phone number, and he promised to look for Zaychek's snorkeling gear. It was hot now, and I was sorry I hadn't worn my bathing suit under my jeans. I decided to go back to Fontana, change, and hit the water, then spend the evening trying to figure out what I already knew and creating an agenda to find out the rest of it.

I parked the moped under some frangipani trees and walked

up the few steps to my bungalow. I'd taken off my tinted goggles in the shade, then walked into bright sunlight, then opened the door to the bungalow and walked into the shade again, and so for a moment or two I wasn't sure just what I saw. And then I was. My eyes were drawn first to the red plasma pop-up screen of the lap-top computer, which was in the middle of the couch and glowing in the dim light of the room. Then I saw the man facing it, kneeling on the floor between the coffee table and the couch. At the same time I saw my briefcase next to it. Everything was exactly where I had left it, but the computer was on, the briefcase open.

I saw it all in a second, and froze.

"Hey," I said. It wasn't eloquent, but it was the best I could do. I hadn't had time to become indignant. Then I warmed up.

"Hey!" I shouted indignantly.

It was Jeff Little, his attention seemingly riveted to the lap-top's screen. He had picked a funny place to blaze the path of the telecommunications revolution. And something else was wrong. He was ignoring me.

I advanced and said *hey* again, but this time quietly. I shook Little by the shoulder. And then I saw that he hadn't been looking at the computer at all; he had simply been on his knees facing the couch, his hands resting at his sides, his back against the low coffee table, looking as if one push would topple him. Which is just what happened. Slowly, like a tree, he fell sideways. I wanted to stop him, but I was paralyzed. His shoulder hit first, taking the brunt of the impact, but his head missed the area rug and crashed against the hardwood floor. The noise scared the hell out of me.

Okay, don't panic, I told myself. First thing to do, check for a pulse. Just like in the movies. Life imitates art.

And *holy shit*, it was there—slight, slow, but there, a glimmer of life under my fingertip. For that matter, he was breathing—wheezing, really. Now that he was lying down, the spittle around his mouth and on his chin had started in a different direction across his cheek.

I asked Little if he could hear me, but he didn't react. His eyes were slits through which slivers of white showed.

What now? Elevate him so he could breathe easier? All those years of writing about science and medicine and I didn't know. I decided not to elevate his head; I didn't want the blood to leave his brain. On the other hand, I didn't want him to suffocate. Shit! I grabbed a pillow from the couch and slid it behind his neck. Then I picked up the phone and dialed the front desk, my hands shaking; in more words than necessary, I told them to send help. Now I could only wait.

I forced myself to be rational—literally talked to myself. And my training took over. I walked quickly into the bedroom and took my Nikon from a bureau drawer. There was no film in it, so I took a fresh box along with me into the living room. I had 800 color; if I turned on the lamps by the couch I would have plenty of light. It was the one thing I had trained myself to do—record events—having learned from experience that memory was too selective to be dependable; there would be things that I would remember and things that I might not even look at—the way a theatergoer might remember a play but be unable to even venture a guess at how many seats were in the theater. After having run into some problems like that back when I worked for the paper, I'd started using a camera and a tape recorder.

But when I started to load the camera I realized how shaken I was. My fingers just wouldn't operate, and after a few tries at threading the film, I gave it up, a dumb idea, and went over to watch Little breathe. If he ran into trouble, I figured, I could try CPR. I'd never taken a course, but I'd written an article about it once and figured I knew what to do.

The doctor arrived before that was necessary, followed in quick order by two uniformed paramedics with a portable EKG and some resuscitation equipment. They might have moved fast, but to me it was like watching water turn to ice.

"Looks like a heart attack." The doctor, a stout, middle-aged guy in a short-sleeved shirt and shorts, stared at the EKG, then at the digital readout of the portable monitor. "Let's get that pulse up; give him a shot of atropine," he said quickly. "And clear away that congestion." One of the paramedics shoved a syringe with a thick hypodermic needle into Little's arm; the other slid a suction tube into his mouth and down his throat, where it made a gasping sound. They worked on him for another minute or so, inserted an IV, then put him on a stretcher and lifted him. By this time, the patio outside my bungalow was populated by a small crowd of hotel guests and employees.

"You know who he is?" the doctor asked.

"His name's Jeffrey Little," I said. "He works for AT&T. He's here on business."

"Are you a business associate?"

"Friend," I said.

"Can you get in touch with his family?" I thought about Little's wife and kids and the female voice in the bungalow.

"I think so." I shrugged. "I can probably track them down through AT&T."

I watched Little's pale face, still as a death mask, as the ambulance doors closed behind him. "You think he's going to make it?" It was a stupid question, I knew, and the doctor just lifted his eyebrows in response. I watched the ambulance disappear around a bend, listened as its siren faded into the thick quiet of a Bermuda afternoon. Then I went back into the bungalow.

A sense of outrage suddenly hit me. What the hell had he been doing in my apartment? With my computer?

The lap-top's screen was still glowing. I sat down on the couch and turned it to face me. The last prompt, still on the screen, was: NEW SEARCH?

What was on the screen looked familiar. Every piece of software, and therefore every data base system, has its own look, its own recognizable on-screen format, and I knew of only one system that used those specific words and looked exactly like what I was now seeing. I typed *@totime*. If this was in fact Stella, that command would make her respond with the total time elapsed since the user—in this case, Jeff Little—signed on to the system. That command was exclusively Stella's; no other system used it. If I wasn't connected to Stella, the response would be a question mark, a statement that I had used an improper command, or no reaction at all.

I hit the return key, and the screen reacted with *194:11:17*. I grabbed a spiral notebook and scribbled the number.

Well, that was that. It *was* Stella, and the connection had been open for 194 minutes and 11 seconds—a long time for a guy who was operating out of somebody else's apartment, and an especially long time to be on-line in computer terms, with data pouring in at 2400 bits per second.

On the other hand, I didn't know how much time he actually spent on-line. It was now one-fifty, which meant that Little had accessed Stella just after ten-thirty—not long after I'd left to meet MacLeod and Chew. But whatever had happened to him could have happened after he was on-line for half an hour. Or fifteen minutes. Or an hour. All I knew for sure was that for the past forty-five minutes Little had been lying on the floor doing nothing. But Stella knew. She would have recorded individual time on and time off for each particular file accessed. Not that it mattered; whatever Jeff Little wanted to know, he had probably found out. But maybe I could learn something by seeing where he had spent *his* time.

One thing I already knew. The little sensor that I'd depended on in the course of so many stories had failed. I hadn't smelled anything, and in this case it was right under my nose.

I suddenly realized how quiet it was. Little was gone, the crowds had disappeared. I sat down on the couch to assess the potential damage, and realized that I had no indication that there was any.

Okay, what was there to worry about? Not whether Little got into one of Stella's data bases; all of the information in there came from other sources anyway. That wasn't much of a reason for lying about an appointment in Hamilton or breaking into my apartment. Now, my *personal* files were something else. Having a rat in your neighborhood is not the same as having one in your house.

I typed @*personal*, automatically connecting to DATABASE, ALEX BLACK; @*listitle* followed by today's date would tell me if Little had been here, and what he'd been looking for. I hit the return key.

The search terms, names of people, started scrolling down the screen. VLADIMIR ZAYCHEK, ALBERT M. AUGUSTUS. And a couple I didn't recognize: ALFRED BUCHNER, and DAVID BORNSTEIB, a last name I'd never even seen. All of them searches made of my personal files by Little.

One thing I'd say for him: he was a fast study. He couldn't get into Stella or my personal file without my password; obviously he'd gotten it by watching over my shoulder as I typed it that morning.

I now knew that Little's first search—for ALFRED BUCHNER, whoever that was—had taken place at 11:14; the last, ALBERT M. AUGUSTUS, at 11:41. That left forty-five minutes unaccounted for *before* those searches had been made, a period of time during which Little had been on-line with Stella. That was a lot of time. How had he used it?

Well, first of all, he had to familiarize himself with the anatomy of Stella, a user-friendly device but one with a decidedly anti-pirating bias. A novice would have been lost. But Little knew his way around. He'd figured Stella contained a tutorial to help new users, and he found it. There he learned the commands for calling up menus and entering files. Once in, he did sweeps for the names, and then opened each file where he got a "hit"—I knew that because Stella records the "last access date" beside the title of every file in her memory, and many of my files now had the current date next to them. Little, though hundreds of miles from Philadelphia, had been an electronic housebreaker—poking through my file cabinet and opening dozens of files, some of them for no apparent reason, the way burglars dump the contents of drawers to find things that aren't where they should be, rummaging, playing hunches. But looking for what?

I said GB to Stella and placed a call to Little's office at AT&T, where a woman identified herself as Ms. Cole, Little's secretary. I told her who I was, where I was calling from, and that her boss was in a hospital with a suspected heart attack.

"Very funny," she said.

"I'm serious," I said.

"Come on. Who is it?"

I told her again.

There was a pause. "Look, I'm busy," Cole said.

"Am I talking to Jeffrey Little's office?" I asked again. "Vice president for sales?"

"Yes."

"Well, I don't know what to say. Why am I not being taken seriously?"

A pause again. "Mr. Little is in his office," she said carefully.

"What?"

"He's in his office."

"Uh-huh. Well, when was the last time you saw him?"

"I'm looking at him now."

"Jeffrey Little, vice president for sales."

"Right."

"I'm holding his business card right in front of me. There's a guy in the hospital here in Bermuda who's been saying he's Jeff Little from AT&T, Basking Ridge, New Jersey. He's married, has two kids, lives in Bernardsville. He's about forty."

"Bermuda?" she asked incredulously.

"That's right."

"What would he be doing in Bermuda?"

"Selling telecommunications systems, he says."

"Mr. Little doesn't *sell*." She said it as if it were synonymous with pimping. "He *manages* a sales *organization*. Just a moment—I'm going to put you on hold."

I waited.

The next voice I heard was that of Jeffrey Little, or so he said.

"What's going on?" he asked.

I went through it again.

"You say he mentioned my wife and kids?"

"Showed me a picture. Doris and Stephanie and Timmy."

"Doris is my wife. Stephanie and Timmy I never heard of; my kids are John and Allison." We were both silent for a few seconds, then: "Wait a second—what *kind* of picture? Can you describe it?"

"An attractive blonde woman standing in front of a blue or green Volvo station wagon with two kids."

"Son of a bitch. Did this guy have a black billfold?"

"I don't remember."

"If he did, it was mine. A few months ago, I lost my wallet. Or it got lifted. Anyway, this is the first I've heard of it since—and that's where that photo was. I can't believe it. This character is apparently posing as *me*. Now, you say he's in the hospital—what hospital?"

"There's only one. King Edward VII."

By the time I'd gotten off the phone, Little, who clearly did not like being in Bermuda without his knowledge, had already told his Ms. Cole to put through a call to Bermudian authorities.

As for me, I had an impostor on my hands. But I didn't know why, or what it had to do with anything.

I sat there for a couple of seconds staring at the red spiral notebook in which I'd been scribbling notes for the past half hour. And then, not all at once but gradually, I realized that it wasn't mine.

Furthermore, I didn't remember where I first saw it, didn't even remember picking it up. Apparently I had done so absentmindedly, which would've been natural for me even if I *hadn't* found a stranger dying in my apartment. In the intensity of the last hour and a half, I had simply appropriated the notebook. And if it wasn't mine, it had to be Little's, whose name I now used with a certain amount of discomfort.

It was a typical spiral-bound notebook, vest pocket size, the kind you'd find in any stationery store. It looked fairly new, and it was: in fact, I was its only subject. That wasn't obvious right away—only two or three pages of the book had been used, and they contained nothing more than a series of numbers and letters—but I knew that the numbers and letters had to *mean* something. From that point I started to see patterns emerging.

It turned out to be fairly simple. My flight number, with an estimated time of arrival in Bermuda. The date I left Philly. A series of hyphenated numbers which, in the most

rudimentary kind of code, simply translated into the nu-
merical positions of the letters of the alphabet and spelled
out "Fontana." My name, handled in the same way. A time
and address, which turned out to be a record of my trip to
see MacLeod. Even my goddamned supermarket shopping
trip—if I was right about having seen Little at the roadside
café with the redhead, he saw me, too. The time of my dinner
reservation—our meeting had been no accident. The cryp-
tography was low-level amateurish, the kind of thing kids
playing spy would have invented.

But there was one series of computer-look letters that I
couldn't figure:

C1K,LJL,MEMO

I tried various combinations to decipher it, but got nowhere.

Then I picked up the phone and called MacLeod.

J eff Little died without regaining consciousness. The weakened condition of his heart, they said, probably exacerbated by the labored breathing caused by pulmonary edema, brought his life to an uncomfortable but quick conclusion. Heart failure, they called it.

I don't like "heart failure"—not without knowing how and why the heart failed. It's the lazy way of describing what happened, usually used by physicians to avoid lengthy explanations they assume laypeople won't understand anyway. Death is *always* heart failure, whether it's caused by old age or a bomb on your jetliner. It may be *true,* but it isn't *accurate.*

In the case of Jeff Little, however, they couldn't give me much more than that without an autopsy. Until then, the most they would do was speculate a possible myocardial infarction, a heart attack. Little had been where he had no business being, trying to do something he had no business doing. That could have sent his pulse sky-high, and if he'd had any coronary artery disease, the tension and anxiety of the moment could've done it. Yes, they'd learn more if they went further, but the coroner would have to decide that. I wasn't worried about that; I simply told the hospital folks that Jeff Little wasn't Jeff Little at all, and the resident in charge said that this fact, plus the suspicious circumstances, would be cause enough for a complete autopsy.

Meanwhile, the body itself would remain on a slab in the

hospital morgue pending identification and notification of next of kin.

I couldn't help them with that, but I did tell them where to ship the wallet.

Okay, forget swimming. The sun was down, and not much lay ahead. Dinner, a drink, bed. Christ, what a day. Maybe I would make it dinner, a drink, another drink, bed.

I took a shower. When I got out, I heard somebody in the kitchen. After what I'd found earlier in my living room, my heart practically jumped out of my chest; I could picture myself lying alongside Jeff Little, a tag on my toe: *Alex Black. Heard a noise. Heart failure.* I wrapped a towel around myself and, hoping it would be the maid—fat chance at 7 p.m.—walked whistling out of the bedroom.

Well, speaking of fat chances, there was a guy touring my refrigerator. I was almost too relieved to be pissed.

"Want a menu?"

MacLeod didn't look up. "Didn't think you'd mind."

"There's beer."

"I don't drink."

"Then close the refrigerator. How the hell'd you get in here?"

He held up a key. "The hotel management. Scene of the crime and all that. I knocked, but you didn't answer."

"What would you have done if I hadn't been alone?"

"I'd have watched." He said it without smiling, then smoothly switched gears. "This is business. I got a call from Devonshire, police community-media relations. Inspector Blake feels that it would be very bad for its image if anything happened to a big-shot American journalist."

"Yeah, well, I feel the same way. Why are you here, Sergeant?"

"Well, Mr. Black, when a person like you comes to Bermuda asking a lot of questions about a death, and when a path has apparently been paved for you to do so, and then when someone using a phony name is found dying in your

apartment having entered the premises illegally, we begin
to think, Well, this Alex Black is not just another tourist,
and we'd better keep an eye on him. Better safe than sorry,
we always say." It wasn't hard to hear the sarcasm.

I turned around and went back into the bedroom. MacLeod's
voice followed me. "Been downstairs?"

"Downstairs. You mean to Little's apartment?"

"Yes."

"No."

"Why not?"

"I don't know." I thought about it. "It's not my apartment."

"Well, you certainly do stand on ceremony," MacLeod
said.

I certainly do. What kind of a shmuck would've worried
about violating Little's privacy? He sure as hell hadn't worried about mine. But old habits die hard.

"Let's go down and poke around," MacLeod said, not
sharing my apprehension.

The downstairs layout was much different from mine—
smaller, it seemed, with fewer windows and square footage,
but with a glass sliding wall that led from the living room to
a patio. It was neat, less a consequence of Little, I was sure,
than of the maid who had been there. A few magazines lay
on a table in a sitting area.

MacLeod started with the bedroom, opening drawers in
a methodical left-to-right, top-to-bottom fashion. "Lots of
clothes here," he muttered, "although I don't know just how
much good that'll do us." He opened the closet, exposing a
sports jacket, some slacks and two suits; on the floor were
a pair of dress shoes and a pair of running shoes. "Check
the bathroom," MacLeod said.

I did. There was a toothbrush, a container of shampoo, a
tube of Crest, a travel tin of Anacin. In the medicine cabinet,
a few toiletries. Two brands of deodorant. A Gillette razor.
Dental floss.

"Ever hear of anyone traveling with two deodorants?" I called to MacLeod. He came in, shrugged as if it were inconsequential, said, "Maybe he was running out." I shook them; both were fairly full. Besides, even if I didn't know much about police work, I knew something about packing. I told MacLeod that, and then about the female voice. He said he'd heard of ladies bringing their own toothbrushes. Maybe this one brought her own deodorant.

"Maybe she was traveling with him," I said.

"Possible."

"And left in a hurry when things went wrong."

"It's all possible. Maybe he just sweats a lot."

"Uh-uh. Where's his luggage? There's no luggage. Not one piece. Ever see anyone arrive at a hotel with clothes, toiletries, travel alarm, socks, underwear—without a piece of luggage to carry them in? Hell, there isn't even a backpack."

I was getting excited. MacLeod just nodded.

"I figure he had one piece," I continued. "Or they had one piece between them. Anyway, find the woman and you'll find the luggage. In my opinion."

"Check under the bed."

"I did."

He looked at me, raising his eyebrows. Did that mean he was amazed that I had the intelligence to look under a bed? It was hard to tell with MacLeod; whatever he did with his face looked threatening. If he had a sense of humor, it was buried beneath years of being black and being a cop, beneath what those years had taught him; if he had an emotion, the most you could expect was a momentary flicker across his face. He was one of those men difficult to picture as anything but a man—there was no vestige of childhood; at any rate, not of any childhood I wanted to know more about. A kid leaning out of his stroller to intimidate Dobermans?

When it came to understanding Little, however—and despite my own considerable confusion at this point—I had an advantage over MacLeod. I *knew* Little—if not what he stood for, at least what he looked like. And I knew, simply because of the attention I paid to the physical and biological worlds, that appearances provide clues to the nature of things. A flounder is flat for a reason. It has both its eyes on one side of its body for a reason. It has a dark side and a light side for a reason. And if you find something swimming that doesn't look like that, it may be a lot of things, but one of the things is not a flounder.

For the same reason, the man I knew as Little was not a likely candidate to have become a high-ranking sales executive at AT&T. To do that would have meant coming up through the ranks, elbowing out some formidable competition. It would have meant looking the part, sounding the part. Little wasn't persuasive or decisive enough. Not the kind of guy who could control a meeting. Not the kind of guy you'd buy things from if you were spending in the millions. Not the kind of guy who would have invited himself to dinner with me. Not the kind of guy who belonged in the same family as Doris and Allison and Jimmy or whatever the hell their names were, or in their station wagon. He was, in addition to everything else, too short: if you thought in terms of stereotypes, Little should have been an organization man, but more entrepreneurial than most, not merely a cog in a corporate wheel. The exceptions only prove the rule.

All of which adds up to a certain belief in stereotypes. I don't deny it. As a rule of thumb, they're pretty dependable. That's how they got to be stereotypes.

My instincts told me all of this, but the props got in the way. The business card, the photograph, the appointment in Hamilton—I'd bought it all. Put enough structure around a lie and it becomes believable, providing there's no apparent reason why anyone should be lying in the first place.

That's why they say hindsight is the only perfect science.

Whoever Little was, he didn't commit it to paper, except for that spiral notebook. No manila folders, no trade pub-

lications, unless they had gone the way of the luggage. We
found a receipt from a restaurant called Sestina and a matchbook advertising a pasta product. We opened the closet and
looked at clothing labels, found a couple of ticket stubs in
a jacket pocket. When we put it all together, we came up
with Chicago.

"Where're his shirts?" I said. "There are no shirts."

"How about the one he was wearing when they took him
to the hospital?"

"Right. We can check for laundry markings."

MacLeod and I spent the next fifteen minutes looking. I
never bothered to ask if the search was legal; if he wasn't
bringing it up, I wasn't either.

Back upstairs, MacLeod asked if I'd ever handled a pistol.
I shook my head.

"Did you ever shoot anything?"

"Yes. Rifle, carbine, submachine gun. All army."

"But no pistol."

"No."

"Well, it doesn't matter. You know, Mr. Black, there are
two ways to think about carrying a pistol. One is that you
carry a little thing that will fit in the palm of your hand so
that no one will know that you have it. The other is to carry
something larger, something that, when you hold it in your
hand, can be seen at a distance. Do you know which pistol
is better?"

"The one nobody can see."

"And why is that?"

"Because then no one will know that I have it."

"And what is the purpose of that?"

"I can take them by surprise?"

MacLeod shook his head. "No, Mr. Black. You don't want
to surprise anyone, because then you would have to shoot
the pistol. And I'm not sure you could do that, at least not
in time, and possibly not well. The larger pistol is better.
Because you *want* it to be seen. The advantage is that you

may never have to fire it, and for someone who has never fired a pistol, that's a definite advantage. A small pistol has no deterrent effect. A large one *frightens* people, gives them time to reconsider. . . ."

"You're right. It's working already."

"In fact, usually the sight of it is enough to discourage the enemy, provided you've left room for him to back off. Of course," MacLeod said, "pistols are illegal on Bermuda."

"So I've heard."

"But we're just talking."

"Right."

"Now, if you had such a weapon, you might wonder how you would carry it without it being noticed."

"I would."

"Inside jacket pocket." I was wearing a jacket, and he opened it. "Cut a small hole in the corner there and let the barrel go through it. It would have a tendency to pull, but you're no fashion plate anyway."

Look who's talking.

"Are you saying that I should have a pistol?"

"Absolutely not," MacLeod said. "I am saying that if you did have one, you wouldn't want to have to fire it. That way, you might never be caught with it."

"Then why are we having this conversation? Are you saying that I'm in some kind of danger?"

"*I'm* in danger," MacLeod said. "They tell me I'm responsible for your safety. I have a career at stake. If you had a gun, it would be for *my* protection." And then he stopped talking about the gun and everything else, and fell silent.

"You want to eat?" I asked, feeling some kind of momentary responsibility for his future. I was instantly sorry I'd issued the invitation; turning a dinner conversation with MacLeod into a cozy chat would take more martinis than I could handle. And I would be drinking alone.

He looked uncertain.

"*World* will pick up the tab," I added, wondering why my mouth kept moving. "Come on. I'll buy you a steak."

On our silent walk to Fontana's dining room, we passed through the lounge, now filled with people enjoying before- and after-dinner drinks; others were dancing on the terrace to a five-piece group playing "Yellow Bird." I hoped we wouldn't be able to hear it from our table.

MacLeod and I spent the next hour finding out what we had suspected all along: there was almost nothing in the world that held our mutual interest.

That night, when I got into bed, something hard and cold struck my shin. It was a pistol, black and long-barreled and large enough to be seen from a distance. It was loaded, the safety on. I stared at it for a long time, then put it on the night table next to me and turned off the light. I lay there for a few minutes with my eyes locked open, pissed off at MacLeod and picturing a farfetched early-morning scene in which I would awaken to go to the john, knock the pistol off the table (causing the safety to slip off and the pistol to discharge) and end up with a bullet in the groin. I turned the light back on and put the pistol on the floor facing away from me. I didn't like that, either—if I forgot it was there, impossible as that was, the maid might find it and turn me in. So I put it into the drawer of the night table, as far back as it would go, and hoped it would disappear.

I didn't sleep well.

It rained furiously the next morning, lashing the roof of my bungalow and cascading down onto the glass-topped patio table loud enough to awaken me. I woke up remembering that Little was dead and I felt lousy about that; somehow I knew that buried beneath the enigma had been a nice guy with a history—family, loves, dreams—and there but for the grace of God, etc. I put up some coffee and called Angel. Again the answering device; I left a very brief message and felt lonely. Where the hell was she?

Okay, I know I don't own the lady and it's her body and she can do whatever she wants to with it, but Christ, everybody's body should spend at least a little time at home. It wasn't even that; it was just that she should have known I'd be trying to reach her and that I'd be reaching the answering device and she was supposed to care about me—and she had to know that I would be worried about not being able to reach her. On the other hand, if I *said* any of that I'd have a different kind of grief. I sat there and stared into space—stared at a dozen possible scenarios, most of them wishful thinking—and when I came out of it, an hour had passed.

When the rain stopped, I left the bungalow. Sleeping had been torture, with me constantly replaying the scene with Little, constantly wondering if better training would have enabled me to save him. I was glad to get out.

I carefully negotiated the moped over wet roads to the

Temple Bay Marina. The air, cooled by the rain, now smelled
like grass, and the water stretched endlessly at my left, turning from gray to a shimmering blue as the sunlight broke
through. Then, around a bend, a dozen or so large craft
came into view, and as I got closer I spotted the white cap
of Carlton Chew bobbing up and down as he wiped the rain
from the chrome of the *Pound-Foolish*. He saw me, smiled
and waved, then disappeared briefly below. By the time I
reached his slip he was topside again, victoriously waving
the snorkel and face mask, bright blue against the white of
the boat.

I took it and looked it over. "Did anybody wash this or
wipe it off?"

"No chance. It's all I can do to keep up the maintenance
on this little wonder without worrying about things like that."
He opened the engine compartment hatch, reached down
and twisted something, closed the hatch again. "You can
keep it—unless you feel like returning it to the hotel. It was
rented." Along the inside of the retaining band of the face
mask and the length of the snorkel the letters appeared in
black: FONTANA.

I drove back to Fontana and dropped the equipment at
my bungalow, then followed the winding path past the main
house to the small private beach. My destination was a freshly
painted, windowless white shack in which was conducted the
business of rentals—everything from one- or two-person sail-
boats to beach umbrellas. If Zaychek had rented the equipment, this was where he got it.

A tall blond kid in a Fontana T-shirt sat behind a wooden
counter reading a paper.

"Is this where I rent snorkeling equipment?"

He gave up the paper reluctantly, watching a few last
words disappear as he slid off his stool, then became perfunctory. "Guest of Fontana, right?" Without waiting for an
answer, he swiveled a well-thumbed blue-lined ledger toward
me. "Just sign out. And I have to see your key."

"I don't want to rent anything right now. I just want to know how it works."

"Okay, not much to tell. For skin diving, it's $2.50 a day for each piece. So with the snorkel, mask and flippers—you want flippers, right—it comes to $7.50."

"Uh-huh. Well, I think I've got some Fontana property that was never turned in."

"What do you mean?"

"A few months ago, there was a guy who died—stung by a Portuguese man-of-war, remember?"

"Oh, sure." Then, wide-eyed and curious, "You have his gear?"

"Yeah. I'll be returning it soon. It's involved in an investigation." I was about to ask him if I could look up the entry. I decided not to ask in quite that way. If you ask permission they check with their superiors. If you don't ask, they don't have to cover their asses. So I didn't. Besides, the guy clearly thought I was on official business.

"Would the entry for that equipment be in here?"

"Should be—although I don't remember the date."

"That's okay. I'll find it." I started thumbing, and I could sense that he was a little apprehensive, but he handled it: he went back to his paper.

I looked under June 17, the date of Zaychek's death, scanning the list of names of vacationers. His name wasn't there. I went back a page, then another. And there it was, the only blank spot in the RETURNED column on the double-page spread. He had rented the equipment a couple of days earlier.

"You have a copy machine here?"

He looked around the small dim space and shrugged his shoulders.

"Where's the closest one?"

"Up in the main house."

"I'll bring this back in a minute." I closed the ledger and started walking out.

That was too much. "Hey, no, wait a second. What am I gonna do if somebody comes in here and wants to rent something? Or return something?"

"Oh. Right," I said. "I'll do it this way." I tore out the page; he gasped, but it was done, and all he could do was stare. "I'll copy it. And I'll tape it back in. I guarantee you, nobody'll know the difference. I really appreciate it. Thanks."

If he thought he was surprised, he had nothing on me. I don't do that kind of stuff. But there was something about the day, the loneliness of it, the rain, the being far from home, the death of that guy I couldn't stop calling Little, the gun that I couldn't get used to and which, to tell the truth, was in my night-table drawer because I was afraid to carry it while riding a moped—there was something about all of this that made me understand that I was on my own and that it was do unto others before they do unto you. It was a crappy way to feel and I kept hoping it would go away, but it had some positive characteristics, one of which was that I was just miserable enough to do some pushing of my own instead of getting pushed. I'd been pushed a lot lately. I wanted to make one goddamn decision of my own.

My style in doing so, I was relieved to notice, was different than Chase's would have been. I was direct; there was nothing manipulative about my behavior. I knew what I needed and I took it, even at some risk, rather than suffer yet another bureaucrat. It was not exactly an act of heroism, but if Chase had to accomplish the same thing, he would have covered his ass six ways. This, in fact, may have made him cannier, but I was happy with the discrepancy between us.

Later, in my bungalow, I looked at the photocopy of the sign-out sheet. There were no surprises except that Vladimir Zaychek had rented snorkeling equipment in the first place. I would have expected a guy like Zaychek to have his own gear, but that was attaching too much significance to what might have been a simple matter of forgetfulness. He could have inadvertently left it back in Philadelphia or, for that matter, in his room at Fontana, which would have been a long walk for a millionaire; Zaychek was not one to worry about $7.50 a day. He had signed out for a full set—face mask, snorkel, flippers—and the signature was unmistakably a match to the sample I had brought along, supplied by Maria. The flippers were gone, but they could have been kicked off—and if Zaychek had been attacked by a Portuguese man-of-war there could have been the kind of instantaneous, flailing reaction to cause that.

Of course, I was making a lot of assumptions. Some of them were colored by Zaychek's widow, like the one that told me that Zaychek was too old for her. That is, *I* was just about right for her, and I was almost thirty years younger than Zaychek. I knew all about May-December marriages and the safety and security that some women find in older men, and it still didn't feel right.

But I was picturing an older Vladimir Zaychek. It was also possible that he'd been, despite those other assumptions, physically powerful, brilliant, eccentric, virile. I factored those characteristics back into the mix, but I was guessing. The only things I knew for sure were that Zaychek was wealthy and influential. After all, I'd never seen him. I didn't even know precisely what he'd done for a living, except that it paid better than what I did.

And then there were the assumptions I *couldn't* make— like why a science editor's little investigation into a rarely noticed toxicological occurrence would suddenly become the focus of attention for a guy like Little. If he'd gone through my drawers or my luggage instead of my data bases, I could have chalked it up to simple burglary. In fact, that would have helped explain the photos of the real Little's family, too; burglars have been known to come up with such stuff.

But Little hadn't been after anything that conventional, and all I really had to go on was a red spiral notebook and,

from Stella, the list of searches that Little had made: VLADI-
MIR ZAYCHEK, ALBERT M. AUGUSTUS, ALFRED BUCHNER, DAVID
BORNSTEIB.

Hell, yes. Why not start there? Why not do what Little
did and at least know what Little knew?

I made myself a martini, which wasn't a bad thing to do
on a day like this, pulled a kitchen chair over to the couch,
opened my briefcase, set up the computer and modem, and
called Stella. I connected, tapped out my password, saw the
familiar greeting glow at me—GOOD AFTERNOON, ALEX BLACK.
YOUR PLEASURE?—and felt connected in a human sense,
somehow, the way someone lost in the woods at night might
derive comfort from a voice or a familiar song on a transistor
radio. I opened a file to save the data, then asked for the
works—the *Wall Street Journal, Wall Street Transcript, Business Week, Forbes, Fortune,* plus a few specialized data bases
to cover older information. Search term: VLADIMIR ZAYCHEK.

Within seconds the data started spilling across the screen
in short bursts—stuff from the fifties through Zaychek's death.
I'd seen it all before, but only cursorily; I'd been more interested in jellyfish than entrepreneurs. Now I looked more
closely.

From what I could tell, Zaychek was phenomenally successful but reclusive to a degree that made Howard Hughes
look like the life of the party; in fact, the *Wall Street Journal*
called Zaychek "a prestidigitator who holds his cards so close
to his vest that he could probably control his holdings—
estimated to be in the hundreds of millions—from the neighborhood deli." The image of the deli was all wrong, from
what I knew, but call it a greenhouse and it would've been
on target.

The earliest mention of Zaychek turned out to be in 1951,
when he emerged already rich; the power came later. Prior
to 1951, nothing; after that, in terms of his origins, only a
few vague references to his having been a World War II
refugee. The lack of earlier information was hard to figure,

although the further back you go into the past, the less you find in data bases—but it was still hard to figure. I kept reviewing things to determine if I had inadvertently typed anything to limit the search; I tried giving him a wild card middle initial so that Stella wouldn't skip over the name if it didn't match perfectly; I tried Wladimir, another spelling for the name; I even guessed at a few other spellings, far-fetched and unlikely. But the fact was that nobody knew much about Zaychek until he gained a foothold in the American financial world, and back then the business press was unsophisticated and undervalued and concerned itself with the news, not with deep background, and if it *had* ever cared, it had long since ceased caring; there were other more important things to worry about, and Zaychek had been, as far as the press was concerned, a fait accompli. The question had never been where he came from, but where he would go next, and now that, too, had been answered for all eternity, and Zaychek was history, and the papers reflected that as his name followed him into oblivion; he disappeared almost as silently as he'd arrived, yesterday's news.

I had Stella save the information and went on to ALBERT M. AUGUSTUS in several combinations, searching for everything from A. M. AUGUSTUS, M.D., to DR. A. AUGUSTUS, but the doctor appeared only in Cincinnati papers, and I didn't find out anything I didn't already know. From there I went on to one of the names that meant nothing to me: DAVID BORN-STEIB.

As it turned out, I stayed on-line with the computer well into the late afternoon, which probably cost *World* plenty—something, I was sure, I would hear about. Nobody had mentioned where the bucks for this dream vacation were to come from, but they were going to get one hell of an argument from me if they expected to apply it to Science's microscopic budget.

I looked—and looked, and looked—for David Bornsteib. Because the name was unusual, I dropped David and just went with BORNSTEIB, checking most of the major papers and American and foreign news services, too, zipping through data bases. If Bornsteib—*any* Bornsteib—had made news in the last ten years or so, he didn't do it in even a small way in any big city in the United States, and he didn't do it in a big way in any small city. Sweeping the newspapers of the entire country turned up only one Bornsteib, a man injured in an apartment house fire. I figured if there's one, there must be others, but I was reluctant to start tapping into telephone systems or state transportation departments to find the one listing, the one driver's license, of David— too much red tape, too much time, too many clearances.

Alfred Buchner, on the other hand, turned up as one of those wonderful guys who, in his own small way, helped bring us the horrors of World War II. He was not a major figure in terms of what faced the court at Nuremberg, but his name did pop up here and there in articles about Nazi

Germany, particularly when Nazi medical experiments were mentioned. Buchner was a doctor who had come from a well-connected political family (except for one black sheep, an older brother who had opposed Hitler and the Nazis), received a captain's commission at the outbreak of World War II, and spent the war running a small clinic outside of Ostrov, Czechoslovakia. He ran it well enough to have been in line for an executive appointment with the government that was supposed to emerge, but Germany lost, and the last anyone knew of Buchner, depending on who you talked to, was that he was killed in a fire or had fled to Canada and then to Paraguay. Then the trail grew cold.

Well, I had a few things to go on—maybe not as much as Little had, but something. I tried to put myself in Little's position: *I'm breaking into a bungalow where I use somebody's portable computer to tap into some data bases, then attempting to search the data bases for a few items, all of this at some, although not much, personal risk.*

The question now became: Why break in? What Little did in my bungalow he could have done anywhere, with any portable computer, phone line and modem—*unless he wanted to access Stella specifically.* For that, he'd need two more things: my password, which I assumed he picked up by watching carefully that morning as I completed the access, nd the special software—what computer folks call a hidden file—built into a chip in my portable. Little had no way of knowing about that because it doesn't appear on-screen as a part of the listing of the contents of the computer's memory, and I certainly hadn't told him about it. But *if* he had tried reaching Stella on his own computer, assuming he had one here in Bermuda, after a few misses he would have realized that something was keeping him out, and that my computer had to be the variable. That would have brought him to my bungalow, and it brought me to my next question: Why was Stella his target?

As good as Stella is, she isn't the only source of the information she holds. Most of what she has in her data bases is in hundreds of other data bases; the beauty of Stella is that it's all in one place. That, and the fact that she's current—her permanent memory gets updated every few seconds—are two of her strong points. Practically everything that had gone over a news wire in recent memory was now stored within her, with more ancient newspaper and magazine files constantly being transferred to her by electronic scanners.

So there had to be something *else* that would have made Little—or whatever his real name was—take such a gamble to find it. And it had to be something that Little didn't want to simply ask *me* for. As soon as that thought occurred to me, I knew what it was.

Little wanted to read my *personal* files—my notes, my correspondence, all the kinds of things that people without computers might ordinarily commit to corkboards or file folders or index cards. I had told Little how I worked, so he knew those files existed. And once into Stella, he could have requested a directory listing of my files, had each *folder,* so to speak, on the screen in front of him. He would have seen titles covering everything from my staff's VACATION schedule to the recently opened PHYSALIA. By using the search terms VLADIMIR ZAYCHEK, ALBERT M. AUGUSTUS, ALFRED BUCHNER and DAVID BORNSTEIB, he would have instantly determined whether I had stored anything in Stella in which those terms appeared—and Stella would have been able to take him to those exact spots in my text. In fact, he wouldn't have had to search file by file, because Stella was capable of doing a global search—that is, automatically sweeping all files for a particular search term, and opening the file where each hit occurred.

So the inescapable conclusion, based on what had happened and how, was that Little wanted to know what I knew about the four subjects in question. But why, once having gotten into my bungalow, would he not have simply taken the computer with him? Why hang around to be a sitting duck when he could have done the same thing in his apartment, undetected? Wouldn't it have been more convenient to steal the computer? After all, Jeff Little, supposedly an AT&T vice president, would not have been a suspect in the disappearance of something he could have gotten for nothing just by asking his company for it.

Obviously he didn't want to steal the computer. He had walked into the apartment with no intention of removing anything—except information. The same subject matter, some of it, that *I* was after.

Maybe he didn't want to slow down my progress by taking my most important tool. Or maybe he intended to do this again and again as my investigation unfolded. Or both.

As for his chances of getting caught—they were there, but they were slim. The maid wouldn't know one guest from another. In the afternoon stillness of Fontana, Little would easily hear my moped as I pulled up in the small courtyard at the side of the bungalow to park. Then I would have to put the moped on its kickstand, remove the key, take off my helmet and lock the whole business up, then walk up about a dozen or so steps to my bungalow level and around the grass to the front entrance—giving him plenty of time to disconnect, put things back as they were and get out. After all, he didn't have far to go: just down the spiral staircase to the floor below.

This theory seemed to make pretty good sense, and it explained his kneeling position on the floor before the couch, certainly not the most convenient position for using a computer. He could have transferred the whole business to the coffee table and sat on the couch. That would have made more sense, but it would have given him one more item to put back.

One of the search terms was ALBERT M. AUGUSTUS. But I hadn't mentioned Augustus to Little, not once. So now it was a matter of recognizing that Jeff Little knew not only more than he should have but more than I did. He was an impostor. He was spying on me. And his presence in the apartment below mine was no coincidence. But why?

Could Little have been a journalist working on the same story, assuming that there was a story there to get? That was not impossible. Little looked a hell of a lot more like a writer than like a corporate vice president. I thought back to dinner that first night, and his curiosity about my mission in Bermuda. I thought about the way he'd obtained the password to my data base—the only way he could have gotten it—not merely by looking over my shoulder at the screen of my computer, which would have done no good at all since the password wouldn't have echoed on the screen as I typed it (a common computer safety feature to keep electronic eavesdroppers at bay), but by watching my fingers to see which keys I hit. I'm not a fast typist, but it would still be no easy feat. You'd have to know your way around a keyboard.

One other characteristic that Little had was what made this entire scenario possible, something no go-for-the-jugular journalist could exist without: acting ability. He'd been totally convincing, completely in character—and he'd been lying through his teeth. That characteristic was precisely what I lacked, and one of the reasons, aside from personal interest, that I preferred to write about science instead of corruption in city government; you can't just walk up to a possibly corrupt official and ask him if he's on the take. Of course, investigative reporters are unlikely to think of themselves as actors; it's less a talent than it is an adaptive behavior, one that enables them to do the job. And it is the social significance of doing the job which makes the behavior somehow acceptable. But call it what you like: it's what you need to appear to be something you aren't, and—journalist or not—Little had it in spades.

MacLeod stopped by. I knew it before I saw him—recognized his knock, not because he'd bothered to observe such courtesies during our short relationship, but because he had a lot of meat between the skin and the bone, and the sound he made was solid, dull and menacing. Like a dead animal tossed onto your porch.

He nodded at me, waited for me to step aside so that he could pass, and tossed a bulky envelope on the coffee table. Then he walked to the kitchen, poured himself some leftover coffee the same color as the droplets of sweat that glistened on his face and neck, and settled into the sofa like a diving bell, sending up a hiss from the pillows. "We have a few things," he finally said in his official manner, removing the well-worn notebook from his jacket pocket. "First, there's the matter of a lady who showed up to claim the deceased."

"Little?"

"Yes, indeed. Asked for him by that name, too. Unfortunately, the folks at the hospital made her a little nervous when they told her some questions had been raised and asked her to take a seat. I don't have to tell you what happened."

"She left."

"Bolted is more accurate."

"Did she give a name?"

"Not that anybody remembers. They handled it sloppily."

"Description?"

"Not a great one, but we did get 'attractive, late twenties

to early thirties, red curly hair.' She described herself as a friend of the deceased."

"Sounds like the woman I saw in the roadside café. That means she's still in Bermuda."

MacLeod shrugged. "Could be."

"Is there any way we can have the people at customs alerted?"

"It's already been done. But all she needs is a wig and she's out. Besides, we don't have any real reason to hold her."

"A wig won't match her passport photo."

He looked at me, expressionless except for an almost imperceptible arching of the eyebrows. "If you know her true hair color, Mr. Black, you must be on intimate terms indeed. Besides, if she's a U.S. citizen, which is reasonable to assume, she won't need a passport."

"Right."

One thing was for sure. The woman was no passing acquaintance. Not only that: she knew where the body really belonged, where *home* was to the man I knew as Jeffrey Little. Where that body would have to be shipped. She knew the things I wanted to know, and she was somewhere on the island. But that could change quickly.

And now she would be even more careful; she had to know that her behavior in the hospital would not have gone unnoticed. My chances of finding her were pretty slim.

"Next." He reached out for the brown kraft envelope and dumped a wrinkled tan button-down shirt with a red pinstripe on the table.

"It's not my birthday."

"That's the shirt Little was wearing when you found him."

I checked the collar for laundry markings. There was only one, four letters long: BORN. In the characteristic shorthand of shirt launderers, short for Bornsteib.

So I now knew the real name of the deceased, as MacLeod

called him, even if I didn't know his identity. I could stop calling him Jeffrey Little.

"What is it?" MacLeod asked. I guessed I reacted in some way when I saw the name. The son of a bitch didn't miss much.

"Little was looking through my data base. One of the search terms he used was Bornsteib."

"Now what's this, uh, search term?"

"It's when you're looking for something, you give the computer the thing, the word, you're looking for, and if it's there, it finds it for you."

"Bornsteib?"

I tapped the laundry mark. "I think it's *his* name. Which means he wanted to know if I had any information on *him*."

"I don't get it. Where does this information come from?"

"What's *this*?" There was a small red dot, almost invisible, on the back of the shirt near the left shoulder.

"A tiny red spot," MacLeod answered.

"Looks like blood, doesn't it?"

"Well, it actually looks like a tiny red spot," MacLeod said. "It could be blood. Or it could be ink, or an imperfection in the shirt. And if it's blood—well, Mr. Black, everybody has some."

"Well, how about running some tests."

"To find out?"

"If it's blood."

"And what then?"

"Hell, MacLeod, I don't *know* what then. When *then* comes, I'll let you know. It's a dead man's shirt. Christ, you can't ignore that."

Of course, I didn't know *what then*—and it didn't matter. I had seen that red spot and had jumped on it more to change the subject than anything. If it hadn't been the little red spot, it would've been the pinstripes; I would have told MacLeod that Little didn't impress me as a man who would wear pinstripes. The point was, I just didn't want to give MacLeod his first lesson in data access. It wasn't *necessary*. He knew zip about computers: to him, a memory was what kept him from screwing up his mother's birthday. And I didn't want to get him off on a tangent, wanted him to keep his eye on one ball at a time. His primary job, as I saw it, was to step in when I needed help, and my experience with Little had taught me that my instincts were not infallible.

I put the shirt back into the envelope. "Okay," MacLeod said. "A test can't hurt. And I think the circumstances are suspicious enough to justify an autopsy."

"Good."

"This could drag out. A pathologist's report, and later an inquest. It could take months."

"I don't have months."

"Well, I know the pathologist. Nice guy, fellow named Thorne. I can talk to him about letting you see the results."

"If it'll help, tell him I'm a science writer."

MacLeod was obviously in no rush. Unlike that first time in his office, when he couldn't give me even a few minutes, he now seemed to have nowhere to go and nothing to do.

Which, now that I thought of it, was probably the case. I was the last stop of the day for a guy who had nowhere to go, no one to be with. Afternoon was quickly turning into evening. And I didn't want to invite him to dinner again; you reap what you sow. He still didn't like me much—a feeling that was mutual, because he was gratuitously hostile—but I could sense that we were both developing a sort of working relationship; grudgingly, we each acknowledged the limits.

"Suppose I wanted to go spend a few hours at customs," I said. "Could you arrange it?"

He looked at me, and in his eyes I could practically read the caption *American who's seen too many movies.* "Mr. Black," he said, "it's busy down there."

"I won't get in the way."

"What I mean is, they process a lot of people—"

"Well, that's precisely—"

"—and they're very careful about eliminating contact between people who have already passed through and people on the other side. Drug smuggling."

"I don't get it."

"I mean that your access to people will be severely limited. You can't move beyond the customs lines. Not even if I intervene for you. Not on this short notice. You can stay on the Bermuda side, but you can't go onto the U.S. side. And understand this: you can't stop her. You have no authority."

"Yeah, but *she* might not know that."

It was a wise-guy answer, the kind of answer that unnerved even me. I'm a guy who comes to a complete stop at stop signs, and I knew I wouldn't be doing anything illegal. But part of me balked at being told once again that my idea, the only idea I had, was something that MacLeod didn't want me to do. I was beginning to think that all my differences with MacLeod were turf issues, a knee-jerk reaction on his part that the cops should do the surveillance and the writers should do the writing.

"Besides, it's too late. No more flights to the States today."

"How do we know she's going to the States? Maybe she's going somewhere else."

And so on. The conversation became an exercise in hair-splitting, and as soon as I realized that, I abandoned it altogether. I figured I would simply go to the airport unannounced and hang around and watch the cabs arrive, and even at that I couldn't stay there constantly, and so my chances of catching her would be slim at best. But it was worth a shot.

Before he left, there was one more thing. "There's another autopsy I'd like to order," I said.

"Who?"

"Zaychek."

"But there *was* one."

"That was before, when it all looked pat. I'm thinking maybe something could have been overlooked. The guy had what looked like a jellyfish sting, and he drowned, or his heart stopped. Well, that's easy; I guarantee you that nobody looked much beyond the obvious. I'd like to see an autopsy performed as if everything was suspect."

"That'll be a little tougher. It'll take an exhumation order. You'll need the signature of the next of kin."

"I'll do better than the signature," I said. "I'll give you the next of kin herself."

If we were going to go to the trouble of digging up what was left of Vladimir Zaychek, I wanted to be sure that somebody would be around who could identify it.

I had arrived in Bermuda on Sunday afternoon; it was now Friday morning and I was looking at the end of a hell of a week. During that time I'd spoken to Maddie a couple of times, but I hadn't been able to reach Angel. At first that didn't bother me—*so I'm alone, so what.* Ultimately we're all alone. Besides, I'd never given her the phone number of Fontana.

Of course, she could have gotten it easily enough.

But that wouldn't have been Angel. Angel doesn't want to need *anyone.* It's not a matter of whether she needs or doesn't need, and it's not a matter of personal philosophy. It's learned behavior. She grew up tough, watching out for herself. If she didn't call me, it wasn't because she didn't want to. It was a response to what she *thought* she should do—her idea of the appropriate handling of a situation. In that respect, she was years behind the times—that was precisely the kind of game-playing most of the women I knew didn't do anymore. Of course, you could ask, "Who is this asshole who thinks he knows what makes people tick," and every once in a while, when I'm playing Freud with Angel, she does ask that question. In those very words.

Well, I figured, I *did* know what made her tick—at least as much as anybody could. It took a while. When I first met her, for instance, she used to do a lot of prowling, but gradually her cruises into the world of casual sex became much less frequent, far more rational: she would now choose to act instead of being forced to react. She was learning to be in control.

I'd been one of the catalysts. AIDS and herpes were the others; warm bodies had become booby traps. But I was most important, because she was learning to trust me, to trust a male for the first time in her life. And there was a lot of incredible warmth and heat generated as a result of it. Sometimes I'd think it was almost there, almost perfect. I'm a guy whose strength is language, and when you're in a relationship you use whatever you have, so I made love to her with conversation, with humor, with fantasy. I gave her what she was missing—the right words, whatever was on my mind—and gradually she missed them when they weren't there.

If I do say so myself.

There was another person I had to think about, and my stomach flipped as I did so: Colin Chase. This was, as I'd told him three weeks ago when this had all started, his party, and now I figured he deserved a progress report. Actually, he'd deserved one earlier, but I couldn't get myself to call him, even though what had once seemed like a simple assignment had changed dramatically. I'd been sent on a one-goal mission—to find some support for the "official" version of Vladimir Zaychek's death, ostensibly to help Maria Zaychek find some peace. That original scenario, however, held up only if I accepted the surface appearance of things. Once I started digging, particularly in view of the constellation of activities that seemed to be taking place around me, it looked like Zaychek's was no ordinary death. Although there was still no hard evidence, nothing that would, say, hold up in court, to indicate that the death was anything more than what it appeared to be.

And yet it seemed to me—as it had to Maria Zaychek—that there were some compelling reasons why the explanation of Zaychek's death did not hold water. Sure, it *was* possible. But you can't create an explanation by forcing a string of possibilities or even *givens* together. Life isn't geometry; you don't want to hold your breath waiting to find a situation as pure as a theorem. The art of understanding human behavior lies in reading *between* the givens—that's where you discover the illogical, the bizarre. They belong in the equation, too. In fact, you can go broke betting on the predictability of the species except for this: when people behave uncharacteristically, there's always a reason.

The question was now one of deciding how much to tell Colin Chase, who was interested in a fast, simple solution to support what he felt, and then in getting me back to *World*. I decided to tell him the facts as I knew them; I owed him that. But only the facts. What I conjectured would remain mine. I placed the call.

One of these days I'm going to do a little essay on how people answer their phones. Take Colin Chase. I'm in Bermuda on an assignment that is basically his wet dream. I talk to his secretary, the kind of person who would be perfect behind the counter in an outrageously expensive boutique where she could look down her nose at you for being unable to afford something that would take her a month's salary to pay for. She says, "Uh, he's quite busy, Mr. Black. Is he expecting your call?"—which is as friendly as she gets. At least to me.

This time I say, "I doubt it. You'll have to ask him." And Prunella pushes the hold button as though she were pushing a switchblade into my liver—it's funny how, from a thousand miles away, you can hear someone's rage in a click—and after a long wait Chase gets on. And what does he say?

"Chase here."

Now here's a guy who has sent me away from my job to toodle through the tropics. He knows it's me on the phone, because Prunella would have told him that. He could have said, "Hiya, Alex. How's it going?"

He says, "Chase here."

It's a game. First the secretary, so that I feel humbled by

having to seek an audience; then the wait, so I won't think he has nothing better to do. Then the annoyed "Chase here," the second word of which is followed by a brief but perceptible sigh that only William Buckley can do better, and which therefore makes the entire greeting sound a little like "Shit, another interruption."

"Black here."

Chase was surprised, he said, that he hadn't heard from me in all these days. I said I was surprised that he'd given me a second thought. He ignored that and told me he was going to send me some copies of the September 9 issue of *World*, which looked terrific—his way of saying that the Science section managed quite well in my absence. I told him I'd already read, and probably edited, everything that could possibly be in that issue, just so he'd know whose hand had been at the helm. He asked me how long I needed to finish up in Bermuda; I told him I didn't know, but that things were moving along quickly, and apparently there weren't any real problems back at the magazine, right? Well, uh, sure, but he really didn't have time to ride herd on it to make sure things continued like that. And so on and so forth.

Between that kind of stuff, I managed to squeeze in the details of everything that had happened.

I knew I'd bought myself a few more days, but I didn't know if it was because I'd merely sidetracked Chase into defending himself, in which case I could get one of those follow-up calls an hour later in which he'd tell me the *real* news, or because he was manipulating me, which would mean that he actually *wanted* to give me those additional days but didn't want me to know that. Talk about paranoia.

At any rate, I figured I would push my luck, told him I would need Maria Zaychek and possibly another person in Bermuda to look at some bodies, told him I couldn't wrap things up without exhumation and another autopsy, pointed out that airfare wasn't that much. I pushed it, and he bought it.

Chase's priority, I had to keep reminding myself, was Maria Zaychek, and not the truth behind the death of her husband. That in itself was interesting. I had speculated early on that Chase and Maria were romantically involved, though this was hard to believe—the guy was such a cardboard cutout. On the other hand, lots of women are happy to spend their lives with cardboard cutouts like that and, as cutouts go, Chase wasn't bad: good-looking, powerful, suits from Savile Row and shoes custom-ordered from Italy, big bucks in the weekly envelope, lunches at the Four Seasons, the right masseur, influential friends, all the perks. And probably totally different outside the office. It could take a Maria Zaychek years to find out what the guy is really like, and—well, what was I saying? This was, after all, the woman who married Vladimir Zaychek.

I figured the redhead would pick Sunday, the worst day to leave Bermuda and the best day for her. She would want a crowd to get lost in.

On the heavier days, the customs inspectors looked through your brain before they looked through your luggage. Far from the customs stereotype of unsmiling, monosyllabic and perfunctory civil servants, these people engaged travelers in apparently friendly conversation while watching for nervousness or guarded responses or eyes that didn't meet theirs, behavior experience had taught them usually meant that something was in the suitcase. Not everyone was searched, but everyone was scrutinized, and decisions were made with no apparent logic. Sometimes suspicious-looking characters were waved through, while typical middle-aged couples were searched. That in itself may have been the rationale—the logic of following no logical course. I wondered if personal curiosity played a role; did they ever open a piece of luggage simply to look at a beautiful woman's underwear?

Scientific inquiry.

I took the moped. It wasn't the best way to go; the airport was at the other end of Bermuda and the day was hot, and after a forty-five-minute ride under a crash helmet on the serpentine roads, my hair would feel like sauerkraut. But I didn't want to go to the main house to find a cab that might not have been there, and I didn't want to wait for one to get there. So I pulled out of the driveway and headed south to Middle Road, then east.

Jeff Little, I now knew, was David Bornstein, not Bornsteib. The name had sounded funny to me from the start; the thing that pissed me off was that it took me so long to figure out that Bornstein had merely made a typing error when he tried to access information about himself. This occurred to me only as I was staring blankly at the keyboard wondering what I might try next; the *b*, of course, sits next to the *n*. Bornstein had the problem any typist might have had—getting used to a different keyboard, in this case a slightly smaller one. Bornstein had apparently been edgy enough and worried enough about being caught in my apartment not to realize that he'd screwed up, hadn't even seen the mistake on the screen. And Stella, like any good computer, did only what she was asked to do; she scanned my personal files for Bornsteib and came up empty.

With that error, Bornstein had concluded that I didn't know he existed. If he'd done the search properly, he would have found that to be not entirely correct; his name did appear in one of my files. But it had been just one of a number of names in some research I had pulled together for a possible story, a name collected indiscriminately because it appeared in an article that contained a search term that I'd used. I didn't find this out until later, and possibly I would never have learned it at all—it was a tiny reference I might have ignored even if I'd gotten around to doing the piece— if it hadn't been for Bornstein's intrusion into my life.

By the time the cab reached the airport, a large round clock on the wall read eight twenty-nine. Customs wouldn't even begin processing people until ten, so I had some time to wait.

I parked the moped and walked into the customs building, a large, high-ceilinged place with several airline counters— American, Delta, Pan Am, Eastern—and beyond them the series of counters and conveyor belts that was customs. If the redhead was going to leave Bermuda for the United States, this is where it would have to happen.

Talk about long shots.

Despite the size of the place and the traffic that it handled, there wasn't room for more than a dozen people to sit, and I took one of the few available seats among the one group of people already there—a contingent of worriers, no doubt, since the first U.S. flight wasn't scheduled to leave for close to two hours.

They were half a dozen elderly women in quiet pastels, probably a flock of widows, maybe a church group. One of them held a piece of luggage covered with decals of Niagara Falls, the Poconos, Atlantic City and Parrot Jungle, and filled the area with her incessant complaining about the prices of ceramic birds in Hamilton. If her husband was dead, *he* was on vacation.

I unfolded a newspaper and started reading. That would cover my face. It would, I soon learned, also make it difficult to see anything.

I wasn't sure I'd be particularly good at what I'd have to do. If you're going to spend a day sitting on a hard wooden bench watching people stand in line, especially in crowds where it's not easy to see every line as the travelers passed through it, you have to have two things: an ability to concentrate, because the work is tedious; and an absolute disregard for what people might think. I was good at the first, untested on the second. I had seen the redhead only from a distance, sitting in the café with Little—with Bornstein— and to have even a small chance of recognizing her I would have to stare into the face of just about every woman young enough to be her. That would be enough, I was sure, to get me arrested.

I am not anything like a private eye. To be a good one, based on what I've read in paperbacks, you have to be cynical above all, assuming the worst of people. You trust no one.

I trust practically everyone, but I did my best. There were a lot of people coming and going, so I had to establish a priority system. I would assume that the redhead was traveling alone, although she might possibly try to look like one of a group. I decided to ignore nuns and, particularly, men, assuming—if I remembered correctly—she would have had a hell of a time imitating one. I would ignore anyone carrying a baby. I would ignore anyone in uniform.

I sat, I walked around, I invented excuses for spending my day at customs, just in case anybody should ask. I went up and down aisles, I stared at women, I got dirty looks from their husbands and boyfriends and from them, too, and before long I realized it was almost one o'clock. The next U.S. flight would leave at one-thirty, and after that Alex Black would leave because he was tired and dying of hunger and thirst. The sun had turned the afternoon into a hot plate; I could look out and see the heat rising from the parking area, diffusing the images of the cabs sitting in line there. I needed a drink, anything cold.

The entrance to the main customs area was a wide hallway, a sort of indoor portico, and when I arrived I had noticed a Coke machine. Now, with a lull in the activity, I decided to go out and find it. There were a few stewardesses using it when I got there, and when they were done, I threw a few coins in and got my drink and zipped off the top. Across from me, one of the stews was taking a swig from a can, and our eyes met for an instant. Pretty, I thought.

I looked at her like I would have at any good-looking woman; right in the eyes. If she'd looked back, maybe I'd have looked again. If not, happens all the time. Brief eye contact; vague interest, but a plane to catch and miles to go before I sleep, so goodbye, sweetheart. But she recognized me and couldn't hide it—and even *then* I wouldn't have put it together if she hadn't assumed that the game was over and, in the vernacular, hauled ass.

I watched her with my mouth open, and that gave her a

good head start. The woman who was fleeing down the hall-way, her heels clattering on the concrete floor, was no red-head now; her hair was short and dark and shaved to a V at the nape of the neck.

With all that was going on in her life she had time to go to a beauty salon?

No, Alex, you asshole, she just took off her wig.

Now I was running too, and fast, but I'd stood around too long. She was already out the door. I could see her reaching a cab, throwing a small piece of carry-on luggage in the backseat. Now I was outside and the car was moving quickly out of the lot.

I know exactly what would have happened next if I'd been writing it. I would have raced across the parking plaza, trying to jump on the cab while yelling something to the driver about police. Or I'd have pulled out the gun, planted myself between the cab and the redhead's freedom as it bore down on me, tires screeching. *Go ahead, make my day.*

Well, you can really get hurt that way. And the gun was still in the night-table drawer. And most important: I *wasn't* the police. I wasn't even sure that I had a right to try to stop the woman. Was she an accessory, a material witness? To what? I didn't know. Suppose I jumped on the cab and it went out of control and hit somebody? I could be sued.

This was my mother's voice in my ear. It's amazing how considerations like these—as opposed to trivial things like personal safety—can intrude on what otherwise might be genuine acts of heroism.

And now *shit, no cab.* Five minutes ago, the place looked like a Honda convention. Now it's the Sahara, and just as populated.

In my panic, I forgot where I'd parked my moped—easy to do, since the rental mopeds all look pretty much the same—and I ran back and forth around the customs build-ing. I watched the cab, in no particular hurry, leave the area.

Okay, there was the moped; as I ran for it, I fumbled in my pocket for the key.

At about this time I started to feel as if I *were* in a movie. The cab was gone, but that wasn't important because there was only one road it could go on, at least until it got away from the airport proper. I was aware that I had attracted some attention; you don't go chasing a stewardess at high speed on a Sunday afternoon without somebody noticing. I looked around and I saw a lot of faces looking at me through the portico's windows. When I was a kid, I got hit by a car, and I remember the faces that crowded around to look at me as they picked me up and put me on the sidewalk. Back then I was too busy getting my leg broken to care if anyone saw me cry, but I was aware of that sea of faces. That's how I felt now.

I removed the lock. The moped, as usual, did not start immediately, but I eventually wobbled out of the parking area to the exit and twisted the throttle all the way when I hit the main road.

After a minute or two on that road, I could see the cab several cars and some distance in front of me, around a bend. I could see that the cabdriver wasn't pushing it the way the ex-redhead would have if she'd been at the wheel, but he wasn't coasting, either—he was clearly trying to get away without doing anything too illegal. That wouldn't be easy because passing other cars was harder in a car than in a moped, and an experienced moped driver could usually make better time than an experienced cabbie.

I was close enough to see the woman turn and look in my direction when we hit a long, steep upgrade. I had a tourist moped, one of the many that had their balls cut off, so to speak, to reduce casualties. I did the best I could, practically twisted the handlebar off, but it soon became obvious that fourth gear wouldn't make it, so I downshifted, and then third ran out, and I was now in second, and the lady in the cab, now far in front of me, turned and looked in my direction one last time as the vehicle disappeared over the crest of the upgrade. Now dozens of vehicles were going past me and I was trying to pedal up the hill into nothing but the clear blue Bermuda sky, wondering what I would see after I reached the top; when I got there I shifted up and accelerated hard and went over the crest and picked up speed as I went around a bend. There I almost collided with the last car in a line of traffic. I hit the brakes, threw out my foot, skidded over to the grass at the side of the road and went down. My lady was no longer in sight.

I sat there on the grass checking myself for wounds, took off the helmet, wiped away some sweat and started to wonder if I'd damaged the moped. I was so preoccupied with that little task that I didn't notice the police car pull up behind me. When the big hand clamped down on my shoulder, my heart, which was already pounding, almost exploded. I saw the gold of the sports jacket.

"Are you hurt?" MacLeod asked.

"I don't know. I'm checking." I looked at my elbows and my knees. "Where were you a minute ago? Jesus, we could have caught her."

"I'm trying to keep you alive," he said. "You're not making it easy. Who was that?"

"The redhead. She was trying to get away. I think she's a stewardess."

He put me on my feet with one hand.

A moving finger, you will learn if you ever put one too close to a denizen of the deep, may look like something to eat; a cluster of your appendages groping along an undersea ledge can easily be taken for an aggressor. It is not a conclusion arrived at through any process of reasoning, but rather as a programmed response to appearances, passed along genetically over millions of years: a shark attacks a swimmer not because it knows the taste of human flesh— few of them have tasted us—but because it mistakes our activity for that of a school of fish. Or so we think. This makes most fish far less intelligent and far more dangerous than dogs or horses or chimps, who would never make that error, although a marmoset monkey once took the rounded tip of my index finger for a grape, and I owned a Siamese cat who in the darkness responded to my toes as if they were mice.

All this may be just as well; in the ocean, nothing suffers by being too cautious.

In the shallow water off the beach at Fontana, as in the water that surrounds most of Bermuda, there is an abundance of life, and you don't have to go far out to see the larger ones. Many species hang around the water's edge, and people often stand only waist-high just four or five feet from parrot fish and hogfish and even barracuda without knowing they're there. The fish give the humans a wide berth, maybe because we don't taste as good as we think we do, or more likely because we're not worth the trouble.

I was tired of the computer, tired of being alone—I didn't count MacLeod as company—tired of chasing things real and imagined. So I spent what was left of Saturday staring at the ocean floor in the water off Fontana's small private beach through a face mask. The sun was warm on my back— I'd painted it with number 15 sun block; the small, crestless ripples that floated toward shore and then out again licked at my shoulder blades, rocking my body; and wherever I looked through the luminescent water was a floor show of green and yellow tendrils. And I joined it, floating facedown, lulled almost to sleep.

I floated. I thought about Vladimir Zaychek and how he'd done that, too, all the way down to Church Bay; I thought about Maria Zaychek, who by this time Monday, at my request, would be in Bermuda; I thought about Tuesday, when, weather permitting (and being Bermudian, it probably would), the body of Vladimir Zaychek would be exhumed; I remembered how the early-morning smell of her had drifted to me, ethereal, a smell I could now conjure up even with my breathing blocked by the face mask. I sparred with a pair of fish of a type I didn't recognize, a bright-red dramatically finny fish and its grayish mate, both around five inches long, who lived in a crack surrounded by thick foliage at the bottom of the small man-made jetty that defined the edge of Fontana's beachfront. There were mussels there, and I thought about Inga Schmidt, the starfish specialist, and the conversation I had to have with her; I had missed her at work on Friday, but the message on her answering machine gave her home phone number, so I would call her this evening. I thought about Angel; as the days passed, she became dimmer, and I worried about that, not wanting to let these few days turn into an estrangement. I missed her companionship and her physical presence and wondered whether she was feeling the same thing. I thought about the opening of the grave and the cast of characters who would appear there, including one person I'd arranged to have show up simply because I had a hunch—the kind of thing you can do when you can pick *World*'s pocket.

Suddenly my vision was filled with splashes of silver: I had become the center of a school of very small fish, thousands of them, that now surrounded my head and body. They glided very slowly alongside me, and I used little pushes of my flippers to regulate my position within that glistening drapery of sequined bodies and tiny black eyes, many of them so close that they almost brushed my cheeks. It lasted for a few minutes, and those minutes were among the most beautiful of my life, enough to make me not care where I was or where I was going. The feeling was more than seductive; it was almost dangerous, like having had one drink or one pill too many. Those moments in the sea, I know, are always within me, buried somewhere; occasionally, when the breeze or the sun or the time of day is right, I can bring them back. And when I'm lucky enough to be able to do that, the rest of the world goes away.

Now I floated facedown in the water and watched the long tendrils of sea grass move below me as I skimmed past and recounted what little I knew about David Bornstein, a guy who'd been struck dead in the act of coveting another man's data base: a high-tech version of divine intervention. Once I had his correct name, I went back to Stella and found that he was no lightweight—a professor of computer science at the University of Chicago who'd designed a nice piece of analytical software that had put some ongoing royalties in his pockets and given him some options. He'd also had a couple of books published. Clearly he'd made some better-than-educated guesses about me: he'd searched ZAYCHEK and AUGUSTUS. He'd also searched BUCHNER, which provided some kind of clue—if only I knew what to do with it. Nevertheless, I had no doubt that I would eventually find out exactly where Bornstein fit in, and why. I knew he had a computer; I was sure he'd committed his entire life to memory. All I had to do was get to that computer and the data base that constituted Bornstein's files.

In my mind, it was easy. Now that I knew where he'd taught, I could find out where he'd lived, and all I would have to do would be to convince somebody that I should have access to his computer. With a little cooperation I could do it all over the phone. I had simplified this to the point where getting into Bornstein's computer was nothing more than a technicality, poetic justice, but I also knew that the scenario that unfolded in my imagination was much simpler than real life. I could go to his house and be denied access. Or find that his computer was at the university. And even if I managed to get to his computer, there was a good chance that a guy like Bornstein would have protected his files from people like me with a password.

This is what you think about when you're facedown in the water and there are no sharks to distract you.

I played and replayed the scene at the airport, which became more and more like a James Bond movie and now featured a cast of thousands: the street-smart science editor cum detective who figured out just what the redhead was going to do; the tough-guy hero who almost wiped himself out on his moped; the stewardesses, one of whom was an impostor and (according to the others) had not even been wearing any airline identification, just a uniform. And finally, the extras: those who'd been hired to stand around and gape as the hero goes off on his cycle; the drivers who witnessed him falling on his ass on the road. And in the final embarrassing scene, a Bermudian cop built like a refrigerator implying that the detective had behaved stupidly even for a tourist and please, Mr. Black, the colony of Bermuda would appreciate it if you don't do anything like that again.

Meanwhile, Mr. Black, on the grass next to his moped, checks himself to make sure everything is there that used to be, happy that nature didn't design him with his private parts on his elbow.

So there I was, floating facedown with nothing but the sound of my own breathing in my ear but unable to stop those little wheels from turning. Snorkeling, except for a blissful minute here and there, was not the same kind of diversion as shooting pool or playing the piano, the two things that I find take total concentration; they exclude everything else. Floating facedown in the water is in some respects like getting your hair cut: there's not much to do except watch what happens, and usually nothing does.

And then suddenly, right in front of me, I saw what I thought was a minnow-sized fish hit the water hard, but it was too hard, not like a fish reentering after having leaped for an insect, and it was quickly followed by another just like it, both with a silvery symmetry, two sudden tracks of bubbles plowing through the water fast for several inches and then suddenly, it seemed, grinding to a halt, dying, tumbling over and over toward the ocean floor. I put my hand out and caught one, and it was heavy and hard.

It was a bullet.

Instinctively I inhaled deeply through the snorkel and put myself against the sandy bottom, anchoring myself with the sea grasses. For a moment I simply sat on the bottom, my heart pounding; it seemed as if my need to breathe had disappeared entirely. And then I used the long tendrils in a hand-over-hand manner to propel myself to the small jetty.

Slowly, very slowly, I peeked out from behind the jetty, all but a few inches of me out of sight of land. I couldn't see anything. I didn't know if the shots had been audible, but if they had, no one had taken any notice. On the beach and the little dock it was business as usual.

It was a long, long time before I left the water, and I didn't do it until I had convinced myself that whoever tried to shoot me probably hadn't stayed around, and couldn't even know that he had missed. I got off the beach fast, blending in with a large group of people, putting as many bodies between me and the hill as possible. When the group dispersed, I stayed close to the walls of the winding paths. The bungalow didn't feel that safe anymore, but I ran to it, my heart pounding, and, it seemed, didn't take a breath until I was inside.

That night I called Angel again.

"Hello?" The word slurred and sleepy; I could hear Puerto Rico in it distantly, the way you hear the ocean in a shell.

"It's me, Angel," I said. "Hace mucho tiempo. . . ." *It's been a long time.*

"Alex! I just woke up. Where *are* you? Just a second. . . ." A few footsteps, water running in the little bathroom next to the bedroom, a silence in which I could picture her face in a towel, her delicate arms moving as she rubbed her face, her hair flying around it, undressed except for her panties, which is how she usually went to bed.

"I'm back." A pause, slightly breathless. "I miss you."

"Yeah, well, I did call. You were out."

"I was gone for a couple of days. I got a call from *Metro*— they had a photographer lined up to do some winter fashion on location in Atlantic City, and he got sick at the last minute, so they called me to fill in. I guess I was the only photographer available on twenty-seven minutes notice."

"How'd it go?"

"Great, if you like shooting furs on the beach in September. I had a ball, but it got a little hot for the models. I get the film back tomorrow and the issue'll be out October fifteenth. I hope it looks okay. They weren't exactly wind-blown."

I felt the tension drain out of me, and I realized I'd been worried about her being off with some guy somewhere. And then I realized I'd been listening—to the water, to her foot-steps—for other, less familiar sounds. I didn't like what I was feeling, didn't like caring that much. Loving her was easy and that's why it was tough; I wanted to possess her. But she didn't want to be possessed.

I hoped that the feeling would pass.

Her voice droned on about the assignment, about her insecurity at never having done fashion before, and I tried to listen, but the other stuff kept getting in the way. It was her body, not mine, I kept telling myself, so why this feeling? And then I knew. It wasn't her body I was worried about. It was her head. If I lost her, that's where it would happen.

I found myself wishing I'd been there to be a part of her first big break, been there when she felt like celebrating and on top of it all. I felt good for her and lousy for me. I asked her why she hadn't at least called me, and as soon as I did, I regretted it. And I didn't get a satisfactory answer.

Of course, it hadn't been my best day ever, and I figured that the attempt on my life had somehow taken its toll. I didn't want to talk about it, but I felt obliged to—I sounded depressed and unenthusiastic, and I figured that Angel had a right to know where that stuff was coming from.

"Somebody tried to shoot me," I finally said, and she instantly knew I wasn't joking, and we talked about that for a long time, and she cried a little and said, "Oh my God, oh my God," over and over, and I guess I needed that, and later I lay in bed thinking of her and the way her fingers moved across her abdomen and toward her sex, as they often did when we made love, the manicured red fingernails gently pulling at her own flesh. And then my fingers intertwined with hers and together caressed an undersea ledge, an object of curiosity to a small red fish and moray eels and a translucent jellyfish shaped like MacLeod whose tiny black eyes watched as my mouth followed Angel's fingers into a dark tangle. And I slept.

The next morning, Tuesday, I gave MacLeod my bullet. I told him I wanted to keep it as a souvenir, but he just looked at me like I was crazy and stuck out his beefy palm, and that's where I dropped it. He had a hard time believing my story, but he had an even harder time believing I would make it up. And then there was the bullet, .30-caliber rifle, he said. Somebody had tried to shoot me, probably from the dense foliage on the hill adjacent to Fontana, but there were no witnesses. I had let the situation grow cold, and by the time MacLeod started asking questions nobody remembered hearing anything. If they had, they'd probably have taken it for the backfire of a car or moped at the time.

I joked about the incident, and even while I was doing it I recognized it for what it was—gallows humor. But MacLeod was taking it seriously. "This is no joke, Mr. Black; a bullet is not funny. This particular one"—he held it up between a thick thumb and forefinger—"happened to hit the water. If it had struck your head, it would have flattened going in and taken enough of your brain out the other side to leave a hole the size of a grapefruit. You are alive today by a foot or two."

For MacLeod, it was eloquent; for me, frightening. It was no joking matter. "What would you say," MacLeod asked, "if I told you to go home?"

"I would tell you I would love to. But I can't now."

"Why not?"

174

"I'm not done, that's why."

"Mr. Black," he said, and I could see the muscles in his cheeks twitching, "you are a fool. Look at this. It is a bullet. A *bullet*. Someone is trying to *kill* you. Get out of here, for God's sake!" It was the most emotion I'd ever gotten from him, and he was almost shouting now, but just as quickly he knew it was pointless, and he drew himself up, quieted down, and walked out my front door without saying a word. Then he turned back.

"One thing," he said, planting himself squarely in the middle of the path and pointing at me. "If you go anywhere—*anywhere*—I want to know about it. I want the option of accompanying you. It's for your own safety. No more business like at customs. Agreed?"

I nodded.

"Okay," he said, a little surprised and suddenly defused. "Okay." And he slowly turned and walked down the path.

Maria had promised to look me up when she arrived in Bermuda. She hadn't given me any specifics; I knew only that it would be some time Tuesday. It was late afternoon when she checked in, and I asked her to have dinner with me. We would meet at Fontana's main house.

I arrived early, so I sat down in the lounge off the dining room and picked up a paper. After I read an opening paragraph five or six times, I surrendered to some vacationers who'd had a few too many pre-dinner drinks. I leaned back on the sofa and tried to shut them out.

Some sounds were unmistakable, however, and even with my eyes closed, I knew Maria was there. There was a diminuendo of the background noise followed by a respectful murmur, the kind of inadvertent tribute people give to things like celebrity, charisma, beauty, opulence. I looked up.

I remember thinking: Jesus.

She stood at the head of the steps, her long black hair loose and just disheveled enough around her face to make her look imperfect, approachable. She wore a bright yellow dress and she wore it well; as she walked toward me she seemed less restrained and softer than the straight-backed lady of the manor I'd met on her terrace. I had seen her only that once, and just as I had watched her calves and the way her feet lifted from the backless slippers as we walked through the huge main hall of her home, now I noticed the front of her. I knew she wouldn't mind. She had to be used to it.

We shook hands. Hers was cold.

We sat in the candlelight of the atrium, the sky turning purple through the glass dome. The place was beginning to fill; over the drone of conversation I could hear the sizzling of steaks and fish, grilling on the burners along the service wall. I felt dressed up, grown up—not the everyday consciousness of being an adult, but the special feeling of wearing a tux to the senior prom. All that was missing was the music.

Despite the unpleasant chore that lay ahead of Maria the next day, I was hoping that she could enjoy herself tonight. But she was tense. When I would say something, anything, she would respond with a perfunctory smile and some pleasant word or two in that slightly Dietrich accent, but then the smile would quickly disappear. She looked around a lot, turned to watch people enter the atrium, started at the scrape of a chair.

I was hoping she would order a martini, just to help her relax. Besides, I wanted a drink but would usually pass it up if I was the only drinker, two slightly inhibited people being somehow more compatible than one who was and one who wasn't.

She ordered Perrier, which I think of as expensive seltzer and which, I'm sure, the French think of as the greatest little con they ever came up with: just take it out of the ground, stick it in a bottle and sell it to yuppies at fifty times the price of oil.

I ordered a gibson, up.

I had to keep kicking myself under the table, reminding myself not to be charming. Maria Zaychek, I knew, as good as she looked, was not feeling all that festive. She hadn't wanted to come in the first place, Colin said, hadn't wanted her husband's grave disturbed. I called her directly, told her it would happen with or without her permission; it was just a matter of when. And besides, I reasoned, if she really wanted to find out what had happened, why not do what she could to accelerate the process? And so she came, but she wasn't thrilled about it.

While we waited for our entrées, she took some things from her small white purse and handed them across the table. "You asked for these."

There was a photograph and a Pennsylvania driver's license. The photograph was old and only about the size of a matchbook, encased in thin plastic. It had to be some decades old—just how many I couldn't be sure—but if Vladimir Zaychek was still physically formidable at sixty-eight, as Maria assured me he was, the photo gave some early hints of what was then yet to come: a trim, muscular young man in his mid-twenties or so, sitting on the rim of a swimming pool, hunched forward like a linebacker. I held it toward the candlelight.

"Vladimir didn't like having his picture taken. This was the only one I had . . . the only one *he* had. He kept it in his desk drawer. It obviously had some sentimental value. I kept asking him if I could have it, and he said no, he would make me a copy. He never did."

It was not possible to tell whether the shot had been taken indoors or outdoors, although there was light coming from above, which gave the impression of sunlight and put Zaychek's eyes in shadow, and there was the sense of a structure in the background.

"Where was it taken?"

She shrugged. "Someplace in Czechoslovakia, probably.

That's where he grew up. Although his parents were Polish nationals. His father was a government official of some kind."

Vladimir Zaychek stared at me, faded and slightly out of focus, smiling almost imperceptibly. His hair could have been light brown or blond; the highlights made it impossible to be sure. He wore dark bathing trunks, barely visible because of the way he was sitting: facing the camera, knees apart, but with his forearms resting on his thighs and his hands hanging easily between his legs. There were some letters, rather fuzzy, behind him—a sign of some kind. I could make out a BA or SA, directly under which was NA. The other letters were gone. In fact, half the photo was probably gone; this vertical sliver had obviously been part of a larger photograph—something I knew not just from the size and the shape but also from Zaychek's body language. After you've done enough editing and photo cropping, you get to know the difference: people who are the sole subjects of photographs tend to occupy their space differently than people in pairs or groups. Zaychek was leaning almost imperceptibly to his left; there had probably been another person or persons in the photo.

"Your husband was a lot older than you."

"Yes. This was taken long before I was born." She said it quietly, like a teenager talking about a forty-year-old lover, which was not that far from true.

The driver's license had expired a year earlier, but it contained a photograph—a typical identification-type photograph shot by one of the instant cameras used by Pennsylvania's Department of Motor Vehicles in their licensing centers. Vladimir Zaychek was staring unhappily into the camera, but then most people do. Licensing centers in Philadelphia are modeled after intake centers in the Gulag, and there are forms to fill out, hard chairs to sit on, long waits. And the reward: an unflattering likeness on an ugly blue background.

Despite that, Zaychek didn't look half bad: he still had most of his own hair as well as a beard and mustache, even if it was losing a battle with the gray. He was not particularly friendly-looking and the pockmarked face, which caught shadows from the camera flash like the craters of a moon, didn't help, but his expression was benign; this was, after all, a mug shot. I wondered how closely his corpse would resemble it.

At the bottom of the license was Zaychek's signature, pretty much as I'd seen it in the snorkeling equipment sign-out book.

"That's not a good picture," Maria said, reading my thoughts.

"And you have no others."

She shook her head. "Vladimir didn't like to have his picture taken. He was . . . "—she searched for the expression—"camera-shy. He was like that about business too. 'Let them write about me all they want,' he would say, 'but no interviews, no pictures.' He didn't trust the press; he called them scavengers, predators. But he was also afraid of being robbed or kidnapped if people knew he was so rich. He could never relax." They'd been married, she said, in a quiet private ceremony in a clergyman's study; there were no photographs then, either.

I told her I wanted to make some copies of the photos, after which I would return them.

Our entrées arrived and Maria picked at hers as she fielded my questions. I prodded her for details about Vladimir—his childhood, references to people and places, memories—about all the things that she had always found mystifying, the inconsistencies that, over a period of more than a decade, would have to become obvious to someone who shared a life.

She didn't know the kinds of things wives usually know. She'd met him around 1974. He never told her much. And she didn't tell me much, either, but it wasn't hard to read between the lines. She had been divorced for a few months, was having a hard time financially, didn't have any skills—

and along came Zaychek. And while she was intoxicated by
the power and the wealth, and while he was a good care-
taker, the age difference was too great; I got the strong impression that there had never been any real passion between
them. That's what I thought, anyway, and maybe it was
what I wanted to think, what with her face in the candlelight, the firmness under the yellow dress, the gin in my
bloodstream.

On the other hand, it was easy to believe. She'd never
been to the cemetery, hadn't attended his funeral. They
shared a philosophy, Maria said. "We did nothing for appearances, nothing unless it was important to *us*. It was not
important for me to watch a coffin lowered into the ground.
Who would have been comforted? Not me. Not Vladimir.
He was buried where he always wanted to be, on the beautiful hillside of an old cemetery here in Bermuda, not where
it would be convenient for me to visit his grave. He knew I
would never do that."

I realized, while she was telling me this, that it was not
something she confessed to often; it would have taken someone equally out of sync with social convention to understand
how she felt. I think she thought I was that person. And at
that moment I was.

"I'm sorry," I finally said. "I've kept you so busy answering my questions that your food is cold." She hadn't
eaten much.

"It's not important. I don't have much of an appetite."

As the time passed, however, her spirits seemed to lift
and she seemed to regret less the reality of where she was
and why she was there. Later, on the terrace, I bought us
after-dinner drinks, and as we sat there the little band took
a respite from its usual Caribbean shit and did a not-so-bad
version of "Embraceable You." She asked me to dance, just
like that.

"I suppose you think it's strange, me wanting to dance
now, here, tonight." I did indeed, but I denied it in the most

nonchalant manner possible. "It's been months since Vladimir died," she continued, "and I haven't been held in all that time."

At this romantic intersection, the gun in my jacket pocket, which I was finally carrying because I had a jacket to put it in, pressed up against her. I explained its presence, feeling silly. "If you complain about my dancing," I said, "you're dead." She laughed; her hand pressed mine. And she no longer felt like marble.

Because of all that, I had a decision to make. She was beautiful and she fit in my arms extraordinarily well, and she was breathing a certain way, and there was that sensational smell of her that wasn't perfume—on her neck, in her hair. I wanted her and I didn't—wanted the her that I held, didn't want the her that enabled her to be so charming and to feel so delicious a few hours before she was going to look at her husband's body. Sure, she said all the right things, made all the right noises, but people are more than the words they use. The more she pressed against me, the better it felt, and the more inappropriate it seemed.

That is what you call looking a gift horse in the mouth.

On the other hand, I was possibly experiencing a woman who felt so alone in the world, so isolated, that she would be drawn to any reasonably attractive and sensitive guy who listened and seemed to understand, anybody who would spend as much time looking at her face as at her breasts.

And then there was the martini, and that goddamn smell of her that drove me crazy.

It reminded me of an old Yiddish expression that Maddie once used when she saw my head swivel to watch the well-endowed wife of one of the big shots at *World* walk past my office: "When the prick goes up to the sky," she said, "the brains fall into the ground."

Little Emma Muriel Buddery, the daughter of Martin and Emma Buddery, didn't get to see much of life. She died in Bermuda on September 21, 1895, and has since lain in a tiny grave marked by a small crucifix mounted on top of three stones, one for each year of her age, along with the poem her parents selected to comfort themselves—and to give those who would see it some rationale for Emma Muriel ever having been born in the first place:

> This little bud, so young and fair,
> Called hence to early doom,
> Just came to show how sweet a flower
> In paradise would bloom.

Today Emma's parents are gone and her brothers and sisters, if she had any, are probably gone, too, but Emma's grave is still there in the Royal Navy cemetery in Somerset, which lies just across the road from the Great Sound. The cemetery was once a busy place, used for officers and sailors and their families who were stationed in Bermuda or worked in the dockyard. While interment on the island was not as comforting as interment back home, it was still burial on British soil, and the old cemetery holds graves of sailors like John Booth of Aberdeen, a twenty-five-year-old seaman at His Majesty's dockyard, who drowned in 1837 after being blown off the Breakwater Bridge, and of those who died in falls from the crow's nest, and of young wives who traveled across the ocean far from their own mothers and fathers to die in childbirth, and of children, like Elizabeth, Eliza and Alex Hamilton, who died between 1830 and 1840, with only Elizabeth making it into her second year.

The children died of almost everything. But mostly the place is a monument to the yellow fever epidemics of the 1840s and the difficulties of life on an insect-infested tropical island, long before anyone dreamed it would become a paradise.

Life on Bermuda wiped out entire families, and all that remains now are the graves, incongruously peaceful reminders of the inconceivable sadnesses that wore their human contents away—just as surely as the weather since then has eroded the thick slabs.

It was in that cemetery that Vladimir Zaychek had been buried. This was uncommon. Once every five years or so an old veteran of the Royal Navy, or someone who had worked at the dockyard, was buried there, but that was usually it, and in the act of being buried there Zaychek had probably become the strangest resident of all, the first who'd had absolutely nothing to do with either.

There is no fence surrounding the Royal Navy cemetery; visitors walk in and out at will. But walking in is a deliberate act; it is not a place you suddenly stumble upon. The cemetery is a grassy, shaded depression of earth about the size of a football field, only more elliptical, suggesting the shape of a teaspoon. On its sloping sides, except for the area fronting onto the main road, hundreds have been laid to rest, their grave markers now like rows of old, uneven teeth, some tilting this way, some that, all originally placed so that the winds and rains that whipped in from the Great Sound would strike their sides, not their faces. Down in the center of the spoon are the more ambitious monuments that need more stability, and those where the entire length of the grave is set off by rails or pillars, an arrangement that wouldn't work on a slope.

To get to the gravesites, one walks down the side of the teaspoon, and so—because the place has long since lost its fascination for local residents, and because few tourists know it's there—the dead usually outnumber the living hundreds of times over. It is a peaceful place, silent except for the chirping of birds and the rustle of the tall trees.

Vladimir Zaychek, Maria had told me, first saw the Royal Navy cemetery years before, during his first visit to Bermuda, and he never forgot it. From the first he was determined to be buried there, would visit it every time he came to Bermuda. Being a guy who'd rather spend an afternoon at an old cemetery than in the best seat at a hockey game, I understood that.

For me, it was all in the inscriptions, the words people used to say good-bye and to memorialize and to talk to the future, and the implications.

Up on the slope was the grave of Lizzie, daughter of William and Alice McAlister, who died at nine:

> Afflicted sore, long suffering bore,
> Physicians were in vain;
> Till God did please to give her ease
> And free her from her pain.

They are the sentiments of the nineteenth century. Back then they put the best face on it, handed the bodies over to God, and didn't question his will. They talked in terms of sending little Charlie "home," sending infant Ira to "sleep in Jesus." The words comfort; science had not yet destroyed Heaven nor looked askance at its supreme resident.

Not knowing may have been better.

When Zaychek first saw it, the cemetery was crumbling and neglected, and it was his magnanimous gift that had enabled the restoration that was now slowly taking place. That gift was also what had made it possible for Zaychek to be interred there—a special dispensation for an American friend—and Zaychek had been unexpectedly accommodating by dying on the very island where he wanted to spend eternity.

It was late the morning after my dinner with Maria when I first saw the Royal Navy cemetery. I had driven the moped there at as high a speed as I could get from it, looking in my rearview mirror more than necessary, suspecting even the flora that lined the way of concealing rifles, weaving as I rode so as not to be an easy target. The cemetery sat under a pale blue sky, and through its cover of tall trees the dancing beams of light flitted about the graves. I left my moped on the grass at the side of the road and walked a few feet to the rim of the teaspoon; it was then that I saw the group at the bottom of the slope in front of me.

I recognized only two of them. MacLeod was there in a white shirt, black tie, black shorts—funereal for him, even with the gold jacket. He saw me but gave no sign of it except to stare in my direction. Maria Zaychek saw me, too, and looked almost as if she were about to raise her hand in some gesture of recognition—which would for her have seemed frivolous, especially under the circumstances. But she didn't. Not that it mattered; I'd have spotted her anywhere: the long black hair; the erect body, a combination of royalty and cheerleader. She wore a bright green dress, full at the skirt; it caught the inland breeze and then released it with a snap. The same breeze touched my forehead and wiped it dry where the helmet had been.

There were others: two workmen leaning on their spades, ready to do that which was an everyday matter to them; a plump, balding cemetery official in a black suit purchased when the man was younger and thinner; and a gray-suited, tight-lipped, mannish-looking woman with an official demeanor, her hair pulled back in a bun. There was also another woman, a pale blonde, in a peach-colored jacket and matching skirt, who could have been as young as fifty-five or as old as seventy-five—it was hard to say which at a distance because her body was well tuned and athletic, like a senior female golf champion. As I drew closer, her face looked drawn and worried and older.

I introduced myself around, got a smile from Maria and perfunctory handshakes from the rest. The cemetery representative, a Mr. Biggs, motioned to us to follow him to Zaychek's gravesite, which was, he said, unmarked as yet. And then we were there, next to an orange-colored mound of earth high on a slope, a mound that had not yet settled.

"You can start digging," Biggs said to the laborers, who did, and then to us: "It will take a little while."

There was the metallic hiss of a spade sliding into earth not yet hardened, and the exhumation began. Maria glanced at me quickly, then turned away.

"I don't like this," MacLeod said. He was standing next to me.

"What?"

"The whole business. Disturbing a grave."

"In that case, you picked a funny profession."

"I try to keep people from ending up here. I don't care much for getting them back. In fact," MacLeod added, wiping the sweat off his forehead with a plaid handkerchief, "this is my first exhumation."

A quiet settled over the group. There is no such thing as small talk when you're about to open a coffin.

I took the older blonde woman aside and told her exactly what was going on, none of which was exactly brand new to her. Getting Mrs. Augustus to agree to come to Bermuda hadn't been easy, but just as the most important thing in her world had been her family, so was getting to the bottom of the strange circumstances that surrounded her husband's last weeks of life—and I told her that her presence would increase the chances of doing that. Of course, *World* would cover all expenses. By this time we were on a first-name basis, Alex and Kate.

She was, in person, more youthful than I had expected her to be, in seemingly excellent physical condition for her age, which I now put at about seventy. For that reason, I was a little less worried about what would happen here, although I wouldn't have bet on her ability to come through unscathed—I hadn't, after all, told her just what it was I thought we would learn.

The laborers worked with fulcrum-like precision; as one spade went down, the other came up piled high. Soon the two men were standing in a rectangular depression, and then there was room for only one at a time to move freely, so they took turns digging. A coolness smelling of earth rose from the hole, and the rhythmic clank of the spades echoed across the vastness of the shallow valley. The birds, hearing it, abandoned their songs.

Maria had wandered down the slope to the floor of the cemetery. I followed her slowly; she had stopped at the grave of John Porter, who shuffled off on September 21, 1845, when he was thirty-four. He had, the stone said, died "Leaving a Widow and 5 Children in Scotland to Lament their Loss." Maria was staring at the words, which appeared on a pitted slab about three feet high that looked almost like a watercolor painting, the weather having changed it from its original pale gray to a darker gray streaked with burnt siennas and dark greens and flecked with large, mildewy spots of white.

"Makes you wonder what her life was like, doesn't it?"

"I don't have to wonder. I grew up in a family like that."

It was the first time she had mentioned anything about her life before Zaychek, and even though she kept her eyes on the grave marker, I could see the tear swelling on her lower eyelid.

I wanted to say something to her, something to commemorate the fact of what had happened only twelve hours earlier. But under the circumstances—standing beside her at a cemetery where we would look upon her husband's corpse— I sensed that anything I would have said would have sounded banal or inappropriate. So I hesitated, and the moment was lost.

I had expected, like in the movies, the sound of a spade striking the coffin. Instead, there was only a small exclamation, then another, no more ominous than voices at a picnic.

Biggs motioned to us, and soon the coffin was open. And speckles of sunlight, which were never again supposed to have touched the body of Vladimir Zaycheck, tumbled in.

If this was MacLeod's first exhumation, he had plenty of company, and our senses were busy. Before anything else there was the smell, not just the medicinal smell of formaldehyde, but a certain sweet, unpleasant smell, just a touch of it, like a dead mouse. In the few months following death, Zaychek had come to look like a not particularly convincing wax imitation of himself, but that was the look of death: cheeks slightly concave, a whitish cast to the skin. His beard and mustache, both pure white, looked bushier than on the driver's license.

From across the grave, I watched Maria. She stood facing the coffin, like the rest of us, but not with her eyes; they looked at the ground, at a tree, anywhere. Finally she turned and pulled them to the body, said "Oh, God," wrinkling her face at her own first real look at death, stared for long seconds, her arched eyebrows knit, her face deathly still as she studied the details of the face that slept under her gaze. Slowly her hand moved toward her mouth. I realized, watching her, that I was barely breathing.

I had positioned myself across from Maria; now her eyes shifted quickly upward at Mrs. Augustus, who was standing next to me. Sensing that something was about to happen, I automatically reached out to touch her arm and back, just in case. She didn't need it; she was bolted to the spot.

I looked back at Maria. She glanced at me and then at Mrs. Augustus, who was looking at the body, her eyes wide, her mouth open, with one hand flat against her chest, fingers spread, as if to feel her own heart beating.

Maria broke the silence. "That's not Vladimir," she said quickly, and then she bowed her head and covered her face with one hand; the other hung at her side like a broken limb.

I could see the shock of that quiet statement travel through the group. They had known only that there was probable cause to exhume, possibly to conduct a more thorough examination of the cause of death. But Mrs. Augustus knew why she was there, although she could never have been adequately prepared for this eventuality.

She was looking at this grotesque thing, and I knew what must have been going through her mind at that moment, knew that her pain and confusion had to outstrip even that which Maria Zaychek was feeling. Maria, after all, had no illusions about her husband; she knew there were places within him she could never touch, secrets he would never divulge. But for Mrs. Augustus, who used to think her husband told her everything and who had until this moment assumed that the good doctor's ashes were mixing with the flowers in her garden in Cincinnati, as he had requested, this was all new.

I turned Mrs. Augustus away from the grave and led her to a nearby tree; she sat, trembling, at its base. From there I could watch MacLeod writing in his little notebook as the two cemetery officials, who seemed upset and embarrassed, asked Maria Zaychek question after question. I could only hear snatches of them: *Are you sure . . . bodies look different after . . . if you weren't here, who identified . . .* I wanted to hear the answer to the last one, but Mrs. Augustus had to be my priority; she was here at my invitation.

"Can I get something for you?"

She shook her head, which was between her knees. She was breathing deeply, obviously trying to compose herself. Inhale, exhale.

"Is that Dr. Augustus?"

"I think so." She shuddered, then looked up at me and the words started to pour out of her. "My life, my marriage—invalidated. *Invalidated.* This is too much. I can't . . . I don't." She wasn't finishing her sentences. She didn't have to.

"Are you sure it's him?"

"He didn't have a beard. But it's him." She sniffed. "Oh, God, how I wish it wasn't."

I knew what she meant. Where she'd thought she knew just about everything about Albert M. Augustus, M.D., she now knew she obviously didn't; at the very least, he was a part of some kind of conspiracy. How much more was there that she didn't know?

Her head dropped between her knees again; at the back of her neck, her blonde hair, gray at the roots, was suddenly matted with sweat. I wondered about her physical condition: was her heart okay?

With the sound of the shoveling gone, the birds had started their singing again, and there in the warmth of that Tuesday noontime I found myself trying to remember everything I'd been taught about CPR.

"Just relax," I said. "There's an explanation."

"I must know—"

"When I know, you will, too."

She started to cry. I patted her shoulder for a moment and, sensing that she wanted to be alone, walked back to the grave, where they were now talking about the autopsy and dental records.

"Who identified the body?" I asked MacLeod. "Who *said* it was Zaychek?"

He pulled his notebook out, thumbed it and closed it. "There was the lettering on the snorkeling gear, you know; that's how we found out where he was staying. Fontana. But it seems . . ." He had a faraway look in his eyes; he was back on that beach. He opened his notebook again.

"Here it is . . . the *doctor*, Dr. Augustus, was the first person to recognize him. Said Zaychek was a friend of his and that they'd actually had a drink or two together here in Bermuda. Then we got lots of confirmation from employees at Fontana. We had several of them who said they could identify him, and did—a maid, a couple of waiters, the woman from the check-in desk, the young man from the equipment shack there—he remembered Zaychek signing out for the equipment. Several positive IDs. Then there was the wedding band he was wearing, inscribed *V.Z. from M.Z.* When I phoned his wife"—he nodded toward Maria—"she said she had given him that ring. It seemed absolutely airtight."

The corpse still wore a wide gold band.

"It looks like what we have here," MacLeod said, "is a serious case of mistaken identity."

"I think what we have here is a crime," I said. "Dr. Augustus was the doctor who was supposed to have pronounced Zaychek dead on the beach."

"And?" MacLeod asked.

"Mrs. Augustus says the body in the coffin *is* her husband."

"What?"

"If she's right, the person who signed the statement you took, the person who sat in your office, couldn't have been Dr. Augustus. Dr. Augustus was dead on the beach, and the guy you met forged the doctor's name. Where I come from, that's a crime."

"Here too," MacLeod admitted. The heat of the afternoon was beginning to get to him, and a damp ring darkened his shirt collar. "Who was the person I talked to?"

He looked a little helpless, and I realized that in the quiet of the cemetery, the balance of power between us had shifted. Now I had some credibility, and MacLeod's eyes were no longer impenetrable.

"Well, I can't be a hundred percent sure, but if you run

your finger down the cast of characters, there aren't too many choices."

I asked Biggs if I could remove the wedding band. "Better leave that to us," he said, flapping the lapels of his pinstriped suit to cool himself off. "Sometimes the skin dries quickly. You could go for the ring and get the finger as well."

Well, since you put it that way, no hurry.

If Zaychek wasn't in his grave, he was probably alive, so at least one of the widows' marital status had suddenly changed. The strain on Maria was apparent, and it wasn't hard to see what the strain was all about—in a matter of minutes she had changed from a widow into a woman whose husband was out there in limbo somewhere, from an heiress to a spouse. And if the body in the ground was indeed Dr. Augustus, which it had every appearance of being, several strong possibilities loomed for Mrs. Augustus. One was that she had sprinkled the ashes of the *Royal Clarion* in her garden in Cincinnati; another was that the good doctor had been involved in something so clandestine as to be beyond anything she could understand; and still another (and to her, most incomprehensible) was that one of his last acts was to lie to her. A guy who is supposed to be dying of cancer in a New York hospital does not suddenly turn up dead in a snorkeling accident eight hundred miles away without having been party to at least *some* deception.

There was no doubt, Maria explained later, that the body in the coffin looked enough like Vladimir Zaychek to have given her pause, which I inferred to mean that it had been selected for precisely that reason. I didn't use that word—"selected"—because what I had, if I had anything, was a victimless crime; after all, whoever died in the physalia incident had been killed by a Portuguese man-of-war or one of its relatives and cared little that he was improperly identified. But Dr. Augustus, if that proved to be him, had indeed been selected—there was Zaychek's wide gold band and the forgery of the dead man's signature on a sworn statement regarding his own death. And all the craziness, some of which I understood, and some of which I didn't.

As for Mrs. Augustus: even though she had never seen her husband with a beard, and despite the slight contraction of the skin after death, she knew. "You don't live with a man all those years," she said, "and not know him by sight. I would have known him by the back of his head." She looked sad. "It's funny. Just saying that, I can picture him at his desk with his nose buried in a medical journal."

It was the following afternoon, and Mrs. Augustus—in part due to her second manhattan—seemed somewhat recovered, even bordering on silliness, the emotional pressure of the last few days causing small eruptions of laughter. The three of us—Maria and Mrs. Augustus and I—were at a table under a large umbrella on the sunbaked terrace of the Henry VIII, a Southampton pub where I'd asked them to meet me. MacLeod was due to pick me up in a few minutes, after which he and I were going to an autopsy. In preparation for that, I downed a shot of room-temperature Glenfiddich.

At first glance, the beard and mustache had confused Mrs. Augustus. "I imagine it's like you hear," she said, "the hair keeps growing after death."

I told her that was a myth. The flesh shrinks as it dries; that makes the hair and fingernails look longer. But after death there is no more growth. "Of course," I explained, "just how much deterioration you'll see depends on the amount of moisture present—you can't stop condensation. Now in this case, the body is a couple of hundred yards from the Great Sound, and even in a few months a lot of damage could occur. That's why they bury people at the top of the slopes instead of down in the depression. Down there it's too close to sea level. And that's why they sometimes enclose coffins in concrete in damp climates. But even at that, I've heard of a case where a woman was exhumed after twelve years and her thorax and abdomen were filled with water."

Mrs. Augustus looked a little green, and I remembered that I was talking about her husband. Sometimes I get carried away.

"Then the beard—"

"He grew it before he died."

"I don't understand," Mrs. Augustus said, shaking her head. "I'm sure it wasn't . . . it couldn't have been . . ." She shrugged and her voice trailed off, and we knew the missing words were *another woman*.

Maria patted her arm. "I'm sure that wasn't it." She glanced at me for confirmation.

"Yeah, forget it." I remembered a poem in which a husband is late coming home and the wife figures there are only two choices: he was killed in a car accident or he's with another woman. So she sits there watching the clock, hoping he's dead.

I changed the subject, finally telling them why I'd asked them to meet me—so that I could say good-bye in person. I was going back to Philly. They were surprised, but I hadn't been—I was expecting it. The order came early that day:

"Alex, Colin . . . Colin Chase. Did I wake you?"

This was not just Colin Chase; it was Colin Chase pretending to be a human being. First, that self-effacing reference, lip service to the ridiculous possibility that I could know more than one Colin who would call me in Bermuda at eight in the morning. Then that did-I-wake-you business.

"No, I was on my way out." Why did I say that? Guilt. I was still in bed, and the boss was working.

"Well, I'm just calling to get an update. What's happening?"

I knew he hadn't called just to ask *that*. The timing was wrong, it was too early in the day to be that casual. And he asked the question almost disinterestedly, like a guy who knew the answers. I knew Chase, and I knew that once something was on his mind, he couldn't rest until it was satisfied. And he needed instant gratification; he would have called me at seven if he'd been up. So now it was simply a question of waiting for the other shoe to drop.

"What do you mean?" I asked.

"I mean, have you made much progress?"

"Oh. Well, the big news is that the stiff isn't Vladimir Zaychek."

"I know. I talked to Maria last night. I guess this wraps it up. At least our part of it."

"Why now? I'm getting close to something here—"

"I'll bet you are." There was more than sarcasm in the way he said it—something new had been introduced. He was on a fishing expedition, and he threw out the line and hoped I'd take the bait. The statement implied a question he couldn't ask and I wouldn't answer unless I knew what he was talking about: was there anything between Maria and me?

"What do you mean?" I asked. Again.

There was silence for a moment. "Just what I said. Maria thinks you're quite the detective."

"Uh-huh. Well, occasionally I get lucky."

"Umm. Look, Alex," he said, "I'm afraid you have to come back. A piece on fiber optics came in and nobody around here understands it and it really needs your touch. Your free-lancers are fucking up left and right—they're so goddamned undependable. I mean, Bernie is doing a terrific job, but he's new at it. Besides, you're a journalist, *not* a detective. Okay, we've confirmed that Maria had something to be suspicious about. So now it's time for her to involve the pros, and maybe it's time for us to assign an investigative reporter to the piece. You did a great job—a *great* job— but we need you back here."

The other shoe had dropped, and I couldn't argue. I do a difficult and largely undervalued kind of writing. If you cover fires or murders you don't have to know a hell of a lot in advance; you just arrive with your brain intact and talk to a cop and a neighbor and the pieces start falling into place. If you do celebrity pieces or one-on-one interviews, all you have to do is research what's already been written and create a list of questions based on the latest dirt. But writing about science is like writing about Wall Street; you can't do it without perspective and a certain body of knowledge. And if you don't love the subject, you can forget it. I knew my department would fall apart without me; it was just a matter of when.

I also didn't like the idea of Bernard J. Bernard, the financial writer who'd been editing the science stuff since I left, complaining that my free-lancers, who I generally found pretty dependable and accommodating, were fucking things up.

When Chase wanted to be ingratiating he could charm the habit off a nun. That was what I distrusted most about the guy; there was no valid litmus test, no way to tell just where he was.

But even knowing that, I was vulnerable—especially since I knew there was some good reason for my going back. I couldn't win a fight if I felt ambivalent about what I was fighting for. So I decided to conserve my strength for the ones I could win.

It was Thursday. I told Chase I'd be back to work on Monday. What I didn't tell him was that I was too involved in this thing to stop.

Now, in the warmth of the afternoon sun, I told the two women that I was leaving. Mrs. Augustus was not particularly affected by this news, wounded as she was by the events of the day before; she, too, was in a hurry to leave. But Maria was clearly upset. Without hesitating, she offered to replace my salary if I would stay in Bermuda and help her find her husband.

"I can't do it alone," she said.

"And I can't help you," I told her. "I'm no detective. The salary has nothing to do with it. I'm just not the right guy for the job. Besides, I've paid my dues and I have a job that I like, a job I always wanted. I'm good at it. It's my career. It's not just a salary."

I didn't tell her that I was edgy, but I knew she could see it. MacLeod had recommended the Henry VIII as a fairly safe place for me to meet the women for a drink, although I doubted that he'd been referring to the café's terrace, which was exposed to the main road. But that's where they were when I arrived, and I would've felt ridiculous asking them to move inside, felt silly about it, so I joined them there anyway, and now I was distracted, watching passing cars, looking into the foliage on the other side of the road.

Later, when Maria excused herself to go to the john, I asked Mrs. Augustus something that had been on my mind.

"Do you have any old photographs of your husband?"

"Some."

"How old?"

She shrugged, not caring much about her answers. "Old. Childhood, teens, early adulthood."

"I'd like to see them. I'll be in the Midwest for a day or two, maybe next week or the week after. I can stop in Cincinnati on the way back. Would that be all right?"

She seemed surprised. "Why do you want to see them?"

"It's just a hunch, a long shot. I think I can clear some things up, maybe answer your questions once and for all."

"I don't know," she said. "I don't remember exactly where they are. And you know, Alex, I would really like to put all of this behind me. I was happier when I didn't know anything."

"But now you do," I said. "And now you want answers. I think I can supply them."

She stared at her drink for a moment. "You say next week or the week after?"

"I'll call you before I come."

"I don't think this will ever end," she said sadly.

"I know. But it will. One more thing, Kate. I'd like to

keep this between the two of us. Nobody else. Agreed?"

I saw MacLeod's white Subaru pull up in the driveway below the terrace, and I offered the two women a ride back to their hotel. Maria took me up on it, but Mrs. Augustus shook her head. "I think," she said, tilting her glass slightly, "I'll just do this for a while."

I put my arm around her shoulder, said, "Good-bye, Kate," and she put her cheek hard against mine.

The exterior of the six-story King Edward VII Memorial Hospital resembled the upper reaches of one of the luxury liners that regularly visit the harbor on Hamilton's Front Street, long and bright white and covered with uniformly square picture windows as close together as staterooms. In fact, with its landscaped parking area, lush foliage and large white canopy over its main entrance, the King Edward could easily have passed for one of Bermuda's large hotels.

Inside, however, those impressions quickly faded. There was none of the activity or opulence of a hotel, and while the lobby was clean and its floor highly polished and its paint recent, it hadn't been refurbished in years, and remained a victim of whoever had once thought white wrought-iron trim and trellises and vinyl patio furniture were just the thing. On this warm, quiet afternoon the lobby was barely inhabited, its sole occupants a mother and her fidgety little boy. The receptionist pointed us toward the elevator, and in a few minutes we got off at the second floor and walked to the autopsy room.

Dr. Reginald Thorne, tall, thin and balding, glanced up when we opened the door. "Come in, come in," he said, motioning with his head, then asked us to forgive him for not shaking our hands. He wore rubber gloves and a transparent green plastic apron and face mask, both with fresh, organic-looking spots and smears on them; in one hand he held a long scissors.

"I'm pretty well along," he said. "Got an early start re-opening him. Figured you wouldn't mind if you missed a few slices here and there."

It was a small white room with an acoustical ceiling, down the middle of which ran a fluorescent light. Aside from that, every other surface was hard and smooth and nonporous, stainless steel and glass and chrome and plastic, an unfriendly world for bacteria. The floor was concrete. Because of this, the sound bounced around so that even a normal hello had a valedictorian import, and everything echoed. On the far wall were a rack and some hooks which held a few items of clothing, a large schoolroom clock that read three-forty, and a blackboard on which some numbers, the weight in grams, had been written in chalk alongside the names of various body parts: brain, heart, r.lung, l.lung, r.kidney, l.kidney, liver, spleen.

"Those numbers," he said, "are from the original autopsy conducted by Dr. Trott. You of course realize that an autopsy was done at the time of death, which is clearly the best time to do it."

The room was filled with a perfumey but unpleasant sweetness, the combination of formaldehyde and death, and there death was, on a rectangular stainless steel table in the center of the room over which Dr. Thorne hovered, his long angular form and shiny baldness and transparent green mask making him look like a bird of prey. At the far end of the table were a faucet and some rubber hoses and a drain, and above the table, suspended from the ceiling, the kind of spring-operated scale that pre-dated the digitals, with a large round dial and a single thin red hand. On the flat tray under the dial was a grayish-pink mass.

Augustus's body—it *was* his, the fingerprints said—now looked like a garbage pail for human parts. The skin had been sliced around the rib cage in the shape of a bib, and that bib had been pulled up and tossed over his face. Then the ribs had been sawed away and the abdominal region sliced open with a long vertical stroke. The body was naked and greasy-looking, and had begun to ooze the soapy adipocere, the fatty substance consisting chiefly of margarate of ammonia generated by bodies after burial in moist places. I saw pieces of my own life go before me, knew I would someday be separated from it the way Augustus was now, knew I would look like this; and at the same time there would be people I knew who were still walking the streets, drinking in the sun, worrying about their jobs and screwing, and, depending upon the cause of my death, somebody might be slicing me open, impersonally, writing down the weight of my vital organs, and I wouldn't know it, any of it, and my face would be covered by the skin of my chest, hair side down.

All of the visual cues were horrifying enough to make MacLeod turn quickly toward the window and to keep me, despite having seen dead people before and having witnessed several operations on live ones, several feet from the corpse. But the scene became even more disconcerting. It was, after all, an autopsy, and in autopsies they don't worry about the little niceties of life. Incisions are not made with care because no one is concerned about scars; neatness doesn't count because the body shell is only a container. A saw is as necessary as a scalpel, and hands are put down into the mess and tear flesh away from ribs with impunity. And forget *sophisticated*, forget *technology*, forget *sterile*. Autopsy rooms are not operating rooms; there are no lives to be saved. When the job is done, the organs get dumped back into the body and the whole package is sent on its way.

The horror was exaggerated by my perspective. A science editor is used to seeing tomorrow. Now I found myself enclosed in a yesterday, a 1930s medical facility with the kind of equipment you might expect to find in a town in Nicaragua. The feeling had nothing to do with Thorne's ability or qualifications or those of the hospital itself—which was, in fact, about to purchase a CAT scan—nor was the autopsy room somehow inappropriate. It had to do with the trappings. It looked old, and the light coming in the windows along the left-hand wall gave a painterly look to everything—Edward Hopper, not Vermeer.

The only modern element in the room looked very modern indeed. A powdered-soap dispenser.

"It certainly looks like the jellyfish sting was the cause of death," Thorne said, "but I can't determine if there was an anaphylactic reaction. Weighing the lungs at this point would be meaningless because the body's been entombed, and evaporation and condensation have occurred. Even with the embalming. So the lungs have probably alternated between light and heavier as they've gained and lost water. Now they're drier, so they're lighter.

"Now, based on the weight recorded at the time of death, they were a little heavier than normal. That could have resulted from the lungs' own fluid, which you could get in an anaphylactic reaction, or from the inhalation of seawater.

"No indication of any kind of coronary incident. No occlusions."

"I wonder," I said, "if I can ask you a few questions."

"Of course. Shoot." He lifted the lungs off the scale.

"A few things have been bothering me. Okay, here's a guy who was supposedly stung by a Portuguese man-of-war. Now, we have no way of *knowing* that—no eyewitnesses—but we figure, okay, it's reasonable to assume that a physalia or some other coelenterate got him because of that jagged purplish marking, and the fact that there are several wheals. So that's at least circumstantial evidence of the cause of death. By the way, do you do any snorkeling?"

"Some," he nodded. "When I get the time."

"Well, let's say you were out there snorkeling and suddenly you were stung by a jellyfish. What's the first thing you'd do?"

"I guess I'd try to pull whatever it was away from my thigh. It would be a mistake. But that's what I'd try to do."

"Okay. Assuming that it was one of a species that causes instant pain, which for several reasons I do assume, we have to figure that our man did just that too. Then why no stings on Augustus's hands?"

"It's a good question. Of course, he could have been immediately incapacitated."

"That's rare in Bermudian waters. But we'll get to that in a minute."

MacLeod, who had been looking out the window, took a deep breath to fortify himself, and turned around.

"Now," I went on, "you've been stung, and you know you're in trouble. What would you do next?"

"I don't know," Thorne said. "But I guess I'd try to make it to shore."

"Goddamn right you would. It's what any normal human being would do—get the hell out of the water. But Augustus here never made it. Now why do you suppose that is?"

"He died first?" MacLeod said.

"Right. Now if we figure he was maybe a couple of minutes from the shore, and he never really got that close to shore, that's a pretty fast death. Faster than any physalia death I've read about. In fact, while there are some deaths attributed to physalia, they're only *attributed*. Lab animals have died after eating extracts from physalia, and back around the turn of the century there was a case of a tribal member who got rid of an enemy by feeding him a soup made with dry physalia tentacles. So it's pretty potent stuff. But there isn't much conclusive evidence that physalia's *sting* ever actually killed anybody. Doesn't mean it didn't happen, but you have to think twice about its ability to kill a man in a couple of minutes."

"Well, then," MacLeod said, "maybe it was some other kind of jellyfish. You said—"

"Now, that's possible. Even if it was, whatever killed him

killed him fast enough to keep him from reaching shore. Or it caused him to lose consciousness, or put him into shock. Now"—I tossed the scenario back to Thorne—"now you're in trouble. You have intense pain, but you also have something else. You have trouble breathing because we know that an anaphylactic reaction is part of this scenario. So what do you do?"

He looked at me blankly. "I don't know."

"Think about it. It's you out there. You can't breathe. It's like you've gotten some water in your lungs—"

"I tear off my face mask?"

"Right. You'd get that fucking thing off your face and you'd get rid of the snorkel, too, because you're suffocating, and having something in your mouth and something else blocking off your nose doesn't help. I don't know for sure that a professional skin diver would do that, although I think that once anybody crosses that line from logic to panic, he reverts to instinct. But I know what an amateur would do. And when they brought Augustus in to shore, the face mask was still intact, and the snorkel was still in his mouth. I say that's impossible unless he died instantly. Or someone put the face mask and snorkel on him *after* he was dead."

"You have some reason to think that?" Thorne asked, his forehead suddenly wrinkled.

"Maybe he did die instantly," MacLeod said.

"Not a chance. We have the mucus. You said it was there when they brought him ashore. But when you die, you stop breathing. If you're not breathing, there's no mucus. And just for the record, the mucous reaction isn't characteristic of cases involving the two jellyfish most likely to cause instant death, chironex and chiropsalmus. But if you have mucus, you shouldn't have the face mask and the snorkel. It's been bothering me from the very beginning. Based on everything I've read, this guy should have been in a panic."

"Why didn't you say something before?" MacLeod asked.

"To who?" He stared at me, and I stared back. "Now

let's look at the last option: shock or unconsciousness. Some jellyfish deaths have been inadvertently caused by one or the other, since both can lead to death by drowning. This brings us to the idea of incapacitation. The guy's incapacitated, he isn't going to be able to concentrate on breathing through a snorkel tube. So did Augustus drown? Is there any way we can check that on a body that's been embalmed?"

"There are two schools of thought on that," Thorne said. "One school says yes. The other says no."

"Which school did you attend?"

"Well, I think it can be determined. If Augustus drowned, there would've been seawater in his lungs. And if there was seawater, there would also be evidence of diatoms, which are microscopic algae that live in the water. So if we take a little fluid from the lungs and there's no evidence of diatoms, chances are no water got in there. And salt-water diatoms are different from fresh, so we don't have to worry about pollution after death."

"What's the other school say?"

"That it's not a dependable test."

"Why?"

"As far as I'm concerned, because they don't know what they're doing."

"Can you do it now? Today?"

"Sure. But where are we going with this?" Thorne asked.

"I don't know. Let me ask something else now. Have you seen many coelenterate stings?"

"A few."

"How about deaths due to them?"

He shook his head. "This is my first, but I probably know as much as anyone around here about mortality due to jellyfish. Because *nobody's* seen a lot of it. We get a few stings now and then, but deaths are rare. At least in Bermuda. I don't know about anywhere else."

"Does that look like the stings you've seen?"

He shrugged, running his fingers along the wheal on Augustus's thigh. "More or less. Maybe a little more inflamed, but that could be consistent with the severity of the sting. This is more blistery, and the ones I've seen were more like scars, like when you were a kid and you carved your initials in a tree. 'Course, one thing confuses me. If he died almost immediately—and it seems he must have, based on everything else—this blistering effect would have been interrupted. The body dies, the reaction stops."

I took a roll of Scotch tape from my pocket and pulled off a four-inch length. "I'd like to make sure."

"What's that?" Thorne asked.

I pressed the tape along the length of a wheal, a procedure that I'd found in a scientific data base. "This is supposed to be a good way to remove the nematocysts."

"What're they?" MacLeod asked.

"The nematocysts, the sting cells. Cellophane tape is the prescribed method. Rubber cement works, too; you spread some on the wound and let it dry, then peel it off."

"Well, I learned something new," Thorne said. "But you don't have to do that. I can cut you a section."

"Can you do that?"

"Sure. I'm the only doctor who never lies when he tells his patients they won't feel a thing." He laughed at his joke, measured off a length of the blistered skin like a guy slicing a salami at a deli counter, and incised a neat rectangle with his scalpel. The layer pulled away like a strip of pressure-sensitive backing, and he was right: Augustus didn't feel a thing.

"Let's get this on a slide and stain it," the doctor said. "And after that—what do you expect to find?"

"I expect to know exactly what I'm dealing with."

We left the air conditioning of the autopsy room and walked up the hall to the pathology lab, two rooms separated by a partition with a couple of windows. In one room were some blue Formica-topped desks; in the other the same blue Formica surfaces into which were built worktables and a couple of stainless steel sinks. It was the second room that contained the microscopes and centrifuges, the chemicals and burners, the vials and bottles. A looseleaf book that held several stained lung samples in plastic sheets lay open on the desk; alongside it, on the top of a stack of books, was a brochure of revised guidelines on HTLV III, the AIDS virus. On one wall, off by itself, was an incongruous little sign: COWS MAY COME AND GO, BUT THE BULL IN THIS PLACE GOES ON FOREVER.

Thorne stained the slides, then put the one with Augustus's lung sample into the microscope's slide carrier. He moved it around, refocused, changed the magnification. "Nothing here," he said. "No evidence of diatoms, so no salt water. In my opinion, he didn't drown." He withdrew the slide and replaced it with the one of the sting area. This time I looked first. I knew what I was looking for: microscopic threads, many of them, on the surface of the skin and penetrating through to the dermis. They would be very specific, and they wouldn't have to have gone very deep to have done their job; an accidental needle stick could go many times deeper.

"I can't find anything," I said.

"Have enough light on it?"

I moved the slide, tilted the high-intensity light. "There's nothing here."

"Here, let me look."

But there was nothing.

"Let's try the Scotch tape," Thorne said. "Maybe I picked up the same section where you used the tape? It's a long shot. . . ."

But there was nothing. Thorne went back and took a few more sections from various parts of the purple sting area, and we looked at them all. Again, nothing.

"This is strange," Thorne said, two, three times.

MacLeod kept looking back and forth at our faces as if he expected some kind of explanation to emerge. "What's it mean?"

"I don't know," Thorne said, his eye still pressed against

the microscope, his fingers negotiating the slide and shifting the lens from one power to another.

"I do," I said. "This is no coelenterate sting."

"That means he wasn't killed by a Portuguese man-of-war?" MacLeod asked.

"He wasn't killed by any kind of jellyfish. You can't have a sting without a nematocyst."

"They have to be there," MacLeod insisted. MacLeod, suddenly a man of science.

Thorne looked up. "They're not here."

"There's something else I'd like to try. Some toxicological stuff. I'd like to check for the presence of a few substances in Augustus and Bornstein."

"What kind of substances?" Thorne asked.

"Thalassin, congestin, hypnotoxin, a few others. They're all associated with coelenterate stings."

"Needle in a haystack," Thorne said. "We don't have that kind of capability anywhere on the island. But if you can identify a lab in the States, we might be able to ship you an organ from this guy."

"Great. Can you throw in a blood sample from Bornstein, too?"

"He's the guy we had as Little?"

"Right. Can you do that?"

"Sure. Should be pretty good, too. He hasn't been pickled yet."

"Okay. One more thing. Can you take a close look at these guys, see if there's any sign of a hypodermic puncture?"

"Sure." Thorne's eyebrows shot up. "You think—"

"I'm covering my ass."

Thorne shrugged.

"And last—is there a good dermatologist on staff?"

"Yep," Thorne said. "Several."

"Somebody who's had some experience with chemical burns, maybe?"

"We have one guy, Kennedy, who knows his way around."

"Great." I told Thorne what I wanted to know.

"I'll get him on it," Thorne said.

"Can we do it fast? I have to leave the country."

That was the first MacLeod had heard of my impending departure. He didn't say anything, just looked at me. Straight at me. There was no angry glare, and I smiled at him. He half smiled back, not unpleasantly, but like a fat, tough Mona Lisa.

It's a two-hour flight from Bermuda to Philly, and every second of it felt wrong. I thought of Mrs. Augustus, a nice lady whose life I had disrupted and who would never forget the results of that. I thought of Maria; we'd said our good-byes quickly—a sibling's kiss outside of her hotel, MacLeod waiting at the wheel. But mostly I spent the time screwing around with the series of letters in Bornstein's red spiral notebook, which had by now all but replaced for me the Sunday *New York Times Magazine* crossword.

I once had an old dog I called Gene (Gene Pool, actually, a reference to his mongrel origins) who loved people but couldn't stand other dogs. It was not just a matter of Gene protecting his turf. He seemed to know that he could be replaced in my affections only by one of his own species. (This sounds ridiculous, but owners of brilliant dogs will understand.) So Gene sort of became a human being to the best of his ability, and hated what he had once been: dog. It drove Gene crazy to see another dog peeing on his sidewalk or to find evidence that one had; he would bare his fangs and strain to get to any dog that came within barking distance. He would have killed or died in the attempt, and he did in fact bear certain scars that had the cumulative effect of making Gene a lot braver on the leash than off—a rather human characteristic in itself. The vet once told me that Gene was getting cataracts, but I found that hard to believe; he could spot a gray Chihuahua a quarter mile away on a foggy night, upwind.

Gene's personal demon finally caught up with him. I was walking him one day when he spotted a kindly-looking Labrador and decided to take him on, tore loose from my grip for the first time ever, and got himself a school bus instead. That fight he lost badly, and I buried him.

People sometimes behave like Gene when the same things are at stake; they adopt the coloration of what they want to

be, which puts them in competition with anything that re-
sembles what they were.

All of this is perfectly understandable to me. No behavior
exists in a vacuum; much of what we do without thinking
we first learned when we exited from the ooze a few million
years ago. In fact, when I fail to respond according to instinct, I start to feel like I'm getting somewhere. And so
when I got back to *World* and heard about Bernard J. Bernard and managed not to feel much of anything, I felt pretty
superior.

Bernard J. Bernard was the associate editor from *World's*
Financial editorial department who had taken over the Science section in my absence and decided that "he liked it
enough to return should the position become vacant." That
wasn't a direct quote—it was Maddie's recollection of her
conversation with him—but it had the ring of truth because
Bernie Bernard was too civilized to come right out and say
what he meant, like "I want the son of a bitch's job."

As for Maddie, she doesn't mince words. Bernie was "that
candy-ass."

Bernard J. Bernard was, I should point out, his byline;
everyone called him Bernie. To me he looked like a laboratory rat, but blame that on my scientific leanings and the
eye of the beholder; others might have described him as
looking like, say, an intellectual revolutionary or a mild-
mannered bookkeeper. He had a light complexion—pale
skin, blondish hair—with a neat little mustache and the stiff,
erect posture of a fascist, and his lips were thin and unkind.
Before he laughed or smiled, he searched other faces to see
what they would do—so much for spontaneity. Both his
forehead and his chin receded. All he needed, really, were
pink eyes, but his were pale blue, small and set wide apart,
as expressionless as colored glass, all of this enhanced by a
pair of simple gold-rims. He was an unpleasant-looking person, but none of that was his fault, and it wasn't hard to see

why Bernie Bernard had turned into something with all the humanity of a memory chip. You could picture the wise guys in the schoolyard pushing him around; you could see the little girls laughing behind his back the way that little girls would, loud enough for him to hear.

It was Thursday night. They weren't expecting me until Monday, but I'd already decided to go in to the office Friday morning, and now I had come in earlier still. There was nothing that couldn't have waited—except me; like Gene, I guess I wanted to see if a usurper had peed, metaphorically speaking, in my office, and then I would want to start mixing my scent in again, putting things back the way they were before I left.

World never sleeps because the world never sleeps; it's always daylight *somewhere*. So at night there's the graveyard shift, a skeleton crew of weirdos who enjoy living nocturnally, are escaping from unhappy marital beds or are doing the job because they need it, plus a few like me who can't stay away. I like *World* at night—like its abandoned look, as if the building had struck an iceberg; like the echo of a solitary keyboard; like the glow of the monitors. And Iris the cleaning lady humming Rodgers and Hart.

"Jesus, I can't believe you're here." Maddie stood in the door of my office holding up a piece of stationery on which she had quickly lettered WELCOME HOME ALEX. "Best I could do on short notice," she shrugged. "But it's the thought that counts."

I laughed and hugged her and said, "Hey, you changed your hair."

"Yeah, got it styled. And chased some of the gray."

"You look terrific." She did.

"Not bad for a cliché, right? 'Middle-aged and desperately afraid,' " she intoned, " 'Madeline Miller offered her hairdresser an eighty-dollar bribe last week—' "

"You should be a writer. What are you *doing* here?"

"Ah, just stopped by to say hello. I called Fontana and they said you checked out. So I took a shot."

Now that was interesting. Maddie at *World* at nine o'clock at night? I had to think about that because Carol used to tell me how women were always coming on to me and how I never knew it, and it would get her all upset, back in the days when Carol got upset about things like that. She used to say that somebody could put a tit in my mouth and I wouldn't notice.

Maddie?

"Hey," I said, "want me to put up some coffee?"

"No, but that's a nice change. Your replacement didn't even rinse his cup."

"You didn't do *that.*"

"Fat chance—I guess Iris did it. But if that guy gets his foot in the door in this department, it's good-bye, Maddie."

"You worried?"

"Well, the guy is *awfully* political, and he's been *awfully* chummy with Colin Chase. I haven't seen this much of Chase since he started working here as I have in the last two weeks. So it's pretty clear that Bernie wants your job. Where else is he gonna go?"

The last question was a reference to Bernard J. Bernard's position in the hierarchy; an associate editor, he was a peg above assistant editor but more than a peg below senior editor, which is where the job began to be interesting. Still above that was executive editor, and since the people who hold the more elevated jobs at *World* tend to do so for decades, Bernard J. Bernard was, as an associate editor in Financial, in a crowded field—even though the crowd was less than a half dozen.

"Forget it. He isn't good enough at writing *or* editing. And he doesn't *know* enough. This is science, not sports; you can't ask a molecule for a postgame wrap-up."

"Alex darling," she put on her best Joan Rivers–

confidential mannerism, "he doesn't have to. Trust me, I've worked here longer than you. If Chase wants to get rid of somebody, he replaces the somebody with somebody else— *fully expecting to get rid of the somebody else.* He's like the Russians—five-year plans, not instant gratification."

"If it ain't broke—"

"He fixes things that ain't broke *all the time*," she said impatiently. "He'll just say he *had* to break it to fix it *better.* Besides, Bernard raises salt-water fish; to the brass around here, that makes him a marine biologist. Don't forget, some of them are still arguing about evolution."

Well, as I was saying: I didn't let it get to me. I felt nothing—at least, no fear, no hostility. *I'm good, I won't starve,* I told myself. And I believed it. But I also knew that Colin Chase was a guy who would get rid of an Alex Black just to make himself comfortable, and that he might not be *capable* of seeing the difference between Bernard and me. That was the *real* danger.

As for Bernie himself, I couldn't blame him for wanting my job—not any more than I would've blamed him for wanting Angel or a sense of humor. I felt sorry for him. He had a lot of nothing, and nature abhors a vacuum.

"Sure you don't want some coffee?" Maddie asked again.

"I'll buy you a cup. Let's get out of here."

I got up early the next morning and spent Friday putting the department in shape. Maddie checked on several free-lance pieces in process. Pete was doing a piece on language-translation software that Bernie had assigned him—Christ, I couldn't believe that. I told him to put it on the back burner and do an update comparing U.S. and Russian technology, since both sides were making noises about nuclear test bans. Then, not wanting to be in the position of depending on anything else Bernard had done, I picked up the phone and made a couple of more or less generic assignments to some free-lance writers.

By midafternoon, I was in pretty good shape. I tapped into Stella.

GOOD AFTERNOON, ALEX BLACK. YOUR PLEASURE?

She didn't ask me if I'd had a nice trip, but there was nevertheless something very much like *coming home* about seeing the message on my own terminal. I bypassed the menu, checked my electronic mail and a couple of bulletin boards for messages, then took out the photo that Maria had given me. A youthful Vladimir Zaychek stared at me from across the decades.

I typed @ATLAS. Stella responded with her map of the world, famous for its detail and updated on a daily basis as countries liberated themselves or changed their names or flexed their borders; for instance, by the time the buses finished emptying Chernobyl after the nuclear accident there, Stella's map showed the area as unpopulated. It was also possible to call up maps by time periods, which showed the world's configurations as they were in 1917 or 1943 or just about any time, going back centuries. And by typing in the numbers for longitude and latitude, you could fix the screen on any part of the world, then magnify the map with the keyboard's plus key and make it smaller with the minus key. Using the plus key while focused on, say, Paris or Munich or Moscow or any other major city would eventually reveal the streets and major landmarks of those cities, although street maps were updated far less frequently than country borders. It was, of course, possible to search by name of place or to ask for an incredible range of specific information, unlimited except by the imagination: a listing of all the cities, say, with populations between 90,250 and 90,275, or where black populations exceeded white, or where the temperature was currently above 80 degrees, and so on.

My request was simpler. On the wall behind Zaychek in that early photo was a sign, and on that sign, somewhat out of focus, were a few letters in the old formal German lettering, but because the photo had been cut out of a larger photo, part of the sign was missing. I typed the few letters that appeared on the photo along with asterisks—"wild cards" in computer talk—to cover the letters that had been removed along with the rest of the photo. And then I hit the return key. I didn't get anything. Then I substituted a letter for one that looked ambiguous and hit it again, and this time the combination worked: I came up with Bad Nauheim, population 25,000. I checked a mid-1940s map of Germany; Bad Nauheim was there.

I'd gotten lucky: the sign could have said anything; the fact that it reflected a town name was a hunch based on its appearance and nothing more. I'd spent a two-year army hitch in Germany as a clerk-typist; I'd seen signs like that, relics that hadn't been demolished during World War II. Somehow I knew it didn't say *No Parking*.

Next I called Inga Schmidt, the marine biologist at Temple University. The phone rang several times before she answered it.

"Sorry," she said. "You caught me with my hands wet. How'd you make out?"

"It's been an education. Listen, two things—you'll get paid, by the way. I hope I haven't been presumptuous, but I'm having a couple of human organs sent to you, maybe some blood. I want to check to see if the former owners could have died from a jellyfish sting. I figured that you might know how to test for the presence of a few of the possible toxins—"

"I don't think I can do it. But I know a terrific toxicologist."

"Swell. Great. Now, something else. I have a section of skin that, according to a dermatologist in Bermuda, may have been chemically burned. I want to find out if that's so, and if there's a way to identify the chemical."

"I don't know where we'll get that. Maybe the toxicologist knows. I think there are devices that can do that kind of detective work—separate out the components, run some tests. I'll find out what I can."

"Thanks. Next, there was a case, maybe turn of the century, where a guy was convicted of poisoning a few enemies by feeding them something with man-of-war tentacles ground up in it—you familiar with that?"

"Sure. Every student is. Pretty creative, actually. You can put those tentacles in anything. I'd use fudge brownies myself."

"Why fudge brownies?"

"It's the only thing I can make." She laughed.

"Suppose you wanted to *inject* physalia venom into a person."

"It can be done. They've done it to dogs in the laboratory."

"And they die?"

"They die."

"Big surprise—what's the point of doing it?"

"Well, back when they did it, which was a lot of years ago, there *was* a point. They were trying to learn about the venom. So they injected it into dogs and crabs and stuff and measured the effects—"

"Crabs?"

"Yeah, there's a certain automatic reaction you see in a crab, an involuntary reaction—something about dropping a leg when attacked. Anyway, when the crab didn't do it, they knew that one of the effects of the venom was to cause paralysis. Clever, actually."

"Tell me about people. How much of a dose would it take to kill a human being?"

"Depends. How big is the person? How allergic? I remember reading about one determination that was made— that once you're stung by a jellyfish, you can develop an allergy to the sting. And a second sting, even years later, even one that wouldn't normally have much impact if you didn't have this allergy, can cause an immediate anaphylactic reaction and kill you pretty fast. But I do know this: if you were trying to kill somebody, you'd be better off using some other kind of venom than that of Portuguese man-of-war. Why use physalia when chironex or chiropsalmus would be much more likely to do the job?"

"If we're talking about someone being killed in Bermuda," I suggested, "availability? Or authenticity? Besides, while the cubomedusae are more dangerous as jellyfish, physalia venom is still three times as toxic as cobra venom. The only reason people don't often get lethal doses is that physalia doesn't often give one. But put it into a hypodermic and it's deadly. And if you're looking for something that also has a paralyzing effect and can cause edema, that's physalia."

"You know somebody who's planning a killing?" she said, joking.

"No. I'm thinking that somebody tried to get *me*."

C olin Chase wanted to see me, but I managed to put it off until Monday, when I found myself once again in my least favorite place: literally on the carpet, a Persian one, in front of Chase's neat, polished mahogany desk. I don't trust desks that look too organized; I remember an editor whose desk was like that, sort of like *The Picture of Dorian Gray*—and it wasn't until he left his job that we learned that all the horror stories writers had told about him were true. Every drawer, and every corner of every drawer, was filled with his sins: unreturned manuscripts, unanswered letters and unprocessed expense vouchers.

Chase closed the door and the clicking of his secretary's typewriter disappeared. He was, of course, cordial, doing his best to appear pleased that I was back. I tried to do the same; it made my face hurt.

At the same time, Chase seemed somewhat preoccupied. There was the typical small talk, the calm before the storm: *hiya doing,* fine, *is everything under control,* sure. Then he asked me how it felt to be finished with the investigation, his way of letting me know that I *was* finished.

"Well, I don't think I *am* finished," I said, trying not to sound defensive. "I got involved in this thing because you wanted me to convince Maria Zaychek that there was nothing funny about her husband's death, and I proved that he's probably alive. Now I have a doctor from Cincinnati—positively identified, by the way—in Zaychek's coffin. I have another guy who died in my apartment while tapping into my data bases. A ton of inconsistencies, and a few paragraphs of subject matter for—" I broke off, suddenly deciding not to engage myself in a plea for a reprieve. Instead I leaned forward in the big leather chair which, because of its high back and weak springs, made me feel like a midget, and stared Chase straight in the eyes. "I don't think it's fair to pull me off this. It's a story. It's *news*. Somebody has to write it."

"True. But it's no longer your department."

"Come on. You know that whoever writes it'll have to spend hours with me anyway."

"It's a police matter, Alex. They solve the mysteries, we write about them."

"This one is different. Without me, they'd hardly know there *is* a mystery. They think they're looking at a mistaken identity and maybe forgery, and they have no idea why, and it happened far enough away that they won't care a hell of a lot. Look, if it's the time you're worried about, you don't have to—you know what kind of hours I put in." Then I steeled myself and said, very calmly, "I'm gonna fight for this one, Chase."

He didn't flinch, but he heard the warning in my voice— and I could see him decide, right then and there, not to push me to the wall. "What's left to do?" he challenged.

"I have a couple of places to go," I said.

"Give me a clue."

"Chicago. Cincinnati."

He became silent, took his eyes from me and shifted them to a clock on the corner of the desk—not to tell time, but to have a place to put them. "Chicago, Cincinnati," he repeated, then shook his head. "I don't like it. My priority has to be this magazine."

"I'll get everything done I'm supposed to get done."

"Who's paying for the trip?"

"I am. My story, my department. My budget. Shit, I don't

spend it on much else. The sports guys travel to hell and back. . . ."

With his last question, I thought I could taste victory: the conversation had shifted from *whether* to *how*. But I knew Chase well enough to know that I wasn't out of the woods.

"What'd you think of Bernie's work?" he asked. Here comes the fancy footwork, I thought.

"Uninspired. Worse yet, irrelevant. He assigned half a dozen stories; I'll probably end up using one of them." It was all true, but under the circumstances my words had a sour-grapes quality about them. I felt myself wanting to add, "And the son of a bitch *doesn't wash his cup.*"

Chase twisted a pencil between his thumbs and index fingers. "Well, he could gradually pick it up."

Oh no he couldn't. "Pick what up?"

"Well, it's a tough job you have there—"

"I'm not complaining—"

"But you have—you've often said you could use a number two person." I *had* said that, actually, in memos and at planning meetings. But I never knew anyone was *listening.*

"Forget it. I'm fine. Besides, if I get a number two person, it's gonna be someone who knows the subject and, more important, is a good writer and a good editor."

"Well, Bernie isn't bad," Chase said. "I've read some of his stuff—"

"So have I. In fact, the first half of every piece he's written, which is as far as I ever get. The guy's as dry as dust, and you know it."

"What's in Chicago and Cincinnati?" It was a question he had wanted to ask, but not too fast. Chase was clever but transparent; I could practically watch his heart rate increase. What I could never figure out was why so few people could see what I saw.

"Some people. A couple of widows, both recent. Augustus's widow in Cincinnati—he's the doctor in the coffin. And Bornstein's widow in Chicago. He was the guy who was passing himself off as the telecommunications specialist."

Chase stopped twirling his pencil and swiveled to face the window. During my absence, Philadelphia had stopped sizzling; from the twenty-fourth-floor office, where the view was much better than mine, I could see Billy Penn's statue atop City Hall overlooking a city of September breezes and temperatures in the mid-seventies. There was a long silence, and finally Chase broke it:

"Well, if you're going to continue with this situation, Alex, Bernie Bernard will have to continue covering for you." He waited, and when I didn't answer, he added: "Even though you're a little defensive where he's concerned, I think you might do the same in my situation. . . ."

I just looked at him and nodded, and he nodded back, as though we had agreed not to agree. And so the meeting ended. Any action I would take now, Chase had managed to tell me, would put into motion an unpleasant chain reaction, possibly culminating in my being fired. Yes, Chase would have a tough time explaining why I got the axe, but he could do it.

I went home early and unpacked my bags, then put a pair of jeans, my lap-top computer and a few other things into an overnight bag and headed for Angel's house. I hadn't seen her in two weeks, and the phone hadn't been of much use. Even in Chase's office, I had to fight to keep thoughts of her from intruding on what I knew was a very serious conversation.

When I got to her house, Angel was waiting for me in one of the rocking chairs on the small front porch, wearing a pair of earphones with her eyes closed. I came up the steps quietly and placed a long kiss on her mouth. A long kiss.

As I stood over her, she shifted the earphones to my head: voices, medieval stringed instruments, a beautiful ancient music filled with implications of summer-green fields and ladies at court and the mourning of the fallen. When we first met she'd listened to a lot of rock and salsa. But after a particularly insensitive remark of mine, she started experimenting with some other forms—Renaissance music and jazz and early Irish and Scottish ballads—and now she was off and running. As for me, I never stopped feeling guilty about it.

"What is it?"

"Music of the Thirty Years War," she replied.

"Oh, yeah. I remember when it first came out," I said, and she laughed. But she knew instantly that my timing was off, and she could hear the worry in my voice.

"It's getting cold out here. Let's go in." She extended her hand and I pulled her up out of the rocker and followed her through the living room and into the small kitchen.

"I made some coffee," she said, pointing to the glass-topped aluminum percolator on top of the ancient four-burner stove. "Figured after two weeks away from this stuff, you'd be in withdrawal." I poured some of the black liquid into a mug. Angel used a cheap, strong supermarket coffee from Mexico; it looked like roofer's pitch, but it had its moments. And it sort of went with her: intense, dark, foreign.

"I missed you," I said.

"I missed you, too." She touched my face and put her head on my shoulder. "Is anything wrong?"

I told her I didn't want to talk about it, but I did: how I'd painted myself into a corner, how I now had to contend with Bernie if I wanted to finish what I'd started, and how I intended to do just that because there was a line beyond which I wouldn't be pushed. She was supportive but practical, and she asked if I'd weighed the consequences, the bottom line of which she saw as the question of whether I really thought I could lose my job.

Had the situation been reversed, I probably would have asked her the same question, but it wouldn't have had the same meaning, because to me unemployment over a matter of principle was a lot different from unemployment per se, and while Angel certainly distinguished between the two, in her world unemployment of any kind had a stigma attached to it; and even though she'd been in that condition a number of times, that was her, not the guy she was involved with. I was not just Alex Black, I was Alex Black the science editor, and that wasn't the same as Alex Black the jobless.

I tried not to think of that.

"I tried to call you several times," I said.

"I know. I did talk to you once."

"That's not much."

"Well, I was away."

"Not for the whole time. And besides, your answering machine has a remote. You knew I called."

"Alex, don't question me."

"I love you—"

"We promised each other we would accept each other—"

"—and you say you love me."

"I do. Why can't you just accept that?"

"Because love is more than declarations. It's behavior. If I call you and you don't call me back, I worry. You know that. And so in order not to let me worry, you should call me."

"I love you and I love being with you. I also need to get away sometimes, to think, to test the waters."

I didn't bother asking her *what waters*. We'd had the conversation before. It never led anywhere. And yet sometimes I couldn't resist raising the same issue. Every time I did it, I would feel completely justified in bringing it up, but I would end up feeling lousy before it was over. You can't make people be what you want them to be; their behavior is their business. All you can do is decide whether it's too expensive to live with, and if it is, you have to get out.

All these things I believed, or thought I did, because I also could see the hypocrisy in them. It was as though I wanted her to behave like I was the most important thing in her life, but I wasn't giving her any quid pro quo. I was expecting her to be exactly what I needed when I needed it, and not to have any similar needs of her own.

That I couldn't get, didn't deserve.

I wanted to ask her if she had been with another guy. I decided not to. She knew in that instant that I wasn't going to, and she put her arms around me and said, "No."

"No what?"

"You know what."

"I didn't ask."

"But I'm telling."

"You don't have to."

"I know."

"I don't want to know. Because someday I'll have to hear *yes*. You have the right. But I don't want to know."

"Oh Jesus," she said, shaking her head and smiling, a smile as warm and caring as I'd ever seen.

I held her to me, and we stayed like that for a long time, pressed together in her kitchen.

Cincinnati has its hills, and Mrs. Augustus lived at the top of one in a cul-de-sac of single homes. Pine Hill Road was long and serpentine and steep enough to cause the cabdriver to hope, aloud, that he'd never have to come back in the snow. The day was Friday; I had spent four intense days and a couple of evenings in the office to carve out the time to come here.

It was a pretty Tudor house with a path that curved around a neat lawn and some well-established trees—spruce and holly and, center lawn, a maple—but with a middle-aged patina, that graying down of the paint job that homeowners of long standing rarely notice. It was a house that looked cozy and welcoming and instantly familiar, the sort of place Central Casting would have wanted for a kindly general practitioner and his brood.

Mrs. Augustus looked less drawn than she had at the cemetery. She wore a silk high-necked blouse and a dark skirt, less casual and clearly more expensive than what she'd worn in Bermuda, and while she was friendly enough, from the moment she opened the door she seemed more reserved than she had been when I last saw her.

There was no reason to expect otherwise. Circumstance creates foxhole buddies; strangers on an island can't be strangers for long. But now she was back on her own turf, and the person she had called Alex was almost Mr. Black again. Although we'd embraced when we said good-bye in Bermuda, now we shook hands.

The living room was just beyond her foyer, and she led me to a colonial sofa with floral-print pillows flattened by living. She sat opposite me in a tweedy wing chair. Then we made small talk: about the changes in her life since her husband had passed away; about her need to find something to do besides play tennis. I asked her if she meant work, and she said no, she didn't need a job—she had savings and Albert's insurance, and she spoke of a large amount of money that her husband said would come to her some months after his death. She spoke halfheartedly about volunteerism and needlepoint. Then, abruptly, as if just realizing she had violated a sacred canon of hospitality, she asked me if I wanted a drink. I said no, and she excused herself for a moment.

When she came back she was carrying a manhattan and a thick beige volume, the word *Photographs* embossed in a heavy script on its vinyl cover. She sat next to me on the sofa, but on its edge, and opened the album on the oak coffee table in front of us.

There on the album's black pages was a lifetime noisy and bustling and sadly in contrast to Mrs. Augustus's now-empty nest, a chronology that ended with fiftieth wedding anniversary photos. It was there that she started, at the album's end, and thumbed her way toward the beginning—going backwards through grandchildren ("Only two, but there'll be more") and the marriages of her own two children ("They're far away now," she said, but she named two states fairly close to Ohio), and college and high school graduations, and beyond that to photographs of a Cub Scout and kids on bikes and a tiny blonde fairy princess in front of a Christmas tree. And then to strollers and bassinets, and snapshots of a new Tudor house surrounded by small bushes, to the marriage and courtship of an elegant-looking blonde and a proud and handsome young doctor. Mrs. Augustus did not slow down as she moved through the album, and there wasn't much of a narrative. It was not so much that she wanted to explain what I was seeing as it was that she wanted me to know it existed, to witness the history within the black triangular photo corners—to know that the lonely woman who sat next to me came with connotations.

At that point, when there were hardly any pages left to turn, she turned to a page with only two photographs and said, "I think these are what you're looking for."

They were. Vintage Albert M. Augustus, or so Mrs. Augustus said. One of them sent my pulse into orbit.

I hurriedly removed the print from the album, and from my jacket pocket took the small rectangular photograph that Maria Zaychek had given me. I put the two side by side.

"Oh . . . my . . . God," Mrs. Augustus said with genuine astonishment. She stared at it for what might have been half a minute. "Where did you get that?"

I told her where I got it and who it was supposed to be. In front of us were two pieces of a photograph that had once been one and now, maybe for the first time in fifty years, were reunited—and with it were joined two boys, one in his teens, I estimated, the other in his early to mid twenties, on vacation, perhaps, in a strange town on a bright summer day, leaning toward each other with a certain kinship but simultaneously affecting the cool indifference that young men like to evoke. And in that opening of the aperture, recording forever their visit to the city announced by the sign behind them: Bad Nauheim. The Augustus portion of the photo was larger at the bottom, so where Zaychek had been cut off just below the knees, the Augustus photo contained another inch and a half. And from that I could now see that Zaychek had not been sitting on the edge of a pool at all, but on a wall a few feet high with a mosaic decoration around the ledge, probably on a main road leading into Bad Nauheim or even somewhere in the center of town. The younger boy at the right of the photo wore a striped short-sleeved shirt and hiking shorts, high socks and a pair of boots. He had a bad case of acne.

On the reverse of the Augustus portion someone had written *June 1935.*

"Your husband was—how old when he died?"

Mrs. Augustus was still riveted to the photograph, and she answered with a voice devoid of inflection. "Seventy-seven."

"That means he would have been—let's see—twenty-five when this picture was taken, right?"

She nodded without doing the arithmetic.

"And here's the person who's supposed to be Maria's husband." I pointed to the young man on the left. "How old does he look?"

"I don't know. Mid-twenties."

"Good. What's wrong with it?"

"I don't know. What do you mean?"

"Look at the photograph. Zaychek was sixty-eight when he died. If this is Zaychek, and this is your husband, why does your husband look like he's in his middle teens—and why does Zaychek look like he's in his twenties? Shouldn't it be the other way around?"

"Maybe that's not Zaychek. Or maybe he lied about his age."

"Then why does your husband look so young?"

"Well, photographs can be deceiving," she began, but then she broke off. Five years can be disguised easily enough later in life, but not many twenty-five-year-olds look like they're sixteen, and vice versa.

"Here's something else. This kid obviously has a pretty bad case of acne. How was your husband's complexion?"

"Fine. No problem. I mean, you saw him at the cemetery." She thought for a moment. "Of course, acne doesn't always leave scars. . . ."

"True enough. But we know that Zaychek *did* once have acne." I pulled the driver's license from my pocket, and tossed it on the album. "This is Zaychek a couple of years ago. You can still see the pockmarks. But the person in the left half of this photograph has good skin quality. So we have a teenager with acne at the right and a smooth-faced young adult at the left."

I removed the other photograph from the book and turned it over. It, too, was dated.

Mrs. Augustus looked at it, tilted her head slightly as she did a quick mental calculation, and nodded. If the date was correct, young Albert would have been about seven when the photograph was taken.

The photograph was of an infant.

"I never even looked at that date," she said. "What does it mean?"

There was no easy way to say it, so I just said it. "The pictures in your album are Vladimir Zaychek. And this"— I held up the small rectangle that Maria had given me—"is your husband."

She shook her head slowly, but she knew I was right. She knew that she was looking into the face of her husband as a very young man.

"Oh my God," she said again.

"You want a drink of water or something?" I asked.

"No, I'm fine. I just have to—I don't know, calm down." She placed her hand over her breast and wet her lips. "I'll be all right. Why," she asked in the next breath, "do we— do I—have photographs of Maria's husband?"

"Your husband was from Germany, wasn't he?" I knew the answer, but I asked anyway. It wouldn't hurt to slow the pace of this down, particularly since Mrs. Augustus was becoming upset.

"Yes."

"Was Augustus his real name?"

"No. His first name was Albrecht. But by the time I met him, he'd already Americanized it—changed it to Albert M. Augustus. M for Martin."

"What was his original surname?"

"I never knew. He said he wanted to forget it, to forget that whole period of his life. He was frightened; he said he'd been lucky to get away from the Nazis. He would get upset every time I raised the issue, so after a while I simply stopped. It wasn't important."

"Your husband had a brother. Did he ever mention that?"

"Yes, many times."

I tapped the driver's license, tapped Zaychek's face. "This," I said, "is him."

She just looked at me.

"That's why both your husband and Zaychek kept those photos—not because they were photographs of *themselves*, but because they were photos of their *brothers*. That shot in Bad Nauheim—it was a moment, and a relationship, they both wanted to remember."

"I think," Mrs. Augustus said slowly, staring at the driver's license, "I think I know this man."

"You do?"

"Yes. I'm sure of it. He was one of Albert's patients."

"You're kidding. Did he use the name Zaychek?"

"No, I'd have remembered that. I kept the books."

"How about Buchner?"

"No."

"How often did he come to the office?"

"Not often. Maybe once a year, like somebody would for an annual checkup. I remember that because Albert usually asked his older patients to come in more frequently, and this gentleman came in only once a year, and I asked Albert why he didn't come in more often."

"And what did Albert say?"

"I don't remember. Probably something about him being in good condition. I mean, Albert made the rules." She shook her head. "Under the circumstances, I think I'd better show you the letter."

"Letter?"

"Yes. I found it in the pocket of my fall coat after I got back from Bermuda. Albert left it there; he knew that around now I'd be getting ready for the change of seasons."

She went to the kitchen, opened a drawer, and came back holding a white envelope. On the outside it said *My Kate* in a shaky longhand. She handed it to me, and nodded for me to open it.

It was not the handwriting of a healthy man, but it still bore a familial resemblance to the writing of Vladimir Zaychek. It was a short letter, only a few words long, and in it Dr. Augustus told his wife that she would be coming into a large sum of money, and it supplied the name and address of a lawyer to contact if she didn't hear anything about it within a few months. A Philadelphia lawyer. I made a note of it.

"I don't understand why Albert wouldn't have told me his brother was alive," Mrs. Augustus said. "All he told me was that the Nazis took him away."

Well, in a manner of speaking, that was true.

I nga Schmidt called unexpectedly Monday afternoon. She was going to be in center city just a few blocks from my office, and she had something to tell me. It had to be the results of the lab reports.

"What'd you find?"

"You'll see."

We arranged to meet at five at the Barclay. I didn't go into the lounge, but sat instead at a small table near a window in the lobby. The two locations were separated by an arch and, under that arch, the Steinway grand. The pianist played appropriate after-the-rat-race music, a sophisticated, upbeat Cole Porter medley; outside, the homebound traffic inched around the 18th Street corner of Rittenhouse Square and crawled past the canopied entrance of the Barclay and its illegally parked BMWs and Cadillacs.

Inga Schmidt arrived halfway through "Night and Day," looking somewhat less scientific than she had when I'd met her. At the university she'd been in blue jeans and an over-sized white lab jacket; today she was in a sweater and slacks, high-waisted and long-legged, with heels. It was her clothing that made the difference, I realized, and the hair, which, while it was still gathered behind her, now flared out instead of being knotted. The tortoiseshell glasses rested slightly forward on her nose.

We ordered drinks and moved into the lounge area.

"Okay, tell me."

She opened a thin imitation-leather briefcase and pulled out two manila folders. One was marked *Bornstein,* the other *Augustus.* The results of the analyses. I reached for one.

"Don't bother," she said. "The light in here is lousy and it'll take you twenty minutes to figure it out. Besides, as you may remember," she laughed, "I don't mind talking."

"Okay. Your Dr. Thorne at King Edward was very cooperative; he forwarded—I guess you know this—some tissue and organ samples from each body. I talked to the university toxicologist, who has a background in forensic biochemistry, and while he never did anything quite like this, he became very interested. In fact, he did the job on his own time."

"We'll pay for it."

"Great. Okay. First he tested for obvious toxins. Found none, but the morbidity to the organ was, he felt, toxicological, so he knew something was there. It was just a matter of isolating . . . Well, anyway, he then looked for the three toxins you mentioned—"

"Thalassin, congestin and hypnotoxin."

"Yes. These toxins are individually identifiable; they have distinct chemical and physiological properties. So he did a little research, found out how to isolate and test for the toxins, and found hypnotoxin in both men—"

"I knew it!" I smacked a fist on the Formica top. The couple at the next table stared.

"Now here's the thing. The human body produces hypnotoxin. But not this much. This had to be externally introduced, my guy says. Which is funny in that Bornstein was nowhere near the water, didn't you say?"

"You bet I did. But I'm not surprised. I knew it, I knew it. It was that spot of red on his shirt. Right then—"

"Spot of red?"

"—I should have known that somebody had stuck a hypodermic into his back."

"You think—"

"He was murdered, of course. I mean, come on—there
are jellyfish in Bermuda, but not in living rooms. He was
murdered, and so was Augustus. By somebody who really
knew what he was doing, somebody who knew the stuff
cold."

"Well, you could be jumping to conclusions. Couldn't
what'sisname—Bornstein—have received only a minor, hardly
noticeable sting from a more potent species than, say, physalia? Then, while the reaction might not have been immediate, it would have simply been a matter of time before it
took effect. He could have been stung an hour earlier. In
fact, there are some species that can inflict a sting that doesn't
feel like much more than a flea bite—you could almost not
notice it—but which can give you a real problem thirty minutes later."

She was talking about Irukandji stings, named after the
aborigines who populate a territory of Australian coastline
where that kind of sting is most common. As for the jellyfish
that causes it: most experts figure it's the cubomedusae, although nobody knows for sure. "But this wasn't Australia,"
I said, "and Bermuda has no incidence of those kinds of
stings. I mean, we can't ignore statistical probability. Besides, you can bet your ass that Bornstein didn't go swimming
that day; he wanted to be right there, on the spot, when I
left."

"I see."

"But it seems to me that we once talked about an allergic
reaction—"

"Right."

"Tell me more about that."

"Not much to tell. It was the dog experiments. They administered sensitizing doses—you know, enough to make
Fido pretty sick, but not enough to kill him. A few weeks
later, after Poochie was back to his old normal self, they
gave him a *lesser* dose. Theoretically, that lesser dose would
have caused less of a reaction. But it didn't. It caused im-

mediate symptoms—vomiting, respiratory trouble, foaming, bloody diarrhea—and death. So it had to be an allergy triggered by the first dose. Now, I don't remember if hypnotoxin alone was responsible for that, or whether it was all three toxins. I think it was the latter, which originally were isolated from the tentacles of an anemone. But hypnotoxin alone can cause death from respiratory involvement." She lowered her glasses and looked over the top of them. "You don't have a dog, do you?"

"I used to. It got killed."

She nodded, then went back to the subject. "Well, what's your interest in the allergic reaction?"

"I don't know. I'm putting together a scenario where Augustus could have been sensitized ahead of time, then given a slight hit. I mean, administered by hypodermic."

"Okay, let's say that *was* the case. You can't just walk into a drugstore and ask for hypnotoxin; the stuff doesn't exist except in nature. Where did your murderer get the jellyfish toxin?"

"I don't know. Extracted it."

"That would've required some lab facilities."

"How complicated?"

"How familiar was the murderer with this kind of stuff?"

"Pretty familiar, I think."

"In that case, a kitchen would've been enough," she said. "There's one other thing. That section of skin with the blistering."

"The sting area. What'd you find?"

"My buddy put it through the mill. He says it's nitrogen mustard. Does that ring a bell?"

"Holy shit, you bet it does. Sure. It's poison gas, the stuff the German military used. It causes blistering—"

"—that would look very much like a physalia sting."

"Right."

We batted it back and forth. Did I know who did it? Maybe. Did I know why? Yes, I thought I did. Could I prove it? Sure, if you believe in circumstantial evidence. The story still had some holes in it, but they were closing, kind of like what happens when you're carrying water in your hands. You don't have to know exactly where the leak is to stop it; you simply squeeze everything a little tighter, and the dripping stops. I didn't have to fill all the holes; all I had to do was increase the intensity of the search and some of them would fill themselves.

"You've been sensational," I finally said, and, with a mixture of gratitude and genuine affection, I leaned all the way forward and kissed her on the cheek.

I went back to the office and asked Maddie to get me on a plane to Chicago, and after that to call Bermuda for me. I sat down in front of Stella, turned her on, turned her off. From here on, I figured, I was pretty much on my own.

The phone on my desk buzzed; I saw the light blinking.

"MacLeod?"

"Ah. The investigative journalist." He said it not without good humor. "I was going to call you. I talked to the pathologist."

"Thorne."

"Yes. I think he's going to call you, but he did tell me the results. He did find a small hole, a needle track, at the base of Bornstein's neck."

"Right. That's it. Remember the red spot on the shirt?"

"Yes. It was blood, by the way, as we suspected."

"Anything like that on Augustus?"

"If there is, it's a needle in a haystack. Apparently he's had multiple injections in the area of the upper arm and shoulder, and some in the forearm. Thorne says the ones in the forearm were most likely from an intravenous drip. Impossible to find the place where the most recent one might have been introduced."

"That makes sense; he was under treatment for cancer. Now, about why I called, MacLeod. I'd like you to think back to that day on the beach. The victim is brought ashore, stretched out near a rock. You immediately run over. So does the doctor."

"Right."

"You administer CPR."

"Right."

"Again, what was the wound like?"

"Like I told you before. Red or purplish welts."

"With some tentacles clinging to it."

"That's right."

"Wouldn't your first reaction—or one of them—have been to remove those tentacles? Because they'd continue to introduce venom until you got them off?"

There was a silence for a moment. "Yes," MacLeod said. "But . . . I think it was already being taken care of."

"By who?"

"The doctor. The one who said he was Augustus. Like I said before. He was shouting at me, something like 'See if you can get him breathing.' And he had a towel and he was using it to wipe down the area of the wound."

"Did you actually see what he wiped off?"

"Never gave it a second thought. The circumstances—"

"So it might not have been tentacles. It could have been, say, thick lines of petroleum jelly. Or something that *looked* like tentacles."

"Sounds farfetched, but I guess so," MacLeod said.

I tried to backtrack from the scene on the beach at Church Bay. I imagined myself as Zaychek on the beach up the coast, somewhere around the Southampton Princess. I imagined him leading Augustus into the water, helping the elderly doctor into the snorkeling gear. I pictured them both going into the water, saw Zaychek plunge the hypodermic syringe into Augustus's arm, pictured Augustus being hit by an intense allergic reaction, something he'd possibly already been conditioned for, the way those dogs were that Inge Schmidt referred to—and then dying fairly quickly and being laid facedown in the water. From there, Zaychek could've gone up the hill overlooking the coastline, a vantage point from which he could watch the body. Maybe he knew what was going to happen. Or maybe he figured that Augustus would simply be swept out to sea. If that were the case, and if the *Pound-Foolish* had interrupted his plan, that would explain the rest of it—not just his presence on the hill, but his presence on the beach.

What it didn't explain was why Augustus was there in the first place.

Finding Karen Bornstein had been easy enough; both she and her husband were listed at the same number in the Chicago phone directory. I dialed it from the airport, heard a woman's voice, hung up and cabbed it to her home a few blocks from the University of Chicago, a large, neat green-and-white Victorian single surrounded on three sides by a wide wooden porch. I used the lion-head knocker, then watched the tiny glass peephole grow dark. I gave my name, and after a pregnant pause she opened the door. The face that greeted me was resigned—it seemed to know, as they say, that the jig was up.

"I like your hair," I said. "Black is definitely better."

"I wondered if that phone call might be you," she said. "I knew you'd find me eventually. In fact, I'd hoped to get to you first. I was going to—but these are not good days. . . ." There were a few streaks on her face that she hadn't quite wiped away, and her eyes were red.

"Can I come in?"

"Oh. Sure." She stepped aside and I walked into a tiny foyer, then a hallway, and followed her into a living room. There was lots of oak: walls, ceilings, banisters, stairs.

"Nice place," I said.

"Thanks. You want some coffee?"

"That would be terrific."

She went back out into the hall and made a right. I followed her into the pantry and kitchen, where she went about the ritual of opening cabinets and being busy.

"I'd like some information," I said quietly. "Can you help me?"

"Well, I don't know. Probably not."

"Somebody will be writing about this, maybe me. Ultimately, we'll try to get it all. But if we don't, I don't want to be in a position of condemning David. And yet I'll have to. I mean, maybe he had a good reason for breaking into my apartment and my files, but if I don't know the reason, I can't justify the act. See?"

"What do you know?"

"I know who your husband is." I should have said *was,* but I let it stand. There are times not to be an editor.

"How did you find out?"

"The *Chicago Trib.* I searched it on a hunch—his jacket was from a Chicago men's store. Fortunately, he's had a little press, too, which made it easier. Of course, I didn't know who he was back when he was being Jeffrey Little."

"We didn't know who you were, either. We had every reason to believe you were a bad guy. We didn't know where you came from, or whose side you were on."

"I didn't have a side. I didn't even know there was a war."

"The war was over a long, long time ago," she said. "But not for David. He used to say that a few of the enemy remained, and he'd assigned himself to mopping up. Every once in a while somebody used to throw that 'Vengeance is mine' quotation at him, and David would go crazy. 'Where was the Lord when they were sterilizing my mother and poisoning my father?' he would say. Anyway, no hard feelings, I hope. Our information was that you were someone who might lead us to Alfred Buchner. But our informant didn't know whether you were hunting Buchner or helping him."

"Who was the informant?"

"I don't know. You have to understand, I was sort of swept into all of this when I married David, and while I feel a similar commitment now—sort of by osmosis—David ran things. He didn't share information without a reason, not because he didn't want to, but because there was so much of it, and it was so confusing, and his obsession just didn't seem to leave time for chatting. Sometimes it was really lonely—like playing second fiddle to a pile of files and old clippings. In a way he was very selfish, but he didn't know it and couldn't have helped it if he did—he couldn't escape his own history. And once I married him I was trapped in the forties right along with him. But you know, I was crazy about the guy." She put the coffee down on a butcher-block table in the kitchen.

"You were talking about the informant."

"Right. He was apparently somebody who had read about David, and he called David one night. And he said he had similar sympathies. He mentioned you—called you Black, said he didn't know your first name. He said the name was probably a phony anyway, but that's how you would be registered in Bermuda."

"He told you where I was staying?"

"No. We got that from the customs form you filled out."

"How did you manage that?"

"We have a friend."

"It's not possible. Your husband was already at Fontana when I was just filling out that form."

"No he wasn't. He got there an hour after you. He barely got everything accomplished in time to bump into you at dinner."

"Then that business about him not wanting to eat alone for the third night in a row—"

She shrugged. "One of the things I learned from living with David, Mr. Black, is that lying is insignificant compared to almost anything else human beings do to one another."

"And how did he get the lower bungalow on such short notice?"

"Just dumb luck. It was available, and the one we wanted wasn't. What we really wanted was a place where we could keep an eye on you. The problem with being in the same building was that we couldn't see the building or your entrance, as you know. But there were other advantages. Would have been, anyway, if it had worked out."

"There were no women's clothes in the apartment."

"I was registered at a hotel in Hamilton. I came back and forth by moped. We had to be careful. Jeffrey Little's wife was supposed to be back in—wherever. So I couldn't appear to be a wife. And David couldn't look like anything but a typical all-American suburban executive. We didn't even sit together on the plane."

"I thought I heard you in the apartment one night."

"You did. That was to have been the only time."

"This informant—did you have any further contact with him?"

"I never had any contact with him at all. But David did. He had a phone number."

"You don't know what it was—"

"No. But I remember that David had some problem reaching it from Bermuda."

"Okay. So the two of you followed me to Bermuda."

"Actually, we preceded you, and waited. We'd arranged a hand signal with our person at customs. We knew when you came through."

"That's incredible. And then David arranged to bump into me at dinner."

"Yes. Watching you was going to be tough, so David decided to get close to you, find out, as I said, just where you stood. But David was kind of paranoid to start with, and after that dinner he said he couldn't take the chance. He said your story about coming to do a book on computers was simply ridiculous; you didn't know enough about them."

"I wish I'd been that perceptive."

"So the next step was to get into your personal data. To find out what you were all about, to see what you knew."

"I didn't know anything. Certainly not about Buchner. I'd never even heard of him until I saw his name on my monitor—where your husband had typed it. Of course, once I found out who David Bornstein was, it was easy to put the pieces together." I took a sip of my coffee. "How do you know you can trust me now?"

"What's not to trust? David's dead. I'm not as paranoid as he was—I was all in favor of collaborating with you. I'm ready to take you at face value. But I panicked after his death, which is why I ran when I saw you."

Her voice thickened. "God, I can't believe it. He was so young."

"Do you know what killed him?"

"A heart attack."

"Who told you that?"

"Nobody. I mean, I assumed it. He had a weak heart— from rheumatic fever when he was a child—and he worried about his heart constantly. And he was in a high-stress situation when it happened. So I assumed." She looked up, suddenly aware that she was missing something. "What are you trying to say?"

"Haven't you heard about the pathologist's report?"

"No. I wasn't exactly available, you know. I called the hospital when I got back here and told them I would contact a funeral director and make all the arrangements, and then I went to be with my mother so I wouldn't have to be alone. They may have tried to call me. But I just got back." She put down her coffee cup and leaned forward. "Tell me."

"The pathologist found no narrowing or blockage of the arteries. It was no heart attack."

"Then . . . what?"

"Fluid in the lungs. He died of an anaphylactic reaction

caused by the introduction of a toxin." I told her what Dr. Thorne had found and what Inga Schmidt's colleague had come up with.

"You mean somebody *killed* David? *Murdered* him?"

"You mean that never occurred to you?"

"Of course not." She was looking at me like I was speaking another language.

"Well, come on, you were playing some heavy-duty games there."

"But nobody knew we were *there*. We told no one. We weren't even traveling under our own names."

"I've thought about that," I said. "I figure there are two possibilities. One, somebody knew. There was that informant; he knew. There was the person at customs."

"But even so—David was in *your* apartment."

"That's the other possibility—that David's murder was a mistake."

"Like how?"

"Like maybe *I* was the target. Of course, I don't know why. But I don't know a lot of things, like why somebody thought I would eventually be meeting Buchner, a guy I never heard of."

We talked for a long time. I told her there would be an inquest, but that it wouldn't take place for several months and that she wouldn't have to attend, unless she wanted another trip to Bermuda. She said she would never go back, no matter what.

She handed me a thick, dog-eared expanding folder. "Look through this. I'll get you another cup of coffee."

It was at least three inches thick and contained yellowed newspaper clippings encased in plastic, documents in several languages—English and Czech and German—old photographs, some Austrian correspondence from the Nazi hunter Simon Wiesenthal. As war criminals went, Buchner was in the minors, but even the sandlot league of the Third Reich was not entirely undistinguished. Buchner had been a young

and brilliant doctor who'd been swept away by the rhetoric
of Adolf Hitler; during World War II he found himself working in a clinic making decisions about members of "inferior"
groups, a designation that included Jews, gypsies and any
other Czech citizens whose politics were questionable. It was
Buchner who, in Ostrov, Czechoslovakia, helped decide who
should be sterilized; later, there were accounts of certain
experiments. When the last days of World War II approached, the clinic and its contents—some of them human—
were destroyed in a fire. Some said Buchner died there.
Others said the fire had been intentionally set to hide what
had been done there. At any rate, Buchner was never found.

Karen Bornstein came back with the coffee. "David was
born in Czechoslovakia in the early forties," she began, "the
only child his mother would ever have. She saw what was
coming and gave David to a non-Jewish maid who used to
work for the family. Soon after that, because of Buchner,
David's mother and father were sterilized and made part of
an experimental protocol run by Buchner. His father died,
but his mother survived—one of about half a dozen people
who lived to talk about it—and was eventually able to re-
trieve David and work her way to Holland and then the
United States.

"Of course"—she shook her head slowly—"there wasn't
much left of her except her memory. She relived those days
constantly, half crazy and obsessed, and she raised David
on Dr. Buchner stories the way kids today get Dr. Seuss.
From the time he was very young, he was programmed to
avenge his parents for their suffering. He started building
this." She tapped the file.

"Okay, run the clock forward. It's a few years ago. David's
in his early forties; his mother is now a basket case, practically catatonic, and she's in an institution. One day, while
sitting in front of a television, she becomes hysterical. She
just sits there and points at the screen and screams and
screams and screams. It's the first real emotion she's shown

in over a decade, and it kills her; she dies an hour later—cardiac arrest—and no one even saw what she was pointing to. 'What channel was on?' David asked. Nobody knew. 'What time was it?' No one remembered precisely, but she died at about six-thirty. Or maybe it was seven? Anyway, David contacted every TV channel, even the cable channels. He had to deal with the worst kinds of bureaucracies and pain-in-the-ass functionaries you can imagine, but eventually he got to look at every piece of footage that had been shown at that time. Gives you some kind of an idea how tenacious David was; he didn't even know if there was anything worth looking for.

"And then, on one newscast, he hit it. He knew what his mother had seen."

"Vladimir Zaychek."

"Right. There *was* a resemblance, and a certain irony about it—if it was true, Buchner had finally killed David's mother after all. But David was going to have a hell of a time proving Zaychek was Buchner. Zaychek had covered his tracks well. He had a real identity. There were no fingerprints to compare, no dental records. And Buchner was small-time—it wasn't like a concentration-camp guard, who could be identified by dozens. Buchner's subjects numbered in the low hundreds, not the tens of thousands. And they rarely survived.

"So what did David have? Circumstantial evidence—and not even that. A crazy woman screams at a television set; with that, you're going to go after one of America's leading industrialists?"

"What did he do?"

"He started building a dossier on Zaychek, a guy who avoided cameras like the cosa nostra. But David had a file on Buchner, bits and pieces that his mother had collected, and they included this picture of Buchner from Hitler's rag, *Völkischer Beobachter*." She put a small, cracked newspaper clipping encased in plastic in front of me. "Then he got a

shot of Zaychek that the Associated Press got on the same
day of the newscast—Zaychek was involved in a takeover
bid that got messy. So he enlarges both pictures and he
compares pockmarks. It's not conclusive, but he has one or
two prominent marks that seem to match. A face print instead of a fingerprint.

"So he writes to the major papers, to the AP and so on,
trying to get other recent photos. It wasn't going that well,
because Buchner had spent as much time getting his picture
taken as he'd spent at, you know, Yom Kippur services, and
furthermore, he just wasn't anybody's top priority. I mean,
most people don't give a shit anymore. But David hung in."

"What happened?"

"Little by little he started piecing things together. He
couldn't come right out and say anything, but he wanted to
ask enough questions to make the media start wondering,
like, here's smoke, is there also fire? He wanted to create a
network without saying anything that would get him sued.
David was very excited, and so was I—I began to think what
life would be like without Alfred Buchner twenty-four hours
a day.

"Shortly after that, Zaychek was supposedly killed by a
Portuguese man-of-war."

"But David didn't buy that."

"No. He thought it was just too much of a coincidence,
you know, he starts asking for information and photographs
of Zaychek, and a few weeks later Zaychek dies and is buried. And outside the United States at that."

I unzipped my bag and took out Vladimir Zaychek's driver's license. "Here's as good a photograph as you're gonna
get," I said, tossing it down beside the old clipping. "Let's
have a look."

I got back to Philly Tuesday night. Angel was in Virginia doing a shoot for a high-priced retirement community there; she called me around nine-thirty.

"Help," she gasped. "This place is filled with the walking wounded." *Filled* came out *feeled*; when Angel was upset, her accent became more pronounced. "Nothing but stroke victims and widows. So the ad agency hired two models that look like Steve and Eydie." She laughed in spite of herself. "The ad agency people are telling me, 'Don't make 'em look *too* young,' and I'm saying, Hell, they *already* look too young. Did you ever try to age somebody through a lens? A tanned, middle-aged golf pro with all his own hair and teeth? And his wife, who looks like she spends her life sailing and doing the Jane Fonda Workout? The only thing she has that I need are crow's feet."

"You're working," I said. "Three months ago you would've killed for this job."

"Even three days ago. It's not that I don't want it. It's just that the people I'm photographing have no relationship to anything you see here."

"Welcome to the world of advertising."

We didn't talk long; it seemed that neither of us had much to say. But her call was the high point of my evening. My apartment, which was no different than when I had left, looked naked and depressing after the week in Bermuda—unlived in, pristine and alien. Sometimes I put a piece of copy aside and then go back and read it several days later, and it seems like I'm reading it for the first time. This distancing helps me see its faults; I compare the processing to sobering up, or the morning after. Now I was looking at my apartment like that—the bare walls, the unhung pictures, the unpacked whatevers that my ex-wife hadn't wanted. The only new piece was three years old, a space-age off-white desk custom-made to handle the computer and its peripherals.

Somewhere at that moment a guy my age was sitting in the family room with his wife and kids, and they were all eating popcorn and laughing at a dumb sitcom. His walls weren't bare and he wasn't lonely. Tomorrow he might go to a job that he hated, but tonight he was home in the real sense of the word.

I decided to spare myself that kind of thinking, poured myself a drink and started editing a rough draft of my column. With everything that was transpiring, I would've expected my concentration to be fragmented, but the last couple of days had shown me that everything blended beautifully. Every question I asked, every conversation I had, took me into another area of scientific inquiry; every inquiry put me in touch with a possible subject for my column. It was science at work in the everyday world, the concrete as opposed to the abstract, and I spent every empty moment writing about it. On my way to and from the Midwest, in fact, I had knocked out several pages of text on the portable.

But tonight it didn't work for long, and so I accessed Stella and figured I would do some research into the toxins that had been found in the organ specimens of Bornstein and Augustus. Since I hadn't found much in conventional searches of the scientific literature, I decided to enlist the help of a gateway network—a two-way data-base-screening program that would question me on-line and would, on the basis of the answers I typed in, decide for me which data bases were most likely to lead to the information I wanted. It's an am-

"And how did he get the lower bungalow on such short notice?"

"Just dumb luck. It was available, and the one we wanted wasn't. What we really wanted was a place where we could keep an eye on you. The problem with being in the same building was that we couldn't see the building or your entrance, as you know. But there were other advantages. Would have been, anyway, if it had worked out."

"There were no women's clothes in the apartment."

"I was registered at a hotel in Hamilton. I came back and forth by moped. We had to be careful. Jeffrey Little's wife was supposed to be back in—wherever. So I couldn't appear to be a wife. And David couldn't look like anything but a typical all-American suburban executive. We didn't even sit together on the plane."

"I thought I heard you in the apartment one night."

"You did. That was to have been the only time."

"This informant—did you have any further contact with him?"

"I never had any contact with him at all. But David did. He had a phone number."

"You don't know what it was—"

"No. But I remember that David had some problem reaching it from Bermuda."

"Okay. So the two of you followed me to Bermuda."

"Actually, we preceded you, and waited. We'd arranged a hand signal with our person at customs. We knew when you came through."

"That's incredible. And then David arranged to bump into me at dinner."

"Yes. Watching you was going to be tough, so David decided to get close to you, find out, as I said, just where you stood. But David was kind of paranoid to start with, and after that dinner he said he couldn't take the chance. He said your story about coming to do a book on computers was simply ridiculous; you didn't know enough about them."

"I wish I'd been that perceptive."

"So the next step was to get into your personal data. To find out what you were all about, to see what you knew."

"I didn't know anything. Certainly not about Buchner. I'd never even heard of him until I saw his name on my monitor—where your husband had typed it. Of course, once I found out who David Bornstein was, it was easy to put the pieces together." I took a sip of my coffee. "How do you know you can trust me now?"

"What's not to trust? David's dead. I'm not as paranoid as he was—I was all in favor of collaborating with you. I'm ready to take you at face value. But I panicked after his death, which is why I ran when I saw you."

Her voice thickened. "God, I can't believe it. He was so young."

"Do you know what killed him?"

"A heart attack."

"Who told you that?"

"Nobody. I mean, I assumed it. He had a weak heart—from rheumatic fever when he was a child—and he worried about his heart constantly. And he was in a high-stress situation when it happened. So I assumed." She looked up, suddenly aware that she was missing something. "What are you trying to say?"

"Haven't you heard about the pathologist's report?"

"No. I wasn't exactly available, you know. I called the hospital when I got back here and told them I would contact a funeral director and make all the arrangements, and then I went to be with my mother so I wouldn't have to be alone. They may have tried to call me. But I just got back." She put down her coffee cup and leaned forward. "Tell me."

"The pathologist found no narrowing or blockage of the arteries. It was no heart attack."

"Then . . . what?"

"Fluid in the lungs. He died of an anaphylactic reaction

license plates—with only twelve thousand or so cars on Bermuda, numbers are enough.

So if Bornstein had been trying to convert those letters to numbers in order to dial them—which he well might have *had* to do—his problem could have been not being familiar enough with the telephone keypad. And reconstructing the U.S. keypad would be far more difficult than you'd think: besides remembering that there are two keys with only numbers, you'd have to know which *letters* are missing. Most people don't, and the absence of one of those letters, *q*, throws off the sequence of the rest of the alphabet, and you would therefore put the wrong letters on the wrong number keys. So Bornstein could have removed what little hair he had left before hitting on the correct number. It made perfect sense—so why was I dialing a nonexistent number?

I sat there and stared at the telephone, my thumb on the disconnect button. Then I realized that I was treating the O in MEMO as the letter O, and I was therefore dialing it as a 6, because the O is on the number 6 key. But suppose it was a *zero*? I tried it.

This time I got a man's voice. It said hello.

I knew that voice, knew that I had reached an unlisted residential number. The voice said hello two more times, then muttered something unintelligible and hung up. *I'll be a son of a bitch*, I said.

I caught the elevator to the lobby, walked across Rittenhouse Square to the Barclay and reserved a room for that Friday in the name of Karen Bornstein.

Then I came back, sat down at my computer and wrote a letter. I reread it as it came off the printer:

> I know who you are and what you've done. I'm in Philadelphia this week and will be at the Barclay Hotel on Friday. If you want to keep this situation

from escalating, come to the Barclay, Room 941,
at 8 Friday evening.

Karen Bornstein

It's one thing to know and another thing to suspect, and
sometimes you have to throw out a little bait to find out if
you're right about what's in the water. If you are, you learn
about the shark before the shark learns about you.

I addressed the envelope and dropped it into the mail
chute in the lobby. Then I went out again, back to the Barclay, into the lounge, ordered another Glenfiddich and,
watching through the tall windows as the late-night traffic
turned the corner of the Square, sat there alone, listening
to David play "Lush Life" on the Steinway.

The knock at the door came at precisely 8:04. From that—factoring in the nature of the beast and knowing this particular one to be a guy who checked the accuracy of his watch every morning—I knew a couple of things: one, the lateness was intentional, probably to create the impression that he was not worried; and two, he was worried, since four minutes late was not late enough, under the circumstances, for Colin Chase. In fact, an unworried Colin Chase would not have shown up at all.

I opened the door. He stood there in his Burberry, his salt-and-pepper hair slightly windblown. Whatever internal virtues he might have lacked he made up for in appearance, as though nature, recognizing his failings, decided to compensate him in other areas. He was the pitcher plant, a sarracenia among executives: attractive and aromatic, but watch out for the secretions. Chase looked even better than usual this evening. He had obviously freshened up and changed his shirt, and I had to assume that he had come prepared to charm the pants off Karen Bornstein. Maybe literally.

But as in the worst-case scenario of "The Lady or the Tiger?" the wrong thing came out of the opened door, and Chase got Alex Black instead. His mouth, which had been prepared to say hello, opened and stopped dead, his lips moving only slightly as his mind tried to negotiate the new twist in the path. Through his eyes, dark and puzzled, I could see that he was straining to get a handle on the situation, to decide *what to say, what to do.*

What he said was "Hello, Alex." I nodded and kept staring—I was fascinated, in a way—and Chase asked, "Well, what are you doing here?" All this in an even tone, maybe more modulated than usual; a larynx hard at work and trying not to sound it.

"I was gonna ask you that. Come on in."

Chase stepped inside the hotel room, a small, pastel-green room with a narrow-topped desk, a double bed, a couple of chairs and a dresser. "Yes. Well, is there a Karen Bornstein here?"

He was going to play dumb. *A* Karen Bornstein, as if he didn't know who she was.

"She'll be late."

"Oh." He looked blank for a moment. "Well, do you know what this is about? Do you think I should wait?"

There's an old interviewer's rule about never asking the subject two questions at once, because that lets him ignore the question he doesn't want to answer. I ignored the first. "By all means. Here, give me your coat." He took it off and handed it to me. I went to the closet and hung it up.

"Have a seat." Chase dropped slowly into an upholstered chair, and I sat in the straight-backed one at the desk. "You know who Karen Bornstein is, of course."

"No. Who is she?" I could see the gears meshing. I could *hear* them. Right about now, he would be wondering if I'd sent the letter. But he'd reject any such notion immediately, knowing me.

"She's the widow of David Bornstein. The guy who died in my bungalow in Bermuda. You were in touch with him just a few weeks ago."

"Doesn't ring a bell," Chase said.

"Your phone bill says different. You called him not long ago. Chicago."

A short, resentful silence. "How'd you get my phone bill?"

"Friends in low places. Anyway, you called him."

"Maybe I did. I call lots of people. In fact, *yes*, I do remember something. There was a guy in Chicago who wrote me a letter—I don't remember what it was about."

"I can help you. It was about Zaychek."

"Yeah, wait, it's coming back. He wanted some photographs or something?"

"That's right."

"Okay, I remember. I told him we didn't have any."

"That was it? You actually *called* him to tell him that?"

"That was it."

"That was very considerate. And from your home phone. Why didn't you just have Prunella drop him a note?"

"Her name's Florence." He looked straight at me and his lips got thin. "You're on dangerous ground, Alex. Why are you cross-examining me? What is this?"

"Hey," I laughed, "you should be thrilled to death that *I'm* doing it; you could be talking to Flick."

Chase blinked. Kenneth Flick was a *World* investigative reporter and, like most of the editorial side, no fan of Colin Chase; in fact, it was Flick's contact at the phone company who helped me come up with Chase's phone records.

"I don't see any reason why Flick should be involved in this."

"It's him or me, take your pick. In fact, I can't promise he won't get involved anyway. It's not my department, as you've pointed out. But there's a story here, and it sort of makes me wonder how *World* would feel if one of its top editorial people was involved."

Chase was sweating. Figuratively, not literally. I didn't really want to make him sweat, but I couldn't let him off the hook, either. Journalism is like that; once you squeeze the pimple, you can't reverse the process.

"This guy Bornstein," I went on, "carried this around with

him." I took the spiral-bound book out of my pocket and handed it to Chase. It was open to the page with the phone number.

He read the notation and shrugged. "What's that supposed to mean?"

"Translated into numerals, it's your home phone number."

His eyebrows went up unconvincingly. "Those letters could mean anything."

"Nope. I've been down that road already. It's your phone number."

"Bornstein had that?"

"Yep."

"How did he get it?"

"The same way he found out what flight I was on. You told him. And you told him just enough—just enough to sound like you didn't know more. You had his phone number, and he had yours."

Chase laughed nervously and started to protest, but I felt a certain fury rising in me, and I leaned forward and slammed a somewhat restrained palm down on the desk blotter. "I could have been killed, you son of a bitch. You *know* who Zaychek is and how desperate he is. You played both ends against the middle; you told both Zaychek and Bornstein where to find me. You know what caused Bornstein's death? A lethal injection of toxin. And you know what Zaychek's specialty was, back when he was Alfred Buchner and experimenting on Jews?"

"I don't know what you're talking about. What do you mean, back when he was Buchner?" He tried to look innocent, but he was fidgeting and looking toward the door, and I knew he was thinking that the longer he sat there, the worse things would get. And it was already too late to go anywhere.

"Look, I don't need your cooperation," I said. "I already have enough to make things uncomfortable for you."

"Don't be dramatic. I haven't done anything."

"You'd be out of *World* so fast your head would spin."

"I don't know what you're talking about," he protested, but his voice fell at the end of the sentence, and I knew that I had struck a nerve. Chase had, after all, shown up here to avoid whatever it was that he inferred from the letter: publicity, further revelations. But he didn't know just yet where I fit in. He was still waiting for Karen Bornstein.

"You know exactly who Zaychek is. What I can't figure out is why you first helped him, then tried to betray him."

"We were casual acquaintances. I know nothing—"

"You're the executor of his will." I had only so many bullets, so I was taking my shots carefully. The trick was to squeeze off just enough to keep Chase wondering how many more were left.

"So what?"

"Some casual acquaintance."

"He trusted me."

"He's a killer, a war criminal."

"I didn't know that," Chase objected. "I *still* don't."

"But you knew who Bornstein was. You got his letter and you checked him out, which wasn't exactly standard operating procedure. That told you why he was so interested in getting information and photos of Zaychek. Hell, Colin, you had access to the same data bases I did, so even if you never suspected Zaychek before, you knew damned well there was reason to suspect him then. So what did you do? Did you report him to the police or the feds? Or even benignly let things take their course? No. You *warned* him. A few days later, he's reported dead in Bermuda."

"I didn't warn him. I just told him I got a letter asking for photographs of him. I thought it was funny because I don't get requests like that, and not from individuals; it's usually another publication or a wire service, and it usually goes through the photo desk. This one was addressed to the publisher, and got passed along to me. So I mentioned it to Zaychek. That's all I know."

"I see the whole thing is suddenly coming back to you."

"And I see no reason to tell you anything," he shot back, clenching his teeth as if to resolve to keep his mouth shut.

"Okay, back to square one. You met Zaychek a few years ago. Two possible scenarios: you like being associated with power and wealth or you liked his wife. Okay, both. So you got pretty tight with them, and Zaychek came to trust you— at least as much as he trusted anybody. Eventually he asks you to be the executor of his will. Of course, you say yes; the closer you get to the money and the power—and maybe the wife—the better you like it."

"Alex, you're making a lot of unfair assumptions."

"Well, what's the harm; I'm probably making a lot of fair ones, too. Zaychek dies, and everybody's sitting around waiting for the will to be probated. Naturally, you see it first, and therefore Maria does, too. And it turns out that a considerable chunk of money goes to a widow in Cincinnati."

At that moment I could see something die inside him. I saw it physically: his shoulders slumped, the air left his body, his face turned ashen. He just looked at me, his brows knit, his mouth slightly open.

"How did you find out about the will?" he said slowly. "Its contents haven't been made public."

"Never mind that, I found out." I'd taken a guess, but it was a reasonable one; the money that Dr. Augustus told his wife she'd be getting had to come from somewhere, and when I got in touch with the Philadelphia lawyer mentioned in Dr. Augustus's letter to his wife, he confirmed that he'd been retained "just in case"—although he had no idea what the will said.

"Okay," I went on, "back to Bermuda. Zaychek is supposed to be dead. If everything goes according to schedule, the will gets read, the property gets distributed, and that's that. But Maria doesn't want the will probated, and you probably don't, either, not with millions of dollars going to

Mrs. Augustus. So Maria throws a monkey wrench into the works. She tells you she thinks her husband died under mysterious circumstances. And you tell me.

"You know what Maria figures? She figures, I'll bring the son of a bitch back to life. After all, if Alex Black starts nosing around, eventually that coffin will be opened, and then we'll all know that Zaychek is not in it. Bang, there goes the will—no will is valid until its author is dead. And under Pennsylvania law, Maria is much better off if the will is invalid, because Mrs. Augustus's piece gets held up. Besides, if Zaychek was alive and Maria knew it—and again, a lot of this is supposition—she would have agreed to link up with him at some future time, and she didn't want to do that. So she sees this as her big opportunity to be free *and* rich. The world would push him so far into hiding he'd never emerge, or they'd find him and try him and that would be the end of it. In the meantime, she'd buy herself years before she'd have to abide by the will, years to put together a good case for contesting it. And even if it all came out the same, it would sit there and earn interest—interest Maria would end up with.

"Now, how much did you know? You sent me to Bermuda. Then you called David Bornstein and told him that if Zaychek was alive, I was the guy to watch. *That* was the phone conversation—it wasn't about his request for a photograph at all. In fact, it was months after you got that letter that you finally called him back, and he didn't know who was calling him. As far as he knew, *World* had ignored him, and you were simply a guy who wanted to see justice done, an anonymous caller in sympathy with his cause. But you couldn't let it go at that—you had to know what was happening—so you gave Bornstein your unlisted phone number, swearing him to complete confidence. He was so damned conscientious about protecting your anonymity, he encoded your number. Which gave me a real pain in the ass."

"You're crazy." Chase was a little red in the face now, and he said it with conviction. Which meant nothing; he was lying. He knew it, and he knew I knew it.

"I can't believe you warned Zaychek. How the hell could you do that? He was an animal—"

"All I had was some guy who *claimed* that Zaychek was a war criminal. I didn't believe it. I thought this Bornstein was a little nuts, and Zaychek was my friend—okay, I told Bornstein to follow you. I figured it couldn't do any harm. I really expected you to lead him to a dead man."

"Chase, you're either the best liar I've ever seen, or the most naive. But I'll give you naive for the moment. You told Zaychek about Bornstein, and Zaychek takes a sudden vacation to Bermuda. And that's all you know, right? He goes to Bermuda, and there's no more contact between you and Zaychek."

"That's right."

"You fucking liar." I said it more with astonishment than anger.

"What?" He moved forward in his chair, thought better about it, then slowly leaned back.

"I have your phone bill, remember? You took two collect calls from Bermuda during the time Zaychek was there. A coincidence? You have friends there?"

"I have friends everywhere."

"Well, just for the record, you didn't call your Bermudian friends this year—and they didn't call you collect—until Zaychek went there. Chase, that's circumstantial evidence in anybody's book. Let me ask you again: could those calls have been from Zaychek?"

"I don't remember. I guess so."

"You don't remember if you talked to him?"

"Well, I guess I did if the phone bill says I got some collect calls."

"Why collect?"

"I don't remember."

"I'll tell you why. It was safer. The calls were made from a pay phone. He couldn't call you from his room at Fontana, because he wasn't *in* his room at Fontana. A guy named Augustus was in that room, under Zaychek's name. Zaychek was registered under Augustus's name at the Southampton Princess. But he couldn't call you from that room, either, because he didn't want Augustus to *ever* come up. So he used a pay phone in the lobby of the Princess. Anybody could have called from there."

"You lost me."

"Come on, Chase."

"I'm telling you, you lost me. He was a strange guy—very secretive. If you called me collect, I'd ask why. If Zaychek did it, I wouldn't even have thought twice about it; he always seemed to be playing some kind of game." There was a certain sincerity in the way he said it, but it was hard to tell if he was just trying to buy time or if he was saying, *Okay, some of the other stuff is true, but now I don't know what you're talking about.* I gave him the benefit of the doubt.

We went on like that. I kept hammering away, filling in the spaces as I opened them. When I could see I was guessing wrong, I veered, changed the subject. I had most of the facts but none of the *truth.* The two calls to Chase were made prior to Zaychek's supposed death; after them, there was no contact whatever. And Chase was absent a motive: Why had he gone to all this trouble? To accomplish what?

"Let's go back to the time Zaychek was supposed to have died. First of all, the timing is incredible—he named you executor only a week before. Next thing you know, you're comforting the bereaved widow, who has an unbelievable face and an unbelievable body and whose fiscal attributes are about to make her physical attributes look insignificant—"

"Hey—"

"Come on. It isn't a bad package. And if you knew Zaychek was alive, it gave you the world's best reason for wanting him dead, *really* dead, or caught. Did Zaychek trust Maria?"

Chase nodded. But there was something funny in the way he did it. I thought I saw him swallow.

"You're saying he did. Okay, satisfy my curiosity—how do *you* know he trusted her?"

"Well, I just assumed—"

"The will. Would she have gotten all her money at once?"

"Actually, no. He wanted it meted out to her. Didn't want her to get it all at once. I think he tended to treat her like a, I don't know, a teenager."

"So the money was going to dribble out gradually. That wouldn't have made you any too happy."

"What do you mean by that?"

"Or anyone who had designs on Maria."

"Listen—"

"Well, it doesn't matter. So I'm off to Bermuda. And David Bornstein is right behind me, thanks to you. Why is that?"

"Like I said, I didn't know what Zaychek was. Eventually, I figured that if he was dead it would do no harm at all to send Bornstein after him."

"Why not just put Bornstein together with me? Why tell him that I can't be trusted?"

"I never said that, not exactly. I just didn't want him . . . influencing you in any way."

"I see. All of a sudden you're a champion of the empirical method. No, the fact is you didn't want Bornstein and me to get to talking, because then I'd put two and two together, and I'd know you were the guy who talked to him, and that would mean I'd know you knew more about Zaychek than you were supposed to know. By the way, how often do you talk to Maria?"

It was a good non sequitur, and he shot back a too-casual answer. "I don't know. Every few days, maybe, just to keep her informed, make sure she doesn't need anything, that kind of thing."

"You're doing it again."

"What?"

"Forgetting my friends at the telephone company. You talk to her every goddamn day. Sometimes twice."

Actually, he *hadn't* forgotten—I could tell—but he'd forgotten that Maria Zaychek lived a toll call away from him, and that those phone calls were a matter of record.

"Colin, I'm tired." It was true; I was physically and mentally drained. "I have a lot of stuff here. It's a story about a shrewd old Nazi and a naive but greedy associate publisher, and the story's gonna come out whether I write it or not. And if *World* doesn't publish it, the *Inquirer* will. And this beating around the bush is pissing me off."

Chase nodded. He sat forward on the chair, his elbows resting on his knees, his hands hanging limply between his legs. His eyes were on the floor. He was sweating—literally—and he looked worried. And suddenly I knew I had him, and it made me sick to my stomach. I didn't *want* him. It probably explains why I can't hunt or fish; I end up feeling sorry for the prey. Besides, Chase was ruining one of my illusions; he wasn't acting like a cornered rat at all. He wasn't fighting. Some animals, in fact, simply give up, expose their necks.

"One last time. If I can't get some straight answers now, I turn everything over to the people who can. Do you understand?"

He nodded again.

"How did Zaychek learn that I was in Bermuda? Why did he come after me?"

"I don't know. I didn't tell him. I swear it."

"Next question. Were you the reason Zaychek didn't quite

trust his wife?" It was apparently a better question, because half a minute went by before Chase finally answered it, sheepishly: "Zaychek suspected Maria of being unfaithful. But he didn't . . . suspect me."

It was as much honesty as I was going to get, but it was enough.

I left Chase in the room. I told him that Karen Bornstein wouldn't be showing up, just in case he hadn't figured it out, and I suggested, not too politely, that he not make any phone calls.

Then I took an elevator to the Barclay's ground floor and walked down the stairwell off the lobby to the public phones. I dialed, and Maria Zaychek answered the phone herself— it was close to ten, and the maid had probably turned in— and we chatted for a minute or two and I said, "I'll tell you more when I get there." Then I dropped off the key in the lobby, told the desk clerk I wouldn't be needing it again, and put the charges on my Visa. This time I wouldn't hit *World* with an expense voucher; it was my party.

There wasn't much traffic on the expressway. I switched on the radio, checked WXPN and WRTI, the college stations, for jazz, and finally settled for KYW's news radio. But it quickly faded to background. I had too much on my mind.

I missed the blind driveway in the dark, and had to make a U-turn to get back to it. But I soon found myself on that long, poplar-fringed drive—only now the poplars were tall black things sewn to a midnight-blue sky, and all I could see was the road. I followed my high beams through the elaborate gate with the number 100 at the top, then along a twisting drive until the face of the large gray house leapt up, its lights, one on either side of the white columns that framed the front entrance, blinking at me through the foliage that surrounded the place and showing off the custom paint job of the yellow Mercedes. I remembered Maria's robe and patio umbrella and her dress that evening in Bermuda, all the same color.

She met me in that silken robe, extended her hands and greeted me warmly. We walked through the center hall to a sitting room, her arm brushing mine as we went. Her eagerness to find out what I knew was almost palpable.

And then we were on a deep sofa facing each other in what could have been called the Maria Zaychek room—a large painting of a younger her over the fireplace and several sketches of her, large and small, on the walls, framed and hung as if they resided in a gallery instead of a home. In one corner, there was a bronze bust that captured that erect, aloof quality that I had noticed the first time I saw her. Nowhere—not anywhere that I could see—was there any similar indication that a person named Vladimir Zaychek had also lived here.

"Tell me first," she said, "do you know where Vladimir is?"

"No. But there's no reason to think he's anything but alive." I was taking it slowly; there was always the possibility that Chase might have called her, and I figured I would wait until I was sure. "Now, where is he? Maybe he came back to the States; in fact, the feds are investigating whether he might have come in as Augustus. Me, I don't think so. He doesn't have Augustus's passport, and the word's out on that name now anyway. He'll probably go, I'd say, to Canada, where it's easy to get lost, or to South America, where he'd probably have friends, on a false passport, or to Australia, where no one would bother to look for him. Also, I wouldn't count on him using his own name. But you know him better than I do. What do *you* think?"

"Vladimir liked Europe—"

"Not a chance. He won't go back there. Not now, and maybe never."

"Why not? What is he hiding from? Why did he leave?" She looked straight into my eyes, and I looked back, trying to find a trace, a glimmer, of deception. How much did she know? The dark green eyes said nothing. In fact, *too* little.

"We'll get to that," I said.

"Aren't you the mysterious one." She smiled.

"Humor me. I want to take you back to the late thirties to a town called Freital. Ever hear of it?"

Maria shook her head.

"Well, there's no reason why you should have. It's a dot on the map just outside of Dresden in East Germany. A family named Buchner lived there—August, a Dresden postal official, his wife, Helga, and two sons, Alfred and Albrecht. Alfred is in his early twenties and in medical school; Albrecht is about thirty, a doctor in a Dresden hospital.

"This is a close-knit family divided on only one issue: Adolf Hitler and National Socialism. The parents and Alfred, the younger, are staunch Hitler supporters—when the bellies are full, some people don't care where the beef comes from. But not Albrecht. He watches with horror as Jewish professors are stripped of their rank, as his colleagues begin to disappear.

"At first he keeps quiet; the camps are already heavily populated by political prisoners. But then he becomes more vocal. He becomes an outcast in his own family, who feel that he will bring destruction down on them. It is particularly painful for him in terms of his younger brother, whom he really loves, and who is moving more and more toward the brink. Look, you've heard this story time and again—the dreams of the thousand-year reich, the concentration camps, the craziness and the atrocities. So Albrecht gets out of Germany just in time, just before the United States enters the war in Europe. He changes his name, starts a new life as Albert M. Augustus, M.D."

Maria hadn't moved.

"Within a couple of years Alfred, who turns out to be a

medical *Wunderkind*, is heading up a research project and ends up sticking needles into people in what is referred to as a clinic but what is, some will say later, actually more like a laboratory for human guinea pigs. Like many German doctors, he's somehow able to reconcile his work with the Hippocratic oath; he writes about the importance of the removal of certain human cancers from the German national body. A real sweetheart. The lab was a few hundred miles from Dresden, just across the Czech border near a small town called Ostrov. Does that name mean anything to you?"

"Ostrov?" She bit her lip thoughtfully. "I never heard of it."

"Well, no matter. Anyway, time passes, the war is over. The clinic burns to the ground—Alfred Buchner with it, some say. Of course, others insist that the Nazis torched the place to get rid of the evidence and that Buchner survived, which would be no surprise, but they're always saying that about Nazis, so who knows."

She had stopped looking directly at me; her eyes were now on her lap, where her long white fingers were folded.

"Okay, let's move ahead a lot of years. Hitler is so long gone that kids don't even recognize his name anymore; National Socialism is a relic; nobody cares about war criminals, since most of them are dead or getting senile in Argentina; and ex-Nazis are helping to run Germany. Who has time to worry about the old Germany? We have enough problems with the new one. Or the new *two*, as the case is. Everybody forgets. Kurt Waldheim lies about his Nazi past and is elected president of Austria.

"So you can't blame Albrecht Buchner for forgiving his brother. After all, blood is thicker, certainly thicker than politics, and all of that nasty business was a long time ago, right?" It wasn't really a question, but Maria nodded. She still did not look up.

"Well, it turns out that Alfred Buchner, who is very much alive and enjoying life in the United States, finds his older brother—no big problem, because Albrecht had kept in touch with the parents and Alfred knew that he was living as Albert M. Augustus in Cincinnati. And while Albrecht despises what Alfred once stood for, he chalks up Alfred's Nazi involvement to his youth and his being swept along, and so on. Albrecht never stops loving Alfred, we know now, and who knows—maybe vice versa. In fact, I think it *was* vice versa, because the brothers kept each other's photographs all their lives.

"I went out to visit Mrs. Augustus. I showed her your husband's driver's license, which caused her to mention one mysterious patient her husband had; he would come to the office once every year or so, but there would be no records relating to him. He was just a hypochondriac, her husband would tell her after he left; there was nothing to write.

"Okay, fast forward. Alfred finds himself being tracked down by a man with a vendetta. Albrecht has incurable cancer. Now, since Albrecht is going to die anyway, Alfred reasons, why not have *his* death appear to be *mine*? Maybe Alfred convinced Albrecht to do this. Maybe Albrecht volunteered. Whichever, it was by mutual consent, and Mrs. Augustus was supposed to come into some money because of this."

I put the two pieces of the photograph in her hand. She looked at them, then at me. "Are you saying," she asked very quietly, "that my husband was Dr. Augustus's brother? And a war criminal?"

Maria assembled the whole scenario as easily as a preschooler's jigsaw puzzle, and she believed it just as fast. She tried to *look* shocked, of course, but. But.

Things happen when people suffer emotional shocks. Respiration changes, the jaw slackens, the eyes widen. The heart rate changes. The blood leaves the face. You have to be one hell of an actor to make it look real; that's why most people can spot a phony a mile away. And that's why the jury system works: spend enough time watching people in a courtroom and you'll know which ones are lying. The system's not perfect, but it's damned good—good enough to enable juries of ordinary, everyday people to come to the right conclusions time after time.

"You didn't know he was Dr. Augustus's brother?"

"Of course not."

"He'd never mentioned Dr. Augustus?"

"Absolutely not."

"Then you never heard the name before you went to Bermuda."

"That's right."

"Despite the fact that your husband's will mentions only one other person, and leaves millions to her? To *Mrs*. Augustus?"

Now I got the reaction she couldn't fake a few minutes ago. She froze, stock still, like a blind person caught in traffic, and started to stammer. Then she stopped, became a statue on the sofa next to me, and her words sounded disembodied, resigned: "So you know about the will."

"I figured it out, and Chase confirmed it. Dr. Augustus knew he was dying, loved his wife, wanted to leave her financially stable. At the same time, he wasn't particularly anxious to prolong his own life—he knew what was coming—and here was a chance for him to leave more money than his wife and children would spend in a lifetime. Plus save his brother's ass. So a deal was struck. Augustus dies, Zaychek lives. Mrs. Augustus gets rich.

"So you knew, at least, that Mrs. Augustus was ending up with an inheritance that you figured should be yours. Of course, you're probably in that will for the lion's share, but that wasn't good enough. So you did hear of Mrs. Augustus before you met her, because it was partly due to her that you wanted the will invalidated. Which is why you had me sent on that wild-goose chase to Bermuda in the first place. You *wanted* me to find out that Vladimir wasn't dead."

"That's ridiculous. Even if I did know that a Mrs. Augustus was named in the will, I had no idea why. I'd never heard that name before, never until this moment put it together with the name of the doctor on the beach. And I had no reason to think Vladimir was alive." Maria had turned icy, and now she just kept glaring at me.

"That's a bunch of shit," I said.

"Look, I—"

"When was the last time you spoke to Vladimir?"

She looked at the ceiling twenty feet above us. "It was the day before he—the day before the death."

"I have a copy of your phone bill for June. You made a call to the Southampton Princess on June sixteenth. You also made one on June nineteenth. That would seem to indicate you talked to Vladimir not only the day before he was supposed to have died, but two days *after*. Did you know anyone else who was staying there?"

"No. Look, I must have called to find out about his possessions—about his clothing and personal belongings." She stammered again, but I had to hand it to her, she was good. Except for forgetting to be indignant about my having her phone bill.

"You called the Southampton Princess on the nineteenth."

"I guess so. I can't be sure of the date."

"To take care of Vladimir's personal effects."

"Yes."

"You called the Southampton Princess—even though Vladimir stayed at Fontana?"

Of course, Zaychek was supposed to have stayed at Fontana. But it was Dr. Augustus, an obscure family physician from Cincinnati, who was at Fontana under Zaychek's name, making sure everyone was getting to know him as Zaychek. And Zaychek was registered under Augustus's name at the Southampton Princess. The only two people who should have known that were Zaychek and Augustus—the brothers Buchner.

If Maria Zaychek called her husband at the Princess, she probably knew everything. And I was talking to a stranger. Our night at Fontana flashed through my mind; no wonder she looked around so much, acted so nervous. Vladimir could have been right there. She called the Southampton Princess not to make arrangements about her husband's personal possessions, but to talk to him—at a time she was supposed to think he was dead.

Augustus poses as Zaychek, Zaychek as Augustus. They walk out into the water at a deserted stretch of beach; there, Augustus is administered a lethal injection of jellyfish toxin—probably not physalia at all, but something more toxic—by his brother. He dies in Zaychek's arms of an anaphylactic reaction. By the time his face mask hits the water, he's gone—that's why there was no seawater in his lungs. Zaychek puts the snorkel in his mouth, turns him onto his stomach, and floats him off. He's found and pulled ashore a short time later; Zaychek, who is now pretending to be Dr. Augustus, says he knows the man and identifies him as Vladimir Zaychek. The snorkel and face mask are marked *Fontana*, and several Fontana employees say yes, this is the man we know as Zaychek. The ring, as well, is on the finger.

As for Zaychek's actual signature in the snorkeling equipment checkout book, that would be easily explainable—both men went in, one talked, the other signed out the equipment. The guy in the equipment shack was half asleep anyway; they knew he'd never remember which one did which.

It didn't say much for Vladimir Zaychek in the warmth and sensitivity department, being able to play that part so well so soon after his brother's death.

It's all over, and Maria calls. I could see Zaychek being furious about that call. I knew he would have warned her not to try to contact him. And yet she called. Why?

She knew she was putting his phone number on the phone bill. And if she did that, she wanted it there for somebody else to find.

I spent my early teens reading mysteries. The parts I remember best had less to do with murder than with women taking off their clothes. That was the kind of situation private eyes apparently found themselves in on a regular basis, but—from the perspective of a horny adolescent—they usually screwed it up; they were, as a breed, hard drinkers and tough fighters but not much when it came to other abuses of the flesh. I remember, for instance, when Philip Marlowe, I think it was, kicked a beautiful woman out of his apartment simply because she got undressed. That was what the good guys did, sometimes because they were tough, sometimes because they had integrity, and sometimes because the books were written before you could do anything else in American detective fiction. I thought they were crazy.

But then the lady was usually guilty of something, and sex was likely to be a distraction or a bribe. So an ounce of caution was necessary. The ultimate inappropriate use of caution in the case of a beautiful woman, I thought, was when Mike Hammer actually shot one in her birthday suit in *I, the Jury*. Of course, Hammer knew she was guilty. And that she undressed only to avoid her comeuppance. But talk about overreacting.

Maria Zaychek did not slip out of her yellow robe when I confronted her with the results of my little investigation. If she had, I don't know what I would have done. That's the truth. Not that it would have changed the outcome much, but it might have delayed things for an hour. One of my problems is that I can't hold a grudge; another is that I don't see good and evil as absolutes. After all, motivation is everything; you have to know why people do things before you know just how much they deserve to be condemned. Take a commandment, any commandment, and you can find certain circumstances under which it can be justifiably violated. I can, anyway.

That's why I didn't become an investigative reporter. I could never go for the jugular. But I knew where it was.

When I asked Maria why she'd called the Southampton Princess, she had no answer. And she offered none. She sat there quietly, biting her lip, and I knew that she'd known her husband was alive days after he was supposed to have died. At the very least, this involved her in some kind of conspiracy. If she'd taken the will to probate, it would have been a crime. But she stopped short of that.

She confessed the affair with Chase easily—I'd caught her in some serious lies, and she was ready to admit to something, almost anything, just to get some credibility back. She seemed embarrassed by the whole business—and embarrassed, I thought, to have been caught by me.

And she finally told me a little about her life with Zaychek. "My husband is much older. He loves me, in a way. And I once loved him. But he treated me like his orchids—an obsession, yes, but one possessed, something to admire. He was hard to talk to; we didn't share much. I knew that someday it would be over, and I wondered if it would be over early enough."

"Early enough for what?"

"For me, I mean. I was—am—still young. When I met Colin Chase, I saw him as the kind of man I should have married, would have married if I had it to do again. I saw him as a person who might help me break away—I have to tell you, in many ways living with Vladimir was like living with a jailer. With Colin, there was—well, I don't want to try to put it into words, but for a while it was all I could think about. It took a long time, many months, before I realized that my money was a lot more important to him than I was. And once I did, I started putting some distance between us. I don't trust him."

"I don't trust either of you, and if Vladimir was here, I wouldn't trust him either. Why didn't you just ask for a divorce?"

"Vladimir would have considered that the ultimate betrayal. I'm not sure I would have been safe."

Vladimir hadn't known about the affair?

"No," Maria said. "He suspected something. But he always did, even when there was nothing to suspect; he always suspected somebody. And yet he didn't suspect Colin. I don't know why."

"Maybe he thought you had better taste."

I knew why she hadn't gone to Vladimir's funeral in Bermuda, and it wasn't because, as she'd originally indicated, she saw it as an event that was without meaning in terms of her life or their relationship. It was because she and Vladimir had arranged her absence beforehand. If she wasn't there, she couldn't be asked to identify the body.

I thought back to the exhumation, remembered how she watched Mrs. Augustus's face, and I realized that she'd been waiting for her to speak up. When she didn't, Maria did so herself.

She didn't tell me any of that. She didn't tell me much at all. She didn't have to. I just kept asking her questions, and it was all there. If it wasn't in the admissions, it was in the denials, and in the dumb things she said when she made them. It was there in the silences. It all kept tumbling out.

She'd known all along that he wasn't dead. But if the world knew it as well, Maria would've accomplished two things: the will would be moot; and Bornstein would get some credibility. There would be a search for Zaychek, which indeed there now was. And Zaychek, or Buchner, would be forced into hiding or be caught and deported—either way, out of her hair forever.

I concentrated on the will first. Why didn't they just destroy it, pretend they'd never found it? Maybe that was where Chase drew the line. Or, more likely, maybe there was no way for them to know if other copies existed, no way for them to know how much Mrs. Augustus knew. Or maybe they just intended to deal with the will later.

Sending me to investigate, and Bornstein to follow me, was a stroke of genius—*if* Zaychek knew I was there. Either Zaychek would come after me to keep me from going too far, at which time he would presumably be spotted by Bornstein, or he would go deep into hiding. In a few years, he'd be declared legally dead. Until then Maria had plenty to live on. She was in no hurry.

The house was in her name, worth a million or two. I figured she would sell it. I figured she would want to get as far from it as possible. It was too isolated; there were no men. And then there were, I was sure, sufficient funds in joint accounts.

I asked her how deeply Chase had been involved. I knew he didn't have much in the scruples department, but I couldn't believe he wanted me dead.

"At first he knew only what I told him," Maria said. "He thought Vladimir was dead, of course. He thought I was being silly."

That would explain why he tried to pull me away from the whole business early on, when he saw that I was buying her story. But that was *at first*. Then he did that about-face, sent me to Bermuda. What made him care?

"I don't know," Maria said. "I didn't tell him anything more than I told you. But he decided not to make the will public until we knew more."

"I'm sure that was fine with you."

She didn't answer.

I thought back on it, tried to put myself in his place. If I were Chase, I would hedge my bets, avoid risks, use marked cards. And I'd be smart enough—smarter than Alex Black— not to put a lot of faith in Maria *or* Zaychek. If I'd been Chase, I wouldn't've been sure of anything.

Along comes Bornstein. He writes his letter to *World*'s publisher, asking about the availability of Zaychek photographs; the publisher passes it along to Chase, who for reasons of his own—maybe to ingratiate himself with Zaychek, maybe to scare him off—tells him about the letter. Maybe Chase had by that time looked into Bornstein and knew just what he was looking for; maybe not. That I might never know. At any rate, a few days later, Zaychek takes off. A few days after that, Zaychek is dead. Maybe the coincidence of that started to take its toll on Chase. Maybe he wanted to be absolutely sure that Zaychek was in the coffin.

So Chase had every good reason for sending me to Bermuda, and for sending Bornstein after me. If he had to dream up a combination of talents designed to get rid of Zaychek once and for all, he couldn't have done better than the two of us: one to find out that he existed, the other to track him down. In order to have Maria—in the fullest way, which included her money—he had to see Vladimir dead or captured. He probably hadn't cared which.

I was sure he had some kind of hidden agenda. He was Colin Chase. What bothered me was that I could never know whether the attempt on my life was part of that agenda.

Again, I gave him the benefit of the doubt.

Of course, they both managed to stay clear of the action. If Vladimir *wasn't* caught, they didn't want to become his target. They wanted to look clean. Neither of them wanted to have to explain anything to Vladimir Zaychek, because there was no guarantee that they'd get the chance to explain.

Maria had pulled the strings but Chase had made the moves, had been manipulated right into them. It was Chase who'd gotten me for Maria, Chase who sent me to Bermuda, Chase who sent David Bornstein after me. Both Chase and Maria had reasons why they were doing whatever they were doing, but David Bornstein had the best reason of all: vengeance. And when vengeance is the best reason, that doesn't say much for the other reasons.

Zaychek killed Bornstein instead of me. He had no idea what a lucky break that was. He killed the only guy on earth who would never have stopped looking for him. As I said, I don't have that kind of staying power. Sure, I hated everything Zaychek stood for. But it wasn't personal. I could understand why he wanted to get rid of me. He'd been warned that I was a danger to him. If I'd known he was trying to do it, I'd have tried to get him first. Like I said, motivation.

Sometimes I think I understand too goddamned much.

What really pissed me off was being used as a decoy; that would have been an act of conscious betrayal, and a dangerous one. Who? Who told Zaychek I was somebody to watch out for?

I asked Maria.

"I don't know," she said. "It wasn't me."

"When did you last talk to Vladimir?"

"I don't remember. A long time ago. Weeks, months."

"Did you mention me at all?"

"No."

"Bornstein?"

"No."

"What did you talk about?"

"I don't remember."

"You have a lousy memory. You talked to Vladimir the day before I got to Bermuda."

"That's not true."

"It's true. And it doesn't feel like a coincidence." I tapped my copy of her latest phone records, the calls for which she hadn't yet been billed.

"You didn't tell him about me?"

"No," she said, and she looked into my eyes with the innocence of a nine-year-old, knowing that I had the facts but not the truth, knowing that there was a lot I would never be able to prove.

But proving is different from knowing. Proof is what you try to give to a jury, but juries have been known to reach verdicts without it. Knowing is internal, personal. And I knew. I couldn't know what she told him, and she wasn't saying, but it was strong enough to get Vladimir Zaychek to make two attempts on my life. Maybe all she had to tell him was that I was there, and that I would eventually open that coffin.

I was the bait. When Zaychek came after me, Bornstein was supposed to go after him.

I remembered the two bullets in the water.

Maria had seen the name of another woman in the will, a woman who was going to end up with part of her pile, and she went nuts. Nuts enough to have been willing to use me to get Vladimir.

"You're my best suspect, Maria," I said, and—although it was hard for me to equate that kind of cold-bloodedness with her warmth in Bermuda—I was coming to know that in her both qualities resided easily alongside one another. She was simply a beautiful liar.

We sat on the couch together, now silent. She looked a little haggard, and I could smell her perspiration, which I had liked from the beginning. At one point, she shrugged and asked softly whether it wasn't all moot anyway—after all, I was alive, wasn't I?

What, Bornstein doesn't count?

When I left it was close to one in the morning. I just got up and walked to the door, and she walked behind me. I unlocked it myself. The last thing I heard from her was my name with a question mark at the end of it: "Alex?" It was full of implications: *who would I tell, what would come of it all, was there any way she could forestall it?* And maybe there was a little bit of *What about us?* Or maybe I just wanted to hear that.

I was glad to get out of there, and I left without answering, without looking back.

"Look, Bernie," I said in what I thought was a reasonable manner, "I don't want to appear unfriendly, but I wonder if you wouldn't mind working out there instead of in here. I have a lot of personal stuff around."

It was the following morning. I got to the office a little late and found Bernie sitting at my terminal.

"Oh, I wouldn't violate your privacy," he said.

"Well, I appreciate that, but this is my office, and you *are* violating my privacy."

"There's no place for me to work out there." He shrugged. "No desk, no terminal." He was right, but it wasn't my problem. And he didn't move. He was acting like somebody who'd taken one of those fucking assertiveness training courses, which, knowing Bernie, he probably had. I mean, here we were in a little office—mine—with one empty chair—mine—and he was in both of them.

"Maybe they'll fire somebody to make room for you," I said. "Now go. *Go.*" I was leaning over him now, only a few inches from his face. He briskly threw his papers together and went.

Maddie noticed it and came in. "What does he do," I asked, "crawl out every time I'm a few minutes late?"

"He says he's supposed to spend a couple of hours a day here."

"What?"

"Chase's orders. He's supposed to get familiar with things, he says."

"What things?"

"I dunno. Your job."

"Well, that's over."

"Are you kidding? Five'll get you ten you haven't heard the last of it."

"You're on. I hope you can afford it."

Maddie looked at me with a certain amount of awe. She knew I never bet unless I had it in the bag.

I have plenty of self-control. This comes from being impulsive, and recognizing it, and doing something about it. I have certain little rules: imaginary samplers embroidered, framed and hung on the walls of my mind, like SLEEP ON IT and NEVER MAKE A DECISION WHEN YOU'RE FEELING LOUSY. These can be very good rules indeed, because they've kept me from quitting jobs before lining up others, but they also have their negative side—I have a hell of a time doing even simple things on impulse, like buying a pair of underwear.

It's hard to end a marriage if you have samplers like those in your head, so I was married for considerably longer than I should have been. On the other hand, if I'd hung those samplers earlier, I probably wouldn't have married Carol in the first place.

The point is, instead of following my initial impulse to tell Colin Chase where he could stuff Bernie, I thought about it for a couple of minutes and realized I didn't have to. Bernie was just a piece of insurance Chase had lined up in case I walked out of the job before he got rid of me. Bernie had never been intended as my "number two person"; he was an alternate number one, and a temporary one at that because he didn't have what it took. If I'd left *World*, Bernie would have gotten my job—and then found himself transferred within a month or two, replaced by another science editor, a competent one. That's how Chase worked, and it always worked for him.

That afternoon I turned everything over to Ken Flick, the investigative reporter. I figured he'd do a good job—the editorial position of *World* would be to let the chips fall, and I knew Flick would be interviewing Colin Chase, who would cooperate to the minimum level necessary. But nonfiction had taught me that the more you dig, the more you unearth, and I'd picked Flick carefully.

Chase, I suspected, would lose interest in reorganizing my department. He would settle for a truce while he wondered how to get through the next month or so. Someday he would send Bernie or somebody like him back to give me some grief, because he wasn't ever going to forget how I'd humiliated him in that room at the Barclay. But until that day I had a sabbatical.

In the interim, Chase would turn back into his old charming and ingratiating self, but instead of only rarely nodding to me on the elevator like he used to, he would prefer elevators that didn't have me on them.

Angel was supposed to have left Virginia at five or so, so I figured I would show up at her place at nine. I was sitting on the porch rocker when she pulled up in her traumatized '78 Dodge.

"How'd it go?"

"Great, if you're somebody who wants to live in a life care community. You have to look at these test shots."

"No I don't." I laughed, but I didn't feel much like laughing. I helped her unload the car.

Later we walked over to the avenue and Nello's Hiya House, a neighborhood restaurant frequented by fast-growing families and senior citizens, a place with a black-and-white-checkerboard floor and plain white Formica tables and lights bright enough, the locals joked, to frighten away *las cucarachas*. We ordered a couple of $6.95 New York strip steaks, the most expensive things on the menu; I found myself thinking of the article *World* ran in April on colorectal cancer.

"What's new with the jellyfish?" Angel asked, brushing aside wisps of long dark hair and looking great even in the brutal light of the Hiya House.

I'd been looking forward to telling her, and so I started, and we talked for a while. But by the time we were done with our meal, I had decided to spend the night back in my own apartment at the Dorchester. "It has nothing to do with you," I said. "It's me. I feel lousy. And I don't want to feel guilty on top of it." Before I knew it I used that expression I promised myself I'd never use: I told her I needed some space.

Angel was terrific. She shrugged, she understood, she didn't even seem to feel bad, which was actually a little disappointing. In fact, maybe that was the problem; maybe I wasn't important enough. Or maybe I was too needy. Sometimes it was hard to tell the difference.

I walked her home and kissed her good-bye, and she stood on the porch and watched me pull out of the street, and I pictured her standing there for a little while after that, too, unlikely though it was. And after that—well, Angel is unpredictable. Maybe she'd go to sleep.

It was none of my business. I'd done the leaving, not her. Maybe *I* was the emotional gypsy. Maybe we both were.

It felt like October, although it wasn't just yet. I like October in Philly, the snap in the air, the smell of early fires, the thought of getting cozy with a room-temperature drink, sex. And that promise of winter, which is always better than winter itself. I drove through the night and opened my window and let the season come in, let it blow through my hair.

And I felt lousy. The problem was that I had seen myself as a sort of scientific detective, a fictional character, and so I expected everything to end the way fiction does: with an ending. A blast of trumpets. *Something*. The guilty get their just deserts. The good guy's problems are over. Maybe he walks off into the sunset with the lady and maybe he doesn't (string section up and out, no matter which), but the music *ends*.

Real life doesn't. In real life, you're always in the middle of the piece, the music's played by a distant French horn, and you can't hum along because you get to hear the tune only once. You get lots of diminuendos, hardly any crescendos. In this case, sure, somebody would look for Alfred Buchner or Vladimir Zaychek or whatever he would call himself next, and maybe he'd even be found someday. But Zaychek would have planned well; he'd have money. And chances were that with the murder of David Bornstein, the only real passion for justice would have disappeared—and Buchner had struck again, this time the son of the father he had killed so many years before, the son of the mother who died when she saw him on television. Bornstein's pain was over, but the picture of David's mother raising her son with tales of Alfred Buchner had become part of my own personal tapestry, there to stay.

Mrs. Augustus would come out of it okay. I called her and told her the whole story: that her husband had given his life because he didn't have more than a couple of months left anyway—and in this manner could go out not only leaving his wife and his children independently wealthy, but also doing something for his kid brother, too. Which was completely in character for the man she knew. I told her about the will. That money wouldn't be hers for a long time no matter what, but Zaychek would eventually die or be declared legally dead, and by that time Maria Zaychek would be hungry enough to push for probate. Even if she wasn't, Mrs. Augustus, under Pennsylvania state law, could push for it herself.

As for Colin Chase, he'd been outmanipulated by a champ who'd figured him out before he got too close. The will, I later learned, didn't provide a fee for Chase's role as executor, so his only hope of getting any money was through

Maria, and fat chance. The chemistry had been there, but Maria was a practical lady above all.

Then there was me in terms of Maria. One of my disappointments was that in my fantasy version of the story, she, not Angel, was the one I pictured myself going off into the sunset with. It wasn't that I felt anything like love for her, it was that I loved the thought of her: glamorous, beautiful, rich and great in bed. That didn't sound bad; it was a way of handling all my problems in one stupid act. But that's the nature of fantasy.

The good part was that I walked away from her with a sense of relief. I was glad not to want her. A little disappointed, as I said, but mostly glad.

It would have been hard to project the next few years for Maria. The real Maria, whatever that was, was somewhere in the future: by the time she was forty, she'd probably be a captain of industry, or, more likely, married to one again.

Her only worry, in fact, was Vladimir Zaychek. She would never be able to relax, and when she felt the wind at her neck she would never be sure it wasn't Vladimir, coming to reclaim everything that was his. She would never know where he was or how much he knew or how much he would surmise once he read the article in *World*, or what she would do if he attempted to get in touch with her.

For that matter, there was nothing to stop him from writing another will. If he did that, I had a feeling he would be far more inclined to keep his word to his brother than to worry about Maria.

Those were the kinds of scenarios I was envisioning when I pulled into the Dorchester's underground garage. But they were questionable at best. Maria would probably not suffer a hell of a lot, thank you. She and Chase had each taken a shot at the brass ring, and neither of them had quite grabbed it. Maria would eventually. Chase wouldn't, but he wouldn't stop trying. And neither of them would lose much sleep over it. They were survivors.

In fact, if anybody was going to have trouble sleeping, it was me. Because I know how journalism works. It's not law enforcement, not a courtroom. Most of what I'd learned and a lot of what I'd given Flick could end up on the editing room floor, and even if it all somehow managed to see print, most news stories are twenty-four-hour wonders. Like the public's memory.

Further, minor characters are inconsequential; too much detail clutters things up. Never, as they say in the business, let the facts get in the way of the story.

Besides, newsmagazines don't print a whole hell of a lot of speculation, and what did I really have that tied either Chase or Maria to anything? What crime, Maria had asked me at one point, had they committed?

In the eyes of the law, there was no crime. They came close, but no cigar.

So I sat in Rittenhouse Square in the cold. I didn't feel like sleeping. I didn't want to be with anyone. I didn't want to be alone. I didn't want a drink.

And I didn't want to freeze my ass off, so I eventually walked the few blocks to *World*, signed in at the guard desk, took an elevator to the sixteenth floor, got off, nodded to a couple of guys on the late shift, thought nice thoughts about Maddie as I passed her desk, closed my office door, turned on the terminal, waited for the beep, mechanically typed in the password, and there was Stella, ready for action at 1:52 a.m.:

GOOD MORNING, ALEX BLACK. YOUR PLEASURE?

Good morning, Stella. Blackjack?